THE MASK HUNTER

ANNA WILMANS

THE MASK HUNTER

Pantera Books
Santa Barbara • California

Published by Pantera Books
Santa Barbara, California

pantera-books.com

28 27 26 25 24 1 2 3 4 5

ISBN: 979-8-9907480-2-6

Library of Congress Control Number: 2024915541

Credits:
Front cover: Great pyramids of Egypt: © Günter Albers/Dreamstime
The Colloseum: © Miroslav Hasch/Dreamstime
Black horse: © Kseniya Abramova/Dreamstime
Back cover: © Steve Elkins

Coin of Alexander the Great: ANS 1944.100.75504. Courtesy of the American Numismatic Society. Photographed by Alan Roche.

Developmental Editor: Megan Records
Copy Editor: Melissa Stein
Proofreader: Mark Woodworth
Logo Design: Mercedes Martinez
Publicity: Hollywoodbookpublicity.com

Designed and produced by: Terri Wright, Book Lotus Productions, www.booklotus.com

Dedicated to the memory of Bucephalus
and all the other great horses of the world

A NOTE TO THE READER

ALEXANDER THE GREAT was a restless meteor who blazed across the ancient world from his birthplace in Macedonia to Babylon, where he died at the age of thirty-two. Along the way he conquered most of the then-known world as far east as southern India and felled the mighty Persian Empire, while at the same time personally, politically, and religiously morphing himself into facsimiles of those whom he conquered. He was Napoleon and David Bowie rolled into a charismatic five-foot-four package.

Although there is no hard evidence that Alexander was laid to rest in Alexandria, the city he founded in Egypt, or that his body was treated to mummification as would befit the Pharaoh he proclaimed himself to be, there are credible ancient literary sources pointing in those directions.

This tempting probability inspired my fictional search into the postmortem adventures of one of history's most compelling and controversial heroes. The Warner is a fictional museum, and the people and events in *The Mask Hunter* are entirely creations of my imagination. However, it has been well documented that many of the archaeological treasures exhibited in the world's most prestigious museums arrived there thanks to the world's second-oldest profession: grave robbing. This poses ongoing ethical and legal questions.

HISTORICAL TIMELINE

20 July 356 BC	Alexander the Great is born, Macedonia, Greece.
326 BC	Bucephalus, Alexander's wonder horse, dies in Pakistan.
324 BC	Hephaestion, Alexander's longtime friend and lover, dies in Iran.
323 BC	Alexander dies in Babylon. His generals divide the Empire. Ptolemy, ancestor of Cleopatra, claims Egypt.
321 BC	Alexander's body leaves Babylon for burial in Macedonia. Ptolemy highjacks the body and takes it to Egypt.
215 BC	Ptolemy IV builds an elaborate tomb for Alexander in Alexandria.
68 AD	St. Mark is murdered in Alexandria.
391 AD	Zealous Christians destroy all pagan temples in Alexandria. Alexander's tomb disappears.
828 AD	St. Mark's body is stolen from Alexandria and moved to Venice.

As of this writing, the remains of Alexander the Great have not been found.

Credit Suisse
Geneva, Switzerland
October 28, 1985

PROLOGUE

The room was about the size of a walk-in closet, with only enough space for two chairs and a small table. It was steel-walled and windowless, standard issue for clients of Credit Suisse who came to view, add to, or subtract items from their safe-deposit boxes. Like the others in this basement complex it was equipped with prominent security cameras, and only one door, locked until the depositor pressed the button at its right side to summon a bank officer.

Usually one and not more than two people used the room at any single time. Today there were four, forcing the two younger and presumably less prestigious members of the party to stand awkwardly behind those seated in the chairs. Both shifted from foot to foot to ease the discomfort caused by the stone floor.

Other than the cameras and the two chairs, the room was bare except for the functional metal table that occupied the center space. The overall starkness served as a perfect counterpoint to the golden mask lying on a velvet pillow in the center of the table.

The mask, which seemed to glow despite the harsh fluorescent lighting, was hammered into the likeness of a man's face. Not just an ordinary face, but that of a young and handsome man with deep-set eyes and cascading waves of hair. The lips were slightly parted, as if to speak.

As though waiting for that to happen, none of the four men spoke a word.

They were an odd group of mismatched ages and nationalities. The one in the chair closest to the mask gave off a restless energy that was apparent even as he sat motionless, a coiled spring ready to explode. His hair, stark white, echoed the flowing locks of the mask, and his eyes were ice-blue and piercing, drawing attention away from the dishevelment suggested by a suit that looked as if it had been slept in. Which most likely it had.

He was the first to speak. "Where did you get this?" He addressed the man across the table from him, ignoring the others. His tone was measured, and the English words carried a distinctive Eastern European accent.

The man he addressed looked to be somewhere in his sixties, wearing a grey pinstriped suit that screamed "Saville Row." A crisp white cuff discreetly sporting a monogrammed gold cuff link peeked out from each jacket sleeve. The cut of the garment cleverly disguised a midsection thickened by years of too many pastries and too little exercise. The man stroked his chin with a manicured hand, meeting the blue eyes across the table with his equally commanding brown ones.

"All in due time, Roman. First, tell me what you think of it."

This wasn't the first time these two old warriors had faced off against each other. The negotiations were a cat and mouse game, proving their testosterone was still flowing.

The blue-eyed man shrugged. "Well, my opinion is only a small part of any purchase the museum makes, and there is much to consider."

His companion seemed to expect that reply. Both of them

knew—in fact all four of the men knew—that the object on the table, literally and figuratively, was the most important piece of ancient art any of them had ever seen, and most probably ever would see. If it was real, and it certainly looked to be, it would be the greatest find to come to light since the opening of the tomb of Tutankhamun in 1922. Maybe even greater.

"Now that you have seen what we have to offer, I will be expecting to hear from you no later than tomorrow. There are, of course, other buyers. Naturally I'd like to see the Mask of Alexander go to the Warner but . . ." He let his voice trail off, but the meaning was obvious.

He stood up, pressing the button for the bank officer as he did so, cutting off any further questions from the blue-eyed man.

Minutes later, in the bank manager's office, all four men donned topcoats in anticipation of the late autumn chill that would greet them as they exited the building.

As they stepped out onto the Place de Bel-Air, they broke into two groups. They shook hands, and the well-dressed man and his silent companion walked toward the lake.

The remaining two watched them go. "What's with that Mafia guy?" Barry Epstein, the younger one, asked, gesturing toward the open-shirted man they had just left. Dressed in blue jeans and a down jacket, he struggled to pull a pair of earmuffs from his coat pocket as he eyed the two departing men.

"You Americans," Roman Zanski, the blue-eyed man, scoffed. "Anyone with a Madonna around his neck and hairs on his chest you call 'Mafia.' You think only Mafia have chest hairs?"

"Most other people know enough to wax it off or cover it up," Epstein defended his position.

His companion had obviously lost interest in the topic, because he did not bother to reply.

He changed the subject. "So what kind of money are we talking here, and how do you know the damn thing is real?"

"I'm sure the trustees will come up with the money, whatever the price might be." Zanski shrugged his shoulders dismissively, as only a transplant from a Communist country could do when the subject was money. "As for its being real. Ahhh . . ." He raised his fingers to his lips as if he had just savored a truffle, ". . . the mask speaks for itself."

Epstein was dubious. "This isn't like the other stuff we've bought from this guy. You'd think that with all that money on the table they'd at least wine and dine us a bit. I was expecting a good meal at Shott's chalet. Instead, we wind up in someplace that looks like a jail cell. No air and nothing to drink. No fun in that."

"I was thinking of that also. It too much reminded me of why I left Russia." Zanski pulled a flask from his overcoat pocket and offered it to his companion. "Drink."

Epstein took the offered flask and drank deeply. Wiping his lips on his coat sleeve, he handed the vessel back to its owner. They drank in silence, passing the flask between them, both avoiding the name that was on both of their minds: Parthi.

Neither man noticed a tall, dark-haired figure watching them from the other side of the street.

PART ONE

1985

Basement storage area, Warner Museum
Beverly Hills, California
September 30, 1985

CHAPTER 1

I didn't hear him come into the room. I realized he was there only when I felt his hand lightly move my hair to one side as he brushed my neck with his lips. I felt a shiver of pleasure.

I put down the terra-cotta figurine I was measuring and turned my face toward him. I saw lines around his eyes that I had never seen before.

"Is everything OK?" As soon as the words were out of my mouth I realized how childish I must sound to the antiquities curator of this world-famous museum where I was a mere intern.

Zanski shrugged. "It's not much. Nothing for you to worry about, Little One. It is just another of the endless problems with the bourgeois trustees I am plagued with. Do they imagine I made them the finest antiquities collection in the world just by snapping my fingers? I have given up hoping they will understand that archaeologists are nothing but fancy tomb robbers, and if they want the most beautiful objects to brag about, they had best get used to that fact." He threw up his hands like a man impatiently releasing a flock of pigeons into the air.

I'd heard that before. Many times. This too would blow over like it always did. The perpetual dance of a bold antiquities curator and a cautious board of museum trustees.

In a flash his mood changed. The lines on his face smoothed out, and he pulled a chair from the opposite side of the work-bench and sat beside me.

"How is your work going with the figurines? You like them much better now, yes?"

"Actually, I do," I admitted. "When I hold one of these in my hand, I can feel what it must have been like to be one of those hopeful women, so many centuries ago, praying her offering would please the gods."

I lifted one of the terra-cotta images from the wooden tray where it was swaddled in cotton with others of its kind. It was one I had not yet measured, but it looked to be about four inches long, just the size to fit comfortably into the palm of a hand. It had been formed in a mold, mass-produced and without distinctive features. Yet there was an unmistakable energy about it that I could not dismiss.

Zanski nodded, as though he read my thoughts. "The woman who placed this little statue at the foot of the goddess so long ago was praying to be blessed with a child. Can you see how the belly is rounded to show the child within?" He ran his right forefinger lightly over the statue's abdomen.

"Yes. I can still imagine her prayer. How much she longed for a child."

He smiled. "All objects, even a humble one such as this, have a life and carry a story. Our job is to listen to what they have to say. You must not forget that, Little One."

"I love the fact that archaeology is now paying attention to the lives of regular people, not just the gods and heroes of antiquity."

"Ah, my dear, it is a sign of our changing world. The

proletariat given a voice."

I was quiet for a minute, awed and amazed as usual by the profound importance Zanski could recognize in the most mundane pieces of ancient art. That was the secret of his rise to rock-star status in the museum world. His magical thinking was legendary. He made not only ordinary people but also other professionals believe stone could speak.

"And you are not so sad that I have asked you to write the monograph on this collection of little figurines the museum patrons donated? People like to see their gifts appreciated, even if they are not such high quality."

I knew what he meant. Publishing a small catalogue on the goddess figurines donated by Max Cherner, one of Zanski's most ardent supporters, would grease the wheels for the next time the curator needed help financing a purchase the trustees balked at.

He continued, "When you are finished with the internship there will be much time for you to follow your heart and look for the tomb of the horse of Alexander the Great. Maybe we can go to Pakistan together and search for it."

My heart thumped. Horses and books had been my refuge during a sometimes lonely childhood. I had been born in Kenya to an American mother and a half-Maasai big game hunter. In Kenya, this was not a problem, but after my father's death, when my mother and I moved back to her family home in Charleston, South Carolina, things were very different. It was not that I looked different from my schoolmates; my hair was straight and my skin more olive than brown. My eyes, in accordance with Mendelian theory, were aqua blue, thanks to my own mother and my father's English ones. Daddy's deep brown Maasai eye coloring was somewhere hidden in a recessive pocket of my genome.

Actually, I thought I was white until I was eight and a mean girl in my third-grade class whose parents had recently returned from a safari in Kenya where they had heard the story of my father, the not-so-white hunter who had shot himself with his elephant gun, retold the story to the entire class. This was the 1970s and Jim Crow was alive and well in the American South.

Girls who had been my friends the day before got up from the lunch table and found other places to eat when I sat down in my usual seat beside them. And then there was the N-word, not shouted, but spoken loudly enough for me to hear.

Mystified by these actions and heartbroken because of them, I begged my mother for answers. All she could do was sell the plantation that had withstood the Yankee troops but could not hold up against the superior forces of an army of eight-year-olds.

We moved to Boulder, Colorado, where no one knew us or about us, a young woman whose Italian husband had recently died, and her pretty eight-year-old daughter.

Charleston had taught me that my peers were not to be trusted. I made no friends in my new school, rushing home every afternoon to bury myself in book after book. I was a pretty good reader, devouring every volume I could, especially those about animals. Then one day I found a story about a horse whose name I could not make out. I took the book to my mother who, realizing I was in a bit over my head, pulled me onto her lap, even though I was now too large for that, and read it to me.

The name of the horse was Bucephalus, which my mother explained meant "bull's head" in Greek. His owner, a boy named Alexander, named him that because of the white marking on his forehead. Only Alexander could ride him, and later they conquered the world together. I was hooked.

Alexander loved Bucephalus so much that when the horse died, he built a temple in his honor.

I remember asking my mother where I could see this temple. She looked at me blankly. Clearly this was outside her wheelhouse. From that moment I made it my mission to find that temple, wherever it might be. Quite an undertaking for someone who could not yet read a map. My quest would have to be in small steps.

The first step was learning more about horses. The Charleston schoolyard trauma, coupled with my father's suicide four years before, had left me with what the psychiatrists now call PTSD. Getting me a pony might help that. Yes!

The pony arrived, and I named him Bucephalus. I was on my way.

"Did you hear what I said? It should make you happy, no?" Zanski was obviously expecting more of a response than he was getting.

I snapped back to the present. "Oh yes! I can't wait! An adventure with you!"

"Calm yourself, Little One. All in due time." He slipped his hand under my T-shirt and guided me to my feet. "It seems so long since I have held you." He led me toward the back of the room, away from the bright light of the work table.

I hesitated. "Aren't you afraid someone will come in? A guard?"

Zanski laughed. "Ah, the element of danger. That will make it all the more exciting."

MY NAME IS PARTHENIA GUTHRIE, but most people call me Parthi. The most exciting thing for me is that I am here at the Warner, one of the world's newest and best-known museums, in the final year of a two-year internship.

I think I was born wanting to be an archaeologist. My earliest memories, the good ones at least, go back to when I was about four, burying pennies carefully wrapped in velvet in a corner of the backyard so people in the far future would find them and know I was here—and when, because of course the pennies had dates on them. Even at that young age I seemed to have sensed how important it was to assign dates to artifacts.

I was a good student, and my reward was this internship at the Warner, a huge step in realizing my dream.

Everything about the Warner, from its name to its commanding location in the center of world-famous Beverly Hills, to my advisor, Roman Zanski, the senior antiquities curator of this new but mega-rich institution, has been designed to impress. Zanski is especially handsome, flamboyant, and brilliant. He's also the love of my life.

There is one problem: I am currently married, and so is he. That happened when I was eighteen and still searching for security and, without question, a male protector. Rumor has it that Zanski's wife is still somewhere in Russia, but we've never talked about it. I think he's ending it, but he doesn't like being nagged about anything, and especially about that. Things will work out. I have faith. The plan is that I will finish the internship, get divorced, and then he and I will be together.

Being a Warner intern is my chance to run with the big dogs of the museum world. There are three of us interns in the museum's antiquities department. The other two are males. Both from the East Coast. One is the trying-to-prove-himself son of a big-time archaeologist, and the other a rather sallow and too-serious Bostonian. Neither seems to have much use for me or for each other.

I have only gradually come to realize the misogyny rampant in my chosen profession. I know I am smart and motivated, but the chances of my being here on my own merits, without the connections of my husband and the protection of my mentor, are tragically dismal. This might change if a woman were to open a major tomb accompanied by splashy media coverage. Even though I am not holding my breath, I still have plans to be that woman.

The Valley of the Kings, Egypt
September 30, 1985

CHAPTER 2

It was warmer than usual for late September in the Valley of the Kings. Most of the tourists were gone and the afternoon was quiet, the sky clear blue.

Two young men sat at a table in a dusty mudbrick building that served as a tourist restaurant just outside the perimeter of the tombs. Neither seemed to have touched the plates of lamb and fava beans that sat before them, the oil and tomato sauce congealing. A fly buzzed. It went unnoticed. The pair were deep in conversation.

"I'll be leaving the dig and going back to the States on Tuesday. The Old Man is stuck on me going back to finish that internship at the Warner Museum. That's in Los Angeles."

The speaker stopped for a moment, studying his companion's face. The other man was about his own age, height, and build, but there the resemblance ended.

Grenville Hopkins, the speaker, was clearly American. Dressed in safari khakis, he carried himself with the ease of privilege. By contrast, his companion, Christos Laventis, was obviously a local, clad in the traditional djellabah favored by men of the desert, with a scarf loosely knotted around his neck. At second look, however, this young man was in no way a typical Egyptian. His skin, under the desert tan, was fair and his eyes a startling gold.

“That internship. Why does your father think it so important?”

Grenville’s smile could easily have been mistaken for a sneer.

“Connections, my friend, and to some extent, experience. And naturally, he’s right. With a Warner internship under my belt, all the other big museums will be fighting each other to offer me a permanent gig. I can see myself sitting pretty as a big noise in a posh museum. Wined and dined, fawned over by the press, and quoted in all the media. Not a bad life.”

“Are you the only person being given that opportunity, the stepping-stone to a secure career?””

“Actually, there are two others in the program, but no competition at all, really. One is a pasty-faced Harvard nothing, and the other is a girl whose only claim to fame is that she’s banging thc boss.”

“Banging?” Christos looked puzzled.

Grenville reached across the table and tousled his companion’s hair. “Fucking.”

Christos blushed. “I still have a lot of English to learn.”

Grenville changed the subject, a bit clumsily.

“You really mean a lot to me. I don’t know how to say it any other way. But I don’t understand you. You have an education. You’re fluent in English. Why did you come back here to this dirt hole anyway? There’s nothing for you here.”

Christos shook his head. “I have already told you. I have my reasons, but I can’t discuss them, even with you.”

“How can we be friends if you keep secrets from me?” There was a tinge of petulance in Grenville’s voice.

“It has nothing to do with you, really. I would tell you if

I could."

Grenville shrugged his shoulders. "OK then, let's change the subject. I'm curious to know more things about you: for example, what's your ancestry, and what religion do you follow?"

The golden eyes flashed a smile. "Those questions I can answer. My family is descended in a direct line from Ptolemy the First, who was one of Alexander the Great's generals, the one who ruled Egypt after Alexander's death. The Macedonians maintained rule under the Ptolemaic Dynasty until Augustus Caesar defeated Cleopatra, the last of that line. I suppose you might consider me a Macedonian."

"I didn't think you were an Arab, but I thought perhaps a Copt. Your name, after all, is a Christian one."

Christos smiled. "Christos is a common Greek name. My parents called me that so I would more easily assimilate into the Greek world I was intended to inhabit."

"So why did you not? I mean, not move to a more Greek world."

"That is something I cannot discuss. It should be enough to say that Christianity is definitely not my religion."

"Then what *do* you believe?"

The tall young man thought a moment. "If you must put a name to it, you might say my family and I worship as Alexander did: a belief in all the gods."

"That covers all the bases, I guess. But to change the subject: as long as you'll be here, you can do something for me."

As he spoke, he ran his fingers suggestively along the length of his companion's thigh.

Christos winced at the touch but kept his body steady and his voice neutral. "Anything."

Grenville smiled. One of the things that drew him to this exotic creature was his compliance. That, and the fact that no matter how he tried to strip it away, there was always that aura of mystery.

"I have a feeling the Old Man is close to finding something."

Christos caught his breath and waited for Grenville to continue.

"I've seen it over and over again for as long as I can remember. It's as if he can smell a tomb or anything else juicy. He acts in the same way he has been for the last couple of weeks: moody and sort of in another world. Then one day he just walks out into the desert, and bam, there it is. Just like it's been waiting for him or something. The find of the century."

Grenville was referring to his well-known father, the archaeologist Benjamin Hopkins, who was the darling of the society pages, famous for the number of Egyptian tombs he had discovered in places that had eluded previous excavators.

"And . . . ?" his companion prodded.

Grenville smiled. "You know how I loathe being under the family's financial thumb. I was thinking if he does find another tomb we could, well . . ."

Here he hesitated, not quite sure how to phrase what he was about to say. "Well," he repeated. "There's a lot of stuff in those tombs, and I know people in Europe who pay big money for that kind of thing. We could, um, rip off a few baubles that the Egyptian government would never miss . . ."

Christos did not reply.

Grenville continued, "Look, Christos, you won't have to do anything but watch my old man, and if he turns up anything good and for some reason you can't reach me, just get in touch with this guy."

He reached into the inner pocket of the safari jacket that was draped over the back of his chair. He pulled out an index card with a name and telephone contact neatly printed on its face. He handed it across the table.

"He'll do the rest. He does it all the time."

"Does what?" Christos asked. He knew the answer but wanted to hear how Grenville would explain it.

"Smuggles the stuff out of here and sells it abroad, of course."

Christos looked dubious. "It's against the law to take antiquities out of the country, I suppose you know."

Grenville laughed. "That's where this guy is a genius. Paints the antiquities to look like tourist crap and sails through customs."

Christos remained silent.

"Well, what do you say? With the kind of money we'd make, I could bring you to the States. You'd like that, wouldn't you?"

"Who *wouldn't* like to see America?"

Grenville rose and slapped Christos on the back. "All settled, then. Let's get out of here. I know a smashing place to watch the sunset."

The Valley of the Kings, Egypt
October 23, 1985

CHAPTER 3

Benjamin Hopkins had been excavating in the Valley of the Kings for so many seasons that he thought of this rock-strewn landscape as home. When he returned each year, he greeted "El Quorn," the pyramid-shaped mountain that seemed to guard the tomb sites, as an old friend. Its similarity to the Great Pyramids of Giza made it clear to him why the Pharaohs of the New Kingdom had chosen this spot to hide their last resting places.

Hopkins, from his pith helmet and safari jacket to his custom-made boots, exuded the aura of an archaeologist created by Hollywood's central casting. So much so that he was often called a real-life Indiana Jones. This comparison made the Harvard-educated Hopkins wince. In his opinion the cinematic hero was nothing but an unkempt pretty boy.

But to stop at Hopkins' appearance would be selling the well-known excavator far short. Over and above the impressive outer trappings, he possessed the *x* factor that separates the successful from the not-so-successful in his world: he found things.

No one has ever explained this phenomenon, and indeed it was a phenomenon, but time after time it happened: two archaeologists could be searching in areas of proximity, and one would consistently come up with a treasure while the other went empty-handed. Hopkins explained it this way: tombs were like shipwrecks; they were found only when they wanted to be.

The canny archaeologist was not aware exactly why he had returned to a previously and exhaustively excavated spot this season, but he had the strong gut feeling that there was still more to be found.

This afternoon he sat in his tent, pitched close to the excavation area, and sipped his usual Earl Grey. Mustafa, the excavation cook, hovered close to his elbow, teapot at the ready, waiting for his employer's nod for a refill.

Hopkins raised his hand, "No more, thank you, Mustafa. I think I'll go over to the dig site and have one more look around, now that it's a bit cooler," he said in Arabic.

Mustafa nodded and replaced the teapot on the tray as he watched his employer rise, remove his jacket from the peg at the door of the tent, and walk out into the afternoon desert sun.

Hopkins' steps led him to the entrance of a semi-royal tomb he had opened several seasons ago. The tomb itself would now be empty, its contents long since removed to the Cairo Museum, but he felt himself drawn toward it anyway.

As he entered the tomb, he noticed how the temperature suddenly cooled. As he walked slowly down the stone corridor toward the antechamber, he paused for a moment, attracted by the activity of a small dung beetle that was squeezing its body into a crevice in the rock wall.

The tomb had been dug into solid limestone, so cracks of any kind were minimal. Hopkins watched the determined creature inching its way into the rock wall. Then his attention turned to the crack itself. It was far too precise to have been made by nature. He ran his hand along its perimeter and traced the outline of a rectangle a little more than five feet high and about three feet wide.

Heart beginning to beat a little faster, he took a pocketknife from his jacket and inserted the blade into the crack. The knife slid in. Not much, but enough to tell Hopkins he had something. He was starting to sweat now, despite the coolness of the tomb.

He ran to fetch the *fellahin* who should be close by, washing potsherds under the supervision of Randall Powderly, the British excavation assistant.

POWDERLY WATCHED as his superior ran toward him. "Something's going on," he thought. He put down the rim of a broken bowl he had been examining, waiting for Hopkins to come near enough to speak. The young Englishman's first thought was a snake or scorpion bite, but he abandoned that idea as soon as he saw the excitement on his employer's face. This had to be something very different.

"I think I've found something! Bring the men and something to move a rock. And hurry it up. Follow me. I need to get this done before we lose the light," he instructed Powderly.

"How many men do you need?"

In contrast to Hopkins' previous excavations, which employed more than a hundred people, this one relied on only five local men to do all the heavy lifting. With no definite site mapped out, this season was only an exploratory mission, requiring a minimum staff.

"These will do," Hopkins replied, indicating the men washing the potsherds.

"*Yallah, yallah!*" Hopkins, unusually agitated, punctuated this order with a gesture toward the pile of picks and shovels that were lying on the ground nearby.

Walking rapidly back toward the entrance to the tomb, the two Europeans had a chance to exchange a few words. "I think it might be an ancillary tomb chamber connected to the old one," Hopkins volunteered. "I think I have just found the door."

"Good show!" exclaimed Powderly. This would be the first time he had witnessed a major find. He quickened his pace to keep up with Hopkins' long strides.

When they arrived at the tomb corridor, Hopkins instructed the men to pry away the stone that he was sure would lead him to another great New Kingdom burial chamber—undisturbed, he hoped.

As the laborers inserted strong picks into the crack in the stone, both Hopkins and Powderly held their breath.

It came away with little resistance, but instead of a passageway, what the great rock had been hiding was a sort of niche into which was wedged a single mummy. A mummy naked except for an elaborate golden mask.

Hopkins and Powderly stood still for a moment while their brains computed what they were seeing.

"This is him!" was all Hopkins could manage. He had recognized the deep-set eyes and flowing locks of Alexander the Great. The mask was somewhat stylized, but still, there was no mistaking the subject.

"This guy looks as though he's been through a few rough

patches," Powderly observed, running his eyes over the soiled linen wrappings that didn't quite cover the whole body. Wisps of the linen dangled from the chest, and the toes were exposed. "I'm guessing you mean that this mask points to him being the great Alexander himself, but isn't this a weird place to have buried him?"

Hopkins replied with more than a hint of condescension, "This isn't a burial, per se. Actually, it must be a reburial. Egyptian priests were known to have removed royal mummies from their original tombs to protect them from being vandalized by robbers."

"So I guess this means those stories about Alexander being buried as a mummy are true," Powderly observed.

Ignoring him, Hopkins carefully removed the mask from the mummy. "This will be safer with us." He covered it with his safari jacket, carrying it in front of him like a waiter balancing a tray of champagne. He headed toward the outer entrance. "Have the men put the stone back in place, and, for God's sake, make sure they understand to keep their mouths shut. Tell them I'll give them extra *baksheesh*. You and I will talk about breaking this news later."

Powderly nodded as he watched the three workmen lift the heavy stone and tap it gently back into place.

"WHERE DO YOU SUPPOSE the actual tomb is?" Powderly asked later when he and Hopkins were seated in the main tent. Hopkins always insisted on a formal evening meal complete with crystal, candlelight, and proper linens. A visitor peering at this spectacle set in the stark landscape of the Valley of the Kings would imagine himself sent back in time to the 1920s instead of the more casual 1980s. But that was of course how Benjamin Hopkins thought of himself: an intrepid and elegant discoverer of great things in the manner of his predecessors.

Hopkins picked up his wine glass, examined its contents in the candlelight, then took a sip. “It doesn’t matter where the damn tomb is or isn’t. I have Alexander, and that’s all anyone is going to care about.”

“Yes, of course. But, sir, exactly what are you planning to do about that?”

Hopkins thought a moment. “Good question, my man. The answer is: nothing at the moment. I need time to think this through and decide the best way to break this news to the world. Of course, the bigwigs in Cairo will have to be involved, but I’ll be damned if I’m going to let them take all the credit for this. Arrogant bureaucrats.”

“So we’re just going to do nothing?” Powderly questioned.

“Yes, that’s the plan. For now.”

THE VALLEY OF THE KINGS, EGYPT
The same day

CHAPTER 4

CHRISTOS LAVENTIS HAD SPENT THE BETTER PART of the past three weeks thinking and rethinking his relationship with the American. Now that Benjamin Hopkins' son had returned to the States there was indeed much to think about.

The friendship had begun as a way for Christos to maintain a close connection with the excavation the elder Hopkins was conducting here in the Valley of the Kings, this one much too close to the sacred resting spot of Alexander the Great. In fact, the presence of the foreign excavation team prevented everyone in the Laventis family from sleeping soundly.

What Christos had not revealed to Grenville, despite the latter's countless prodding, was the centuries-old secret that preordained he would remain in this remote area for the rest of his life.

The Laventis family was almost pure Macedonian, descended from one of the loyal followers of Alexander himself. Their duty was to guard the remains of the great ruler for all eternity, in a line of succession that passed from father to son or closest relative, male or female. No outsider could ever know this, or where Alexander now lay.

Christos himself had fallen into his current position as

guardian by default: his older brother, who normally would have been tasked with guarding Alexander, had been killed in a military training mission five years ago, forcing Christos, who was then in medical school, to return to the desert and take up the family mandate.

Visiting with Grenville almost daily at the dig site had provided the perfect cover to watch what the father was doing, and thus make sure the sacred burial was left undisturbed. But that convenience came with its own set of complications.

Despite the American's great charm, Christos had always sensed something disturbing about Grenville. As the weeks wore on, it had become obvious that the relationship was headed in an uncomfortable direction, for Christos at least. While he had no moral or religious scruples against same-sex intimacy, not being either a Christian or a Muslim, something troubling about Grenville himself made the golden-eyed man uncomfortable.

Grenville's request, basically an order, that he patrol the dig site for saleable antiquities was nothing short of repugnant. Stealing from both the dead and one's own father was totally abhorrent to someone like Christos, who held duty to the family sacred.

Christos therefore had no intention of helping Grenville smuggle even a potsherd out of the dig. Yet he continued to watch the excavation closely, for his own reasons. With Grenville no longer a cover for his repeated visits to the dig site, Christos forged a friendship with the camp cook, Mustafa.

It was this vigilance that brought him tonight to the communal excavation staff tent set somewhat apart from the more comfortable accommodation occupied by Hopkins and his assistant.

As Christos drove to the camp the desert night was, although warm, pitch-black, illuminated only by stars winking in a clear sky. The headlights of the aged Land Rover alerted the tent's occupants to his arrival. Mustafa hurried outside to greet him, shielding his eyes from the glare.

"*Marhaba! As-salaam alaikum!*" He shook the visitor's hand warmly. "Come inside, please."

Christos followed the cook inside the tent, where the other men were sitting cross-legged on the bare floor. He took a bottle of the local anise-flavored liquor from a bag he carried over his shoulder and placed it on the floor in the center of the circle of men. They eyed it eagerly.

"Ah," said Mustafa. "This *is* a treat. I will get glasses and we shall toast. It is a perfect evening to do so."

Christos looked up sharply. "And why is that?" he asked.

Mustafa quickly tried to cover his gaffe. He and the others had just been discussing the strange mummy Hopkins had found in the rock wall that afternoon, but they had been warned by the master not to mention it to anyone. With the promise of *baksheesh* on the table, no one wanted to expose the secret find. "Nothing in particular. I just meant a visitor is a special occasion."

"But I visit often," Christos probed. "Why should this evening be different?"

Mustafa had no answer, so he busied himself with pouring a generous amount of the clear liquor into each glass. In general Muslims do not drink alcohol, but this was a rule often broken, he felt, especially when the alcohol was free.

"*Fisehatak!*" Each man drained his glass in a single swallow.

"Ah, that is good!" Ibrahim, one of the laborers, sighed, clearing his throat.

"Please, have another," Christos urged. No one refused.

The night wore on, the bottle emptied, and the tongues loosened.

The golden-eyed man was careful not to drink as much as the others. "I must be careful driving back," he explained. "My car is old and the road is dangerous."

His companions nodded in agreement.

"What were you saying earlier about this being a special evening?" Christos reframed his original question when he sensed the men had drunk enough to abandon discretion.

His question brought giggles from Mustafa and two of the men. They looked from one to the other.

"What harm to tell him?" Mustafa asked. "After all, the effendi will never know."

No one disagreed—actually two of the men had already nodded off—so Mustafa continued. "Professor Hopkins discovered a mummy today, a very special one. Not in a tomb but stuffed into the rock."

Christos felt a cold chill pass through his body, and he could feel his heart begin to race. "Is that all?" he managed to ask.

Mustafa, who had a gift for the theatrical, threw up his hands in a dramatic gesture. "No! The rest of the story is even more interesting. The mummy was wearing a golden mask, and nothing else. Very strange! The effendi thinks it's not a Pharaoh or even an Egyptian. A famous Greek, I think." He stopped for a moment, waiting for Christos' reaction.

So this is it.

The event he had been fearing for so long had at last come

to pass. For centuries the great Alexander had rested in safety, nestled into the rock, carefully watched by a long succession of loyal countrymen. But now, on Christos' watch, it had all come crashing down.

Mumbling something about having to get up early in the morning, the golden-eyed man took leave of the tipsy laborers and made his way back the way he had come over the dark road to the village.

He now had a frightening and unpleasant task before him.

The Valley of the Kings, Egypt
October 24, 1985

CHAPTER 5

A potato might not seem like much of a murder weapon, but for the tall man with the golden eyes, it was perfect. From that first moment the night before when Mustafa had relayed his story of Hopkins' find of the magnificent mummy, his brain had snapped into overdrive.

He had to do two things and do them quickly: the first order of business would be to make sure that news of the find, as well as the find itself, would never reach beyond the confines of the small excavation camp. Secondly, he had to return the mask to Alexander.

Mustafa had not specifically mentioned it, but it stood to reason that Hopkins would have removed the precious mask and secured it in his tent. There was no way he would have permitted such a spectacular treasure out of his sight or his hands.

Last week Christos had roasted the most recent batch of potatoes, tightly encased in foil covers, and carefully stored them underneath a pile of dirty clothes, where he left them in peace to generate the toxin that was so potent that a mere bite of food infused with it would cause death. It was a simple process to create the poison: all that was needed was the host, in this case the potatoes, an airtight condition, and two or three days at a temperature that was neither excessively hot nor too cold. Nature would do the rest.

Like the other potatoes before them, roasted each week since the excavation team had arrived several months ago, he had expected these to remain in their hideaway until they shriveled and were dumped in the garbage. Not so this batch. These were destined for greater things.

Contemplating what he was about to do, Christos began to shake. Although he was a young man, he was usually calm and self-possessed beyond his years. The shaking seemed out of character, but then, he had never killed before, and, in truth, wasn't looking forward to the deed.

If only fate had dealt him a different hand, he would be a physician today, and his brother would be faced with this duty. But Georgos' helicopter had crashed into the desert, and Christos was left to clean up the mess Hopkins had created. There was no use lamenting that now. He had a duty to perform.

Hopkins, Professor Benjamin Hopkins, Grenville's father, was obviously the principal target. He was expendable enough. Christos didn't care for him much more than his son did. He was a flamboyant, arrogant man who had the personal means to fund his own excavations, and unfortunately, for Christos at least, he also had that inexplicable knack for finding tombs. The serious young man had to credit the foreigner with that. In previous years he had uncannily unearthed four semi-royal tombs practically under the noses of his fellow archaeologists. Both young men, however, had sensed that this time Hopkins was about to unearth a treasure so wonderful that it would make all his other finds irrelevant. Not a moment could be lost.

THE FOLLOWING MORNING, Christos rose early and prepared the potato salad carefully in the Greek manner, with plenty of olives and garlic, and enough feta cheese to disguise any possible off-taste of the potatoes.

It actually looked quite appetizing, he thought, with no detectable scent betraying its lethal contents. He placed the pan carefully on the seat of the Rover, steadying it with his right hand as he drove with his left.

He arrived at Hopkins' campsite just as the sun was climbing above the sand. Mustafa was stoking an outdoor fire in preparation for the daily cooking.

"This is something special from the restaurant: Professor Hopkins' favorite salad. I thought it might be a nice way to honor the special find. I brought enough for the workers, too. And you, of course."

Mustafa took the flat aluminum pan that was held out to him. He pushed the tinfoil covering aside and was about to dip his index finger into the mixture when Christos stopped him. "No, my friend, the first bite must be for the master. It would be bad luck otherwise."

Mustafa shrugged. "If you say so. Do you have time to stay for tea?"

Christos shook his head. "Sadly, I must get back to work. We will visit tomorrow."

With those words, he climbed back into the aged Land Rover, waited for it to sputter to a start, and headed it back along the dirt trail toward the village.

The Valley of the Kings, Egypt
October 26, 1985

CHAPTER 6

Christos knew something had gone wrong with his plan when Powderly, Hopkins' assistant, sped into town in the excavation jeep early the next morning. He was hysterical, demanding to use the restaurant telephone, the only one within one hundred miles. He was also alive. That should not be. If things had gone according to plan, everyone at the excavation site would be dead by now.

Without calling attention to himself, Christos listened to the call the Englishman was making. He was not sure who was on the other end of the line, but the drift of the conversation was very clear: Hopkins, the cook, and three of the workers had taken sick in the night. At first it was stomach cramps, vomiting, and severe diarrhea. However, toward morning, all five had begun gasping for breath. Powderly said he had done what he could for them, then rushed for help.

By the time the local medical personnel, such as it was—an elderly doctor and his youngish daughter—arrived, the original five victims were dead, and the remaining two workers beyond help.

The deaths were attributed to accidental food poisoning. That Powderly had escaped was explained by the fact that he detested potatoes, and therefore had not eaten any of the salad. From the assassin's point of view, that was more than a bit of bad luck. However, no one seemed to be asking about the source of the potato salad, assuming it had been prepared by the cook. So that at least was one bright spot in Christos' gloomy day.

He would have to come up with another plan to dispose of Powderly, the last witness to the discovery of the mask. But first he had to get the mask.

DESPITE REASONABLE EXPLANATIONS for the outbreak of botulism, rumors of a curse, like those that had plagued foreign archaeologists before, quickly echoed through the valley. Therefore, no one would find it strange if the sole survivor of the mass deaths left abruptly.

Given the rocky road and the Rover's age, Christos drove as quickly as he could to the excavation camp, where he found everything to be eerily silent. Cautiously he entered the main tent of the complex, where he was surprised to find Hopkins' elaborate silver tea service and expensive china in their usual place just inside the opening flap. He had thought these would be the first things removed by looters. The fact that they were untouched spoke much more to the primitive fear of supernatural reprisal than to any moral scruples. After all, in Egypt ever since the deaths associated with the opening of Tutankhamun's tomb, any sudden death surrounding an excavation was regarded as the work of some ancient curse, and everything attached to the unfortunate victims was best left alone.

That tent appeared to be just as it was when Hopkins' lifeless body had been carried away. The cot was still covered with soiled and rumpled sheets. A sweat-stained pillow had fallen to the floor. Christos' eyes darted around the canvas enclosure. In one corner an armoire looked promising.

He quickly scanned its contents: two leather suitcases, three pairs of boots, various items of safari clothing, and a pair of binoculars—but no mask. Nor was the mask to be found on or around the carved wooden desk, or in the miscellaneous cardboard boxes of small finds, mostly potsherds, that were stacked beside it. There was nowhere else to look. With a buzzing in his head, the man steadied himself and exited the tent. He entered the slightly smaller canvas structure adjacent to the one he had just vacated. This one, presumably Powderly's, was, as he had feared, empty of all personal items.

The buzzing in his head louder, and his hands sweating, he was forced to accept the obvious: Powderly had taken the mask with him. The logical place he would go was Cairo, the largest nearby city. Christos would follow and take care of him there.

Cairo, Egypt
October 27, 1985

CHAPTER 7

Randall Powderly knew time was of the essence. He was not as dense as Hopkins had assumed. To the contrary, he was uncannily perceptive. On the seven-hour drive to Cairo, he kept looking in the mirrors at the empty road behind him. Call it a hunch, but he was convinced the deaths at the excavation camp were no accident, and certainly not the result of any curse. Someone else must know about the mask, and that someone was obviously willing to kill to get it. He had no doubt that he himself had also been targeted as a victim, and only the sheer luck of a finicky appetite had saved him. He shuddered. But for that, he too might now be waiting alongside Hopkins for transport out of the desert in a body bag. He felt little emotion for Hopkins' death: the man had paid him poorly and bullied him constantly.

Powderly thought about the mask nestled in his dirty laundry. Alone at the excavation site, he had recognized the chance of a lifetime, and his decision to steal the mask was quick and surgical. It was obvious that in his position, Grenville would have done the same thing. In Hopkins' tent, the mask lay carefully cradled on a pile of bedsheets. He had not noticed earlier how beautiful it was. Even a young man like Powderly who was not given to emotion could not help but be affected by its presence.

The drive gave him time to figure out exactly what he was going to do once he got to Cairo. The thought that he was a thief never crossed his mind. The mask he carried was worth a fortune, and all he had to do was get it to Geneva, the clearinghouse for illegally excavated antiquities. And fast, before whoever might be coming after him could close the distance between them.

Grenville Hopkins had shared Powderly's disdain for the elder Hopkins, and during the weeks the archaeologist's son was a visitor to the dig, the two younger men had, on several occasions, sat up long after the older man had gone to bed, drinking his imported wine and taking turns imitating his pompous attitude. A favorite skit was a scene at the dinner table, with no one permitted to raise a fork until the master picked up his.

During one of those late-night drinking bouts the conversation had turned in the direction of the antiquities trade and how ridiculous it was to warehouse all those valuable objects in the bowels of the Cairo Museum, never to be seen again. Any scrap from an Egyptian tomb went for big money in the private sector, so how much better to circulate them among those who could appreciate them—and pay for them.

Grenville had mentioned an art student he knew in Cairo who ran a profitable business disguising antiquities with a coat of gaudy paint and smuggling them into Switzerland as touristy baubles. He had gone as far as writing on a scrap of paper the smuggler's contact information as well as that of the Swiss dealer who sold the goods once they were safely out of Egypt—miraculously, Powderly had kept it.

Grenville had never asked Powderly directly to pilfer objects from the excavation site, but it didn't take a rocket scientist to decipher his subtext. The young Englishman smiled to himself. Grenville would have no part of this deal.

STAYING AT MENA HOUSE in Cairo would be a nice bit of luxury after the spartan accommodations at the dig site, but Powderly forced himself to be practical. A hot spot for tourists would be the first place his pursuers, whomever they might be, would look for him.

The Englishman sighed, thinking of the soft beds and the swimming pool at the Mena but, knowing that would be the first place a pursuer would look for him, he settled himself in an out-of-the-way clean but nonspectacular establishment close to the Khan el-Khalili souk, his next stop before catching a plane to Geneva.

If someone had told him two days ago, back in the Valley of the Kings, that he would be here today, checking into a one-star hotel with the golden mask of Alexander the Great tucked into his duffle, Powderly would not have believed him.

But this chance was too good to pass up. A once-in-a-lifetime way to make sure he never again had to play babysitter to the likes of Hopkins. Refined and somewhat unremarkable, Powderly was not a born thief. But here he was. There was no going back. The moment he had driven away from the dig with the mask, the die was cast.

Powderly stopped outside the hotel, his eye on a rack of shopping bags for sale on the sidewalk. They were made of burlap, and most were embroidered with scenes of pyramids and the mask of Tutankhamun. The colors were bright and garish, and just what he needed.

He selected a large one with sturdy handles, paid without haggling, and climbed the short flight of stairs to the hotel lobby, taking care not to bump the soft piece of luggage against the pink-washed wall.

Inside his room he gently removed the precious mask from the confines of the duffle and transferred it to the shopping bag. He did not want to risk leaving it in the room, so he nestled it under his arm. He was ready for shopping.

The Khan el-Khalili, the largest and most famous souk in Cairo, sold everything. It was a must-do for every traveler to this part of Egypt, a shopping experience like no other.

The moment Powderly entered its confines, the intense aroma of the cardamom that flavored the Arab coffee assailed his nostrils. Brightly colored shirts and dresses flapped merrily on rope lines at eye level. Men dressed in white djellabahs beckoned him into darkened shops, and shoppers of every nationality bargained for goods. All around him his senses were bombarded with the sounds, smells, and sights of the Middle East.

It occurred to him that any one of the throng of people, Egyptian and foreign, who brushed elbows with him could be the person who would be pursuing him and the mask. He held the shopping bag and its well-hidden contents a bit closer to his body. He needed to find what he was looking for and leave this place where he felt so vulnerable.

He had no idea what the Arabic word for *paint* was, but, in a place like this, where so many languages were spoken, he suspected he would have no trouble locating a shop that sold artists' gouache paints. He was correct. With only one turn into an alley just off the central passageway of the souk he found what he was looking for: small jars of water-based paint in bright colors, and three brushes.

Powderly quickly made his purchases and hurried out of the souk. Instinct told him he did not have much time.

Back in his hotel room, the newly minted smuggler carefully removed the precious mask from the shopping bag and laid it on the floor. The thought of covering this glowing object with cheap and vile paint was an unpleasant one, but he didn't have much choice.

With quick strokes he covered the entire surface with a coat of gold paint, changing its appearance immediately from a breathtaking royal artifact to a mundane copy. For a finishing touch he took the smallest brush and copied the stylized eyes and eyebrows embroidered on the shopping bag to imitate those of Tutankhamun.

Powderly surveyed his handiwork. Grenville's contact could certainly have done a more convincing job, but there was no time, and involving no one else was a much wiser strategy in the long run.

THE FOLLOWING MORNING Powderly took a cab to the Cairo International Airport for the early flight to Geneva. He'd decided to leave the excavation jeep where it was on the street outside the hotel, where he hoped the local criminal element would make it their own. On the slim chance that did not happen, and the vehicle turned up in the legal sector, there was still nothing to worry about because the authorities would be expecting him to run from the scene of an ancient curse, not abscond with a national treasure.

He carried the mask in the shopping bag along with a fez, several strands of worry beads, and a couple of cheap T-shirts printed with the pyramids and the Sphinx. It was a convincing jumble of touristic treasures that he hoped would pass through customs without incident. Nonetheless, his heart was pounding as he presented the bag for inspection.

He was in luck. The agent barely glanced at the bag as he ushered him through the packed line of passengers, most of them Europeans returning from vacation.

Once on board the plane, the shopping bag carefully stowed under his seat, he allowed his breath to fully escape his chest. Then Powderly smiled to himself. If he'd known smuggling was this easy, he would have taken it up long before this. But no matter, this one coup would keep him fixed for some time.

For the first time he began to think about the actual sum the mask would fetch from the dealer in Geneva. By anybody's standards, this thing was unique, and therefore priceless. In the millions for sure. He had to weigh in the dealer's commission, which might be about forty percent, although that was just a random guess. Anyway, he was sure the mask would net him at least a million pounds, nothing to be sneezed at.

Cairo, Egypt
October 27, 1985

CHAPTER 8

The first day after Hopkins' murder, Christos the Mask Hunter had been certain of finding the fleeing assistant, Randall Powderly, and with him the mask. Even in a city the size of Cairo, the thief's obvious preliminary destination, an Englishman could be tracked down, if one knew the right people. And the golden-eyed man knew those right people.

However, by the time Christos reached the capital, the slippery fellow had already left the country. Christos' contacts were able to furnish him with the man's destination: Geneva. So, armed with a newly minted passport and a modest amount of cash supplied by his uncle, he took a flight the next day.

He was seated between two European ladies who appeared to be tourists returning from a holiday in the Middle East. Prior to takeoff, each deposited bulging carry-ons into the overhead bin. The Mask Hunter, who was carrying only a small satchel, politely crammed it into the farthest corner of the space. Neither woman thanked him. Both donned eye masks and settled themselves into as comfortable sleeping positions as were possible in tourist class.

Christos smiled to himself. He had no intention of sleeping. It was his first time in the sky. He looked past the hulk of his seatmate and down at the puffy white clouds that floated outside the small oval aircraft window. It was as though he was floating with them, separated from time and space. He was familiar with the concept of flight from TV shows and the weekly movies that were shown in the village. But those had not prepared him for this. This was extraordinary. It made him wonder why the Pharaohs of old had chosen to transport themselves to the realm of the gods in mere boats, when such a magical conveyance was so much more appropriate. How much they had missed, living so long ago. Alexander also. What would they all think if they could see him now, soaring so far above the earth? Or perhaps they could. Perhaps they were smiling. And perhaps Alexander himself, the mightiest of all the Pharaohs, was leading him on this wonderful journey. Despite his determination to savor every minute of the experience, when the flight attendant dimmed the lights in the cabin, he was lulled to sleep by the steady droning of the jet engines.

WHEN THE PLANE LANDED, he opened his eyes to a totally different landscape. Passengers were anxious to deplane but maintained a civilized order. Once outside, the cleanliness of the Swiss airport was dazzling. The man from the Valley of the Kings found himself propelled through a sea of grey and black well-tailored suits. For the first time he was aware of his own clothing that screamed he did not belong here, in this land of opulence and order. He noticed a child, clad in a miniature version of her mother's soft cashmere coat, staring openly at him.

Even her young eyes recognized that, although he had traded his customary djellabah for Western clothing, he still did not belong. The trousers and sleeves of the borrowed suit were too short, and the heavy-soled brown shoes only heightened the illusion that she was looking at some sort of alien scarecrow. Her mother quickly grabbed her hand and propelled her in the opposite direction from the offending sight. The man felt the pain of the outsider. Clearly the world was a larger place than he had ever imagined long ago when Cairo had represented the pinnacle of all things large and grand.

But he had no time to contemplate this new and frightening world. He needed to focus on the reason he had come to Switzerland. He followed the line of passengers hurrying in the direction of the sign marked *Étrangères.*

GENEVA, SWITZERLAND
October 28, 1985

CHAPTER 9

THE FIRST THING POWDERLY DID when his plane landed was to make a call to Irving Schott, the antiquities dealer.

According to Grenville, Schott was the man to do business with if one wanted to buy or sell important pieces, no questions asked. It was rumored he was connected to the Mafia and also provided a major source of exceptional antiquities for big-money private collectors and museums like the Warner in California. The dealer was reportedly pretty much immune from the law.

Schott answered the phone himself, both friendly and businesslike, polite but wary. “What can I do for you? And who may I ask referred you?”

“I have something fresh you might be interested in.”

Powderly had no intention of revealing anything prematurely that might point to the origin of the mask. He had been around the archaeological world long enough to know that using the term *fresh*, the code word in the antiquities world for a newly—and most often illegally—excavated object, would spark Schott’s attention.

Schott’s tone changed. “My gallery is always interested in purchasing special objects. When would I be able to see what you have?"

"Actually, I'm in the airport now."

"Oh, how convenient. Where are you coming from, and by the way, what did you say your name was?"

"Give me your address, and I'll be there in twenty minutes."

POWDERLY STOOD IN FRONT of Schott's upscale gallery on Rue du Rhône. The door was closed, and the sign BY APPOINTMENT ONLY discouraged browsers. He rang the bell. Schott answered it himself. He was very much as the Englishman had expected from Grenville's description: polished and intimidating.

"Mr. Sykes, I presume?"

Powderly had had the foresight not to give his real name on the phone. This transaction had to be fast—and anonymous. He nodded and followed Schott into the interior of the gallery. It looked much like other upscale galleries he'd visited. There were glass cases displaying Roman coins and clay lamps, and the perimeter was dotted with pedestals holding Greek and Roman pottery. Nothing remarkable. Nothing to alert the casual visitor to the fact that this was the abode of one of Europe's most notorious dealers in rare and stolen artifacts.

"Please come into my office and let me see what you have brought." There was mild interest but no eagerness in Schott's voice.

Powderly followed him into a well-lit, thickly carpeted room, furnished with Italian sofas and a wide glass coffee table.

"Sit down, please."

Powderly sat, placing the pyramid-emblazoned shopping bag at his feet. First, he removed the fez, then the worry beads.

Schott's eyebrows raised a notch. "Been shopping in Egypt, I see?"

"This seemed to be the best way to carry this artifact to you," replied Powderly, aware he was probably keeping Schott guessing whether he was just a buffoon or in fact a seasoned smuggler.

"Do you have a bathroom?" Powderly asked his host.

"You can freshen up in there," Schott informed his guest, gesturing to a door on the right.

Powderly picked up the bag and headed into the bathroom. He bent over the sink and began to scrub the mask with his hands. The sink filled with murky water, some of which spilled onto the tile floor.

"Have you got a rag or something? I'd hate to mess your linens," he called out.

"Yes, may I help in some way?" Schott asked politely, sounding a little concerned.

"If you'd like. Yes, that would be jolly good."

Schott's calculated demeanor slipped when he saw the glint of gold. He took a monogrammed hand towel from the side of the sink and handed it to Powderly. "Here, use this."

Powderly rubbed most of the remaining paint from Alexander's face.

The seasoned art dealer was clearly impressed. "May I?" he asked as he picked up the mask and headed back into the office.

"Be my guest. Look at it carefully. It's one hundred percent genuine."

"I can see that. Where did you get this?"

Powderly smiled the indulgent smile one gives to a child. "You know I can't tell you that."

"I'm not sure how you got this into the country. You should know that every piece I sell has to be first cleared by the people in charge of exports." He clearly did not mean the Department of Antiquities.

"This is my first time doing this," Powderly confessed, "and as long as we were not in Italy, I didn't think the Mafia would have to be involved."

Schott put a finger to his lips. "The first thing you need to learn, my young friend, is that we never use that word."

"What shall I call them then?"

"I usually refer to them as *facilitators*, for want of a better word."

"Fine, facilitators. Now can we get down to business? I'm leaving the country tomorrow, and I want to finish this matter up."

"Of course. I quite understand. Since you are in a hurry, let's get to the bottom line. What do you want for this mask? And do you have other objects from the tomb? I suspect you've located it, but there's been no mention of it in any of the news reports."

Powderly ignored the last question, replying, "One million sterling."

Schott removed his glasses and polished them as he spoke. "That's a lot of money. I would need to have a secure buyer before committing so much of my capital to one piece."

"We both know the Warner will jump on this in a flash. It's the find of the century."

"Agreed. But making the sale might take a bit of time. I could give you a down payment today, say fifty thousand pounds, and the balance payable to you when the deal is complete. Oh," he added, "there is absolutely no way I can offer more than five hundred thousand total."

That was not the number Powderly had hoped for, but he was in a hurry, and this was a fast sale.

"OK. Could you give me a receipt or something?"

Schott smiled. "Of course. Your name again?"

"Sykes, Jerome Sykes."

"Address?"

"I'll be traveling, but I'll be in touch with you."

Schott crossed the room and took a roll of bills from the safe. He counted them out as he handed them to the young man.

Powderly pocketed the bills along with the receipt the dealer handed him, and taking one last look at the golden mask on the table, he picked up his duffle and prepared to leave the gallery. "You may keep these," he offered, pointing to the shopping bag, the fez, and the worry beads.

Randall Powderly went directly to the hotel the airline employee had recommended. As soon as he was in his room, he kicked off his boots and flopped on the bed. In a few minutes he'd take a shower, go out for a good meal, and then think about leaving tomorrow for somewhere comfortable for a few weeks. Perhaps the south of Spain. He'd heard it was lovely at this time of year.

Rue du Rhône
Geneva, Switzerland
Five minutes later

CHAPTER 10

Irving Schott sat looking at the wonderful object in front of him. It was definitely Alexander the Great's death mask, but a death mask the likes of which he had never seen before. For one thing, it had clearly not been cast from the dead man's face as one might expect. It was larger than life size, made of much thicker gold, and suggested an Egyptian sarcophagus ornament rather than something from a Greek burial. Perhaps the stories were true, and Alexander had been laid to rest like an Egyptian Pharaoh.

Now that the tomb had been found—and this mask strongly suggested it had—and not by legitimate archaeologists, who knew what other wonders would be arriving on the market in the near future?

But he had calls to make. This deal had to be completed before word of the mask's existence leaked out. He reached for the phone and punched in a number he had on speed dial.

"Dr. Zanski's office," a chirpy female voice answered.

"Zanski, please. Schott calling from Geneva."

"Of course, Mr. Schott. How are you? I'll connect you right away."

Scott barely had time to light a cigarette before Roman

Zanski, curator of ancient art at the Warner Museum in Beverly Hills, came on the line.

"Irving, my friend, you never call me just to say hello. I think you have something for me?"

"You think correctly, Roman—this one makes the bronze you bought last year pale by comparison."

"Please continue. You know I am interested. What is it that you have?"

"The funerary mask of Alexander the Great."

There was silence on the other end of the line for a long moment, then Zanski replied.

"My friend, if what you say is true, this could be profitable for both of us. And the museum, of course."

Schott smiled to himself. Zanski, the old fox, would be demanding his kickback for securing the sale of the mask to the Warner. That was the way it worked with him. All the dealers knew that if they wanted to sell anything to the Warner they had to pay the curator his pound of flesh. It was a system that worked for everybody.

"Shall I send photos for you to show the trustees?"

"I think not this time, Irving. I would rather show the trustees the mask itself. Put it in front of those capitalist fools at the annual board meeting. It should be good propaganda for my yearly raise." He laughed.

"That sounds like just your kind of dramatic gesture, Roman, but I won't be able to let you take a piece this important out of Switzerland without a sizeable deposit."

"But of course! I'll bring my money man with me, and you shall have your security."

Schott, who himself operated largely outside the law, was

perpetually amazed by the convoluted way Zanski conducted business, but it always seemed to work. "All right. When shall I expect you?"

"Let me have two days and I'll be there."

"Very good. We'll meet at the Credit Suisse. I'm going to put this mask in the vault as soon as we're off the phone. It's much too valuable to keep here in the gallery."

"A very wise plan."

The call ended.

SCHOTT WAS MORE THAN SATISFIED with the call to the Warner. It promised a quick sale for the mask and quick money for him.

A tempting thought crossed his mind. The young fellow who had sold him the mask had none of the earmarks of a runner working for the organization. He probably hadn't come into Switzerland via Italy, either. That meant there was a good chance the syndicate knew nothing about this mask.

His arrangement with the many-tentacled crime family that controlled the flow of illegal antiquities in southern Europe was a long and profitable one on both sides. It ensured that all major antiquities sales were funneled through Schott's gallery. This worked well for both parties: Schott received access to the juicier fruits of illegal excavation and the Family a laundered end point for their wares.

The organization was powerful and tightly run. Crossing these people carried serious consequences. No, the risk of taking on this mask as a side deal away from the jurisdiction of the

Family was too great.

Irving Schott picked up his phone and dialed a number in Rome to a man he had never met, but who had been his designated contact for the past dozen years. He knew him only as Mario.

"Schott here," the dealer announced himself.

"Ah, my friend in Geneva. What can I do for you?" Mario's voice was warm and hearty.

"Have you heard anything about a Greek tomb being found? An important one. The tomb of Alexander the Great."

"What? You pull my leg, as the Americans say. No, I have heard nothing. How did you hear about it?"

Schott knew it was best to come totally clean. One could never be sure what the other side knew, and in this business, it was better to be safe. Healthier, also.

"Funny thing. An Englishman just walked in here and sold me Alexander's death mask."

"Just like that? Walked in and sold you such a thing? Did he say where he got it?"

"No, so I was wondering if you knew."

"My friend, if I knew of such a thing, I would be the one contacting you."

The Roman end of the telephone line was silent while Mario thought for a moment. "This could be very big business for all of us. I'll check all our runners and see if I can get any information. In the meantime, do you have a buyer for this piece?"

"The Warner curator will be here the day after tomorrow. They always want first crack at the newest pieces we find. I think part of their joy in acquiring an important object is the thrill of beating their fellow museums to the punch."

“A fast sale is always the best,” Mario added. “Before any governments get involved. That tomb should be filled with major pieces we can move for millions. I am liking this very much.”

“I am also. Now, to some business: how should we handle the financial part? I’ve always bought directly from you in the past, so your commission was taken care of on the front end. This time, since I’m the one in actual possession of the mask, let’s agree on a percentage right now so there will be no misunderstandings down the line.”

Mario deliberated, but finally answered, “We might consider that. What numbers do you have in mind?”

“I paid the Englishman fifty thousand pounds already and promised him another four hundred and fifty when the sale goes through. I calculate the Warner will pay somewhere in the neighborhood of three million US dollars, so the profit will be around two and a half million in US currency. So what if I pay you a million?”

“You paid so much? I’m expecting larger profits in the future when we locate the tomb this man is mining, and then the percentage will change.”

“Agreed.”

“One more thing,” Mario added. “There is a young man in our organization who we think has great promise. I’ll be sending him to work as an apprentice in your gallery. It would be good for him to learn all the steps in moving our product from ground to museum, and your gallery is an important link in that chain. He will be arriving in Geneva tomorrow. His name is Brazzi. I hope this is satisfactory to you?”

Schott knew he had no choice but to agree.

Warner Museum
Beverly Hills, California
Five minutes later

CHAPTER 11

Roman Zanski put down the telephone. He had a plan to maximize both his profit and his fame as a star-level curator. And keep the trustees off his back. One phone call would do it.

Barry Epstein always had ready cash and the need to make more. Zanski dialed his number and was just about to leave a message when Epstein picked up the phone.

Zanski did not bother with a formal greeting. "We need to go to Geneva right away."

Epstein, an ambitious twenty-something investment banker who supplemented his lavish lifestyle by bankrolling Zanski's risky antiquities ventures and sharing the profits, was used to this. "OK. I'm in. I suppose I need to buy the tickets?"

"That would be very kind."

Yeah, right, as though you ever paid for anything, Barry thought. Aloud he just grunted.

"I'll explain the details on the plane," Zanski continued. "Oh, and you should be prepared to bring at least two million dollars. This is a big purchase."

Barry gulped. "This had better be good. And I'm going to need a bigger cut this time."

"We'll discuss all that in good time," Zanski evaded.

The two men, colleagues but certainly not friends, agreed to meet at the airport the following day.

Barry Epstein's home
Malibu, California
Minutes later

CHAPTER 12

Barry Epstein returned the telephone to its cradle. Zanski was up to his old tricks again. No telling what this one would involve. Barry liked to think of himself as a bad-boy adrenaline junkie, but this Russian had him beat in that area for sure.

He absentmindedly tapped his finger on the desk, thinking back to the caper the two of them had pulled last year selling that fake marble Athena to the museum. A low rumble was already beginning to be heard in the scholarly world about that one. The truth was going to come out sooner or later. That in itself should make the old boy more cautious, but he seemed to be heading in the opposite direction. Also, it didn't sound like he was even telling the museum where or why he was going this time. Not a good sign.

Intuition told Barry this trip to Switzerland was not going to end well. But hell, it might be fun along the way.

He reached across the desk and buzzed his secretary: "Mandy, book me two first-class seats to Geneva tonight. And then a hotel. Something on the lake. Two suites."

"Yes, sir." Barry liked Mandy. Never asked any questions. Just did her job.

The next order of business was to tell his wife, Parthi, that he would be out of town for a few days. Not that she was likely to even notice he was gone. Ever since she'd taken on that internship at the Warner she'd been buried in some pile of potsherds or other. He preferred not to imagine what part of Zanski she was also buried in. But he called anyway and left a message with her answering service.

That about took care of things. He'd throw a few items in a bag when he left the office, then off to fun and adventure with the Mad Russian.

Barry slapped the side of his head. "Almost forgot," he mumbled to himself, then buzzed Mandy again. "I'll need a cashier's check for two million before I leave the office."

"No problem, sir. I'll have it at my desk when you leave today." Her voice conveyed the impression that this was an everyday request. Of course, it was not.

Warner Museum
Beverly Hills, California
Later the same day

CHAPTER 13

I listened to Barry's telephone message with equal parts of exhilaration and annoyance. After four years of marriage, I was used to my husband's frequent out-of-town trips, usually in pursuit of fast money or a faster young thing, often both. Yet a part of me mourned for what might have been. Perhaps if we hadn't been so young, perhaps if Barry had known the meaning of fidelity . . . perhaps if Zanski hadn't come along. Who knew? Yet even I could not deny a failed marriage at the age of twenty-two was nothing to be proud of.

But the exhilaration! Barry's message had said he would be out of town for a few days, was unsure of his exact return, but would call and let me know. That gave me at least one, and most likely two, delicious nights with Zanski.

I lost no time in running to his office to tell him the good news. His door was closed, but Fiona, his secretary, hardly looked up as she nodded for me to enter. She'd become accustomed to my frequent unannounced visits to my mentor, and whether or not she suspected what was going on, she never let on.

Zanski was shuffling papers around the teetering stack of books and papers that was his filing system.

"Guess what?" I bounced across the room and stood by his desk. "Barry will be gone for a couple of days, starting tomorrow. Your place or mine?"

"Ah, Little One, such a wonderful thought, but I too am committed to being away."

He obviously saw the disappointment on my face because he continued, "This is just the opportunity I have been waiting for to put those insufferable trustees in their places." He raised both hands to the sky, "Thank you, Great Zeus!"

I wasn't excited, but I pretended to be. "Tell me about it."

"I cannot do that, my dearest, but when I return, you will be so happy. I am on the edge of something great."

"Can you at least give me a hint?"

He shook his head like a patient father refusing to reveal the hiding place of a Christmas present. "No, not a thing. You will just have to be patient, which I realize is a challenge for one your age."

I turned my face away, hoping to hide the redness I felt creeping into my cheeks.

Zanski stuffed a few papers into his briefcase and snapped it shut.

"Now, my dear, I am afraid I must excuse myself. You will understand everything in a few days."

He kissed me, but I felt he was already gone to wherever it was that he was headed in such a hurry.

International Airport
Geneva, Switzerland
The same day

CHAPTER 14

Tracing Powderly to his hotel room had been easy: the customs official was a middle-aged lady susceptible to Christos' exotic looks. He was a handsome man despite his inelegant attire. His hair was dark, but not black, and his skin would have been fair had he not spent his entire life in the desert sun. Apart from his height, which was far greater than that of his countrymen, there were those amazing golden eyes, reminding the woman of a hungry leopard.

Preening girlishly, the lady customs official was most willing to check her records from the previous day and come up with the information Christos needed.

When the Mask Hunter arrived at the Englishman's hotel, he sensed his streak of good luck had ended. Once more he was too late.

He would always remember the sneering look of recognition on the young Englishman's face when he opened the door.

"I know you. You're that filthy peasant who was always hanging around the dig. How did you get here? Get out this minute before I call hotel security."

Odd, the Mask Hunter remembered thinking, how the thief had seemed unaware of the danger in front of him.

"Where is it?"

"What are you talking about?"

Christos kept his voice calm and soothing, like a cobra hypnotizing a mouse. "I need to take the mask back to its home," he said simply.

As Powderly quickly realized that the man of the desert who now stood in front of him was someone to be contended with, he put on a show of false bravado. "You're too late, my man; it's safe where the likes of you will never get it."

Christos seethed inside, despite his outward calm. His instinct was to end the matter right now: beat the insolent dog to death. But he restrained himself, for the moment. "If you will just please give it to me, I will leave here and bother you no more."

It was then that Powderly recognized the menace in his visitor's eyes, and he drew back, just a step. "Try your luck at Credit Suisse. I'm sure whatever primitive weapons you're carrying will be very effective in opening a bank vault. Oh, yes, and I would not lose any time if I were you. I've already sold the damn thing, and it'll soon be on its way to an American museum."

How could all that have happened, and so fast? The wheels of greed certainly turned rapidly.

There was only one thing to be done. Christos turned and walked toward the door.

"I think I left my hat on the table," the Mask Hunter murmured as he turned back into the room.

As Powderly glanced in the direction of the console where he expected to see the hat, his foe quickly removed the coiled leather strap he carried in his pocket. A quick garotte to the smaller man's throat netted the intruder the assurance of his victim's future silence. The packet of bills in his luggage would make the ongoing quest for the mask more comfortable, even though its current location in a steel vault put it temporarily out of reach.

Boardroom, Warner Museum
Beverly Hills, California
October 28, 1985

CHAPTER 15

Twelve powerful men sat on both sides of a long conference table in the boardroom of the Warner Museum. Each man was a force in his own right, and together they composed a formidable union. Oddly, a much younger man occupied the chair at the end of the table, putting him in a command position in full view of each of the trustees.

The young man was Henry Templeton, an honors Harvard graduate, and one of the three future curators the Warner had selected for a two-year paid internship program in the area of ancient art. All three fell under the jurisdiction of Roman Zanski, the chief curator of antiquities.

Henry was a serious-looking young man of medium height with dark, wavy hair. He looked down at the notebook in front of him, obviously to avoid eye contact with the group.

The door was closed, and the secretary's chair was vacant. There would be no recording of this meeting. It would be as if it had never happened.

Galen Stonecraft, the museum director, opened the conversation. He addressed the uncomfortable young man.

"Mr. Templeton, or may we call you Henry?"

"Henry, please."

Stonecraft smiled in an attempt to put the youth at ease. "We need you to do something for us." He paused for a moment, as though unsure about whether he should go on. A few breaths firmed up his determination, and he continued, "But before I even tell you what it is, I must have your word that nothing we are going to tell you will leave this room."

Henry looked surprised. He hadn't known what to expect when the museum director had called him and asked him to meet with his colleagues later that day.

"Oh course, sir, you have my word."

"Very well then. I'll get right to it: you may or may not know that your advisor, Dr. Zanski, has for some time now been compromising the integrity of this institution in ways that can no longer be ignored."

He stopped momentarily, assessing Henry's reaction. When he was satisfied the young man's demeanor signified acceptance, he continued. "I do want to say up front that we all highly respect Dr. Zanski and the expertise he has brought to the Warner but, as I said before, actions of his have come to light, and they must be dealt with."

Henry nodded.

Stonecraft continued, "You may have heard rumors about the Athena being wrong . . ."

Wrong was the word museum people used when what they really meant was *fake.*

HENRY HAD INDEED HEARD those rumors. Just about everyone in the museum world had. Now the larger-than-life-sized marble statue of the goddess Athena that the Warner had purchased for a price exceeding five million dollars was on the brink of being outed as a forgery by the mainstream media.

Experts from New York, Rome, and Berlin had already voiced their doubts about the impressive piece of sculpture. It was only a matter of time before the world followed suit.

Henry wondered where this was all going.

Stonecraft explained, "As embarrassing as this is, there's more. The Italians are about to pounce on us about that head of Jupiter they claim was stolen from the dig in Morgantina." The museum director mentioned the name of a well-known archaeological site in central Sicily. "This red flag will point the press to more of Zanski's shenanigans, enough to bring this whole place down around our ears."

The older men nodded, looking grim. Henry could not help but look surprised.

Stonecraft drew a breath. "Now I'm coming to the crux of the problem, and it's something we have to take care of at once. It's the matter of the large influx of donations of totally insignificant objects that we have been receiving. That in itself would not be a problem, but the fact that Dr. Zanski has personally written receipts to the donors valuing them at ten times what they should be is most definitely our problem."

At this point Peter Metcalf, an oil executive and newly minted Warner trustee, entered the conversation. "If the IRS gets wind of this—that we're deliberately creating false paperwork to give donors larger tax cuts than is legal—we can kiss our tax-exempt status goodbye."

"And then we might just as well close our doors." Another trustee, a middle-aged man in a well-cut suit, someone Henry did not recognize, completed the director's thought.

Henry himself had wondered about this, but Zanski had passed the legal concerns off as "stupid capitalist nonsense," and who was he to question his mentor?

Henry sat quietly and waited for the next shoe to drop.

Stonecraft was back in the conversation. "I gather you interns type up those appraisals for Zanski. Am I right?"

Henry nodded, "Yes, sir."

"What I am about to say may come as a shock, but we need to find a way to get rid of Zanski before he sinks us, and we were hoping you could help."

"How could I do that, sir? Can't you just fire him?" As soon as the question was out of his mouth Henry realized how naïve it sounded.

"We tried that, and with a golden parachute, but the man's got an ironclad contract, and what appears to be a grudge against us, God only knows why."

"And you want me to do what?" Henry asked.

"I asked Zanski's secretary to search his office, but she wasn't able to find anything on those inflated appraisals anywhere. She's sure he's keeping them in that safe next to his desk. The problem is, she doesn't have the combination. We were hoping you do."

"Yes, I have that. And what exactly do you want me to do?" Henry had a good idea, but he wanted to hear it aloud.

"Get into that safe and see if there is anything we can use to hang the bastard." Henry noticed that during the relatively short space of this conversation, Zanski had gone from being referred to politely as "Dr. Zanski" to the present insult.

Henry thought a moment before answering. "I do need to ask you, why me? There are two other interns besides me who can get into that safe just as easily."

"We know, but Grenville Hopkins recently lost his father in a tragedy in Egypt, so we didn't want to put any more pressure on him. And as for the other intern, Parthenia Guthrie, well, she just wouldn't be a good candidate for this job."

Morton Paley, a bright-eyed octogenarian with an impish face and nothing to lose by ignoring political correctness, snorted derisively. "Whose bright idea was it to pick a female intern anyway? And to work for a dirty old dog like Zanski? We all know what's been going on there."

"This is the 1980s. Women have to be represented or all hell breaks loose," Stonecraft replied in a neutral voice.

"But couldn't somebody have found an ugly one somewhere?"

No one answered.

Henry was feeling more uncomfortable by the minute, anxious to be away from the room.

"When do you want this done?" Henry was above all else practical, and this was a practical question.

"Today, if possible. Zanski's out of the office for the next few days, who knows where or doing what, so this is our window of opportunity."

Henry gulped. So soon. Well, he had no choice. If he refused this "request" from the higher-ups, he was sure it would end his hopes for a career in the museum world.

He stood up. The men did the same, passing by where he was standing, and shaking his hand in turn.

"Good luck, my boy. We're counting on you." Stonecraft put his arm around Henry's shoulders as he guided him from the room.

Hallway outside the boardroom, Warner Museum
Beverly Hills, California
The same time

CHAPTER 16

I'd watched Henry as we sat on either side of the library. I observed both him and Gren often, knowing each of them would be on the lookout to take any opportunity that might raise their stock in the eyes of the museum's upper crust. This was a cutthroat place, and even though I had Zanski in my corner, I had to be vigilant. These two would like nothing better than to undermine my credibility as a scholar, or to do the same to each other.

Usually, Henry would be so absorbed in whatever it was he was reading that nothing less than an earthquake could cause him to look up. But today, something was different. He thumbed pages distractedly and looked at his watch incessantly. Something was surely afoot.

So when he finally closed the volume of Greek architecture and rose to leave the room, I was compelled to follow. Discreetly, of course.

His path led to, of all places, the boardroom. This could not be good. I saw him knock lightly on the door, which was immediately opened by none other than Galen Stonecraft, the museum's director. Henry entered and my heart sank.

There could be only one possible reason a lowly intern

would be welcomed into the inner sanctum of the higher-ups: they must know about me and Zanski and were about to throw me out and reassign my monograph to Henry.

They had obviously chosen a time when Zanski was away from the museum and would not be there to defend me.

There was no clause in my contract forbidding a relationship with my mentor, but perhaps it was understood? Were we doing something illegal? Would my plans to become an archaeologist and discover Bucephalus' tomb fall dead on the boardroom floor?

I needed to think. And wait to find out how bad things were—but that would not be easy. And I also needed to talk to Zanski. Immediately.

Zanski's office, Warner Museum
Beverly Hills, California
Later that day

CHAPTER 17

Henry Templeton twisted the dial of the old-fashioned safe. He knew the combination by heart, having opened it often for his advisor during the many evenings when, the rest of the staff having left for the day, the two were alone in the office.

The young man felt a pang of guilt at what he was about to do. He was familiar with every document in the steel container, and he knew exactly which one would give Stonecraft and the trustees the ammunition they needed to oust the mentor who had taken him under his wing these past months.

Zanski was going to be quietly removed no matter what, so Henry might just as well play ball with the men in charge to make sure he himself did not go down with the ship.

He removed the single sheet of paper from the safe, and walked down the hall to Stonecraft's office, carrying the document that would ensure his future and end Zanski's.

"DID YOU FIND ANYTHING?" Stonecraft's eyes probed Henry's face expectantly.

"Yes, sir, I did. And I think it's even better than you hoped for."

"Looks like we got him! I'll be arranging a nice little reception committee for our arrogant friend when he gets back tomorrow. You have done well, my boy. Don't think I'm going to forget this."

Place de Bel-Air
Geneva, Switzerland
October 28, 1985

CHAPTER 18

The golden-eyed man stood outside the Credit Suisse and waited. He'd been watching this place closely since the Englishman, Randall Powderly, had let it slip yesterday that the mask was now housed in that institution.

Thanks to a receipt Christos had found in Powderly's pocket, he knew the name of the dealer who now owned the mask: Irving Schott. Schott's gallery had not been hard to find, even for someone as unfamiliar with Geneva as the Mask Hunter.

On the way to the shop, Christos had stopped briefly and purchased a black overcoat and shoes. Even though the new attire made him less conspicuous then his previous rustic clothing, he had not risked ringing the entrance bell. But luck had been with him. As he stood indecisively in front of the gallery, two men had come out. One was probably in his sixties, grey-haired and well-dressed, and the other much younger, wearing a black leather coat. The older man appeared to lock the door, then both turned and walked in the direction of a taxi stand.

The Mask Hunter had followed, his own taxi depositing him here in front of the Credit Suisse. Although he was not prone to emotion, Christos' heart pounded as he waited for the pair to emerge.

His wait was longer than he had expected, and when the men at last emerged they were accompanied by two others. But he could see no mask.

That was puzzling. The four men shook hands and parted. The Mask Hunter watched as the two recent additions to the group, Americans by the look of them, stood outside the bank talking. Then they too walked away.

Christos felt sure the mask was still in the bank, but where would it be taken next? The Englishman had mentioned an American museum, but why, he wondered, had the Americans not taken the mask when they left?

For the first time since he had left Egypt the Mask Hunter was unsure of his next move. It had never occurred to him that he might fail in his mission, fail to return the mask to Alexander's mummy so that his *ka* might eat and breathe. Without that, Alexander would have no glorious afterlife. Actually, no afterlife at all—the worst possible fate for a soul. And he, Christos, was now in charge of preserving the great ruler. If he failed in this task, he would also be denied an afterlife, and worst of all, afterlives for all of his family: past, present, and future. This was an unimaginable fate.

Christos' head throbbed, his legs could feel no connection to the pavement beneath him, and his heart sounded a drumbeat against his ribcage. Gasping for breath, he lost his balance and sank to his knees, oblivious to the fact that this might attract attention from passersby. He closed his eyes, and the story he had heard repeated so many times played before him in cinematic detail.

It was 391 AD, and the scene was Alexandria. A young boy with golden eyes like his own was hurrying through the war-torn city as an angry mob of militant Christians, at the behest of the Roman Emperor Theodosius, destroyed the pagan temples. His destination was the mausoleum of Alexander the Great, the Pharaoh whom he and his family had protected since it was decided this was to be Alexander's final resting place.

He arrived at the marble mausoleum, frightened, panting, and out of breath, just in time to help his uncle, the current guardian of Alexander's mummified body, obscure the remains at the bottom of a small donkey cart bound for the Valley of the Kings. The pair, in anticipation of this day, had carved out a niche in the wall of a previously used royal tomb as a humble but safe resting place for their Pharaoh.

The old man had stripped Alexander's mummy of its funerary finery in a shrewd plan to deter the soldiers from desecrating it should they be stopped as they left the city. Seeing this, the boy was horrified, fearing that without his mask Alexander would not be recognized in the afterlife as the Pharoah he was. He quickly retrieved the golden funerary mask from the mausoleum floor and concealed it inside his tunic.

Christos was snapped back to the present by a light tap on his shoulder.

"Are you all right?" a well-dressed elderly woman asked in English.

Embarrassed and still partially in his dream, Christos nodded as he jumped to his feet.

Satisfied, the woman smiled and continued on her way.

WITH NO OTHER PLAN IN MIND, Christos decided to station himself outside the Credit Suisse the next day. His hunch paid off. Minutes after opening time the four men he had been watching the day before reconvened outside the bank and entered as a group.

The white-haired man and the younger American had been carrying overnight bags. That could mean only one thing: after this meeting they intended to go directly to the airport.

An hour later they emerged. This time the man with the white hair was carrying a parcel. The quest was over.

The golden-eyed man would keep his quarry in sight until opportunity presented itself.

BOTH TAXIS ARRIVED almost simultaneously at the airport. The Mask Hunter trailed the white-haired man and his companion at a safe distance. They were headed in the direction of the KLM flight to Los Angeles.

The airport security was intimidating. Christos could not yet risk taking the mask. By a stroke of luck and some of Powderly's cash, however, he was able to secure a standby first-class seat on the same flight.

He waited for the older man and his companion, seated two rows ahead of him, to nod off. When they did, he just might be able to remove the mask without anyone seeing. But no luck. Despite a steady refill of what looked to be straight vodka, both men kept the precious cargo securely wedged between them, and their eyes wide open.

CHRISTOS WASN'T PREPARED for the large number of subtle but highly recognizable security guards that patrolled customs at LAX as the two men passed through. Reluctantly, the protector of the mask decided to wait a bit longer.

Waiting, even though there seemed no other option, proved to be his undoing.

LAX
Los Angeles, California
Minutes later

CHAPTER 19

Roman Zanski and Barry Epstein were waved through customs without incident.

Once outside, waiting for Barry's limo, both men sighed in relief, followed by a high-five.

"Yep, we did it!" Barry chortled. "Nobody gave us any trouble."

"They all know who I am," Zanski said, making no attempt to look modest.

"Well, however it went down, we just pulled off a helluva caper."

The limo pulled up to the curb, and the driver got out and opened the rear doors for both men.

"Tell your driver to take me to my house," said Zanski.

Barry felt a little nervous. "Sure you don't want to tuck that expensive bauble away in the museum first?"

"I'm planning for, as you Americans say, just the right moment to present our treasure to the museum capitalists."

"Just so long as you remember it's my money that's tied up in your little coup."

Zanski reached over and patted his companion on the shoulder. "Not to worry yourself, my friend. All will be well. You will see."

They had reached the driveway of Zanski's Pacific Palisades house. The older man got out of the car and walked toward the front door. That was the last Barry saw of either his colleague or the Mask of Alexander.

Director's office, Warner Museum
Beverly Hills, California
October 30, 1985

CHAPTER 20

Galen Stonecraft paced from window to desk and back again. John Morris, an officer from the INS, was seated quietly in an armchair, drinking a cup of coffee.

Security had informed the museum director an hour ago that Roman Zanski was back from wherever it was he had been and had just entered the building. Stonecraft had then left word with the Russian's secretary that he needed to see him at once. How like the arrogant curator to ignore his superior!

"How will his deportation take place?" Stonecraft could no longer ignore the elephant in the room.

"Don't worry. Very smoothly. We do this every day. I do wonder, though, how he was able to fly back and forth to Europe with an expired visa."

Stonecraft laughed. "I don't know how he does it either, but . . . he's done it."

"For the last time. We have laws in this country, and I am here to make sure this one is no longer violated."

"I'll just let you deal with him, then."

Myra Standish, Stonecraft's secretary, tapped lightly on the door, then opened it a crack. "Dr. Zanski to see you, sir."

Stonecraft's heart gave a thump. He was about to be rid of his nemesis at last, the man who was turning the Warner into a place of scorn and notoriety, yet the next minutes would not be easy. Confrontation had not been part of his job description. He took a breath.

Zanski, as was his habit, did not wait for an invitation to enter.

"Ah, my friend, I have just come back from a most successful trip to Switzerland. You will be astounded at what I have for the museum." Zanski stopped, suddenly aware that he and the director were not alone.

"Ah," Stonecraft began, "there is a gentleman here who has come to see you."

Morris was now standing in front of Zanski, hand outstretched. He introduced himself in the smooth manner of a diplomat rather than an agent of extradition.

Zanski was taken by surprise, but not for long. "What kind of capitalist plot is this? Who are you working for, the KGB?"

Morris was prepared for the outburst. "I assure you, Dr. Zanski, this is only a formality. As soon as your papers are sorted out in Russia, you will be welcomed back."

Zanski turned toward Stonecraft. "You did this to me. I have known for some time you were jealous of all the fame I bring to this museum. It was I who built you a collection like none other. And this is how you reward me? Swine."

Morris interrupted the tirade in a smooth voice. "There is a car outside waiting to take you to the airport. We have arranged to have your belongings packed, and your family will be waiting for you in Moscow."

Zanski looked toward Stonecraft, who had taken refuge behind his desk, making himself look as small as possible. Clearly there was no help there. Zanski had little choice but to follow the INS officer.

Malibu, California
The same day

CHAPTER 21

Xandra Guthrie, my mother, had arrived in town unexpectedly last night, just about the same time that Barry returned from his trip. Both were in excellent humor, and Xandra had her heart set on breakfast at the Beverly Hills Hotel, then shopping on Rodeo Drive.

I hadn't slept at all. Possible reasons for Henry's visit with the trustees playing over and over in my head, it was no surprise that neither of my mother's planned activities interested me, nor did time with the woman herself, and her uncanny knack for making me feel inadequate. She would have had a field day with my current problem.

"I would love to, Mother, but I really should go into the museum and work on the goddess project."

"Let's compromise, then. We'll go to breakfast, then you can show me around the museum."

That option was even worse. I had no intention of letting my mother within shooting distance of my lover, should he have returned—and I was certain he had—and definitely not today.

Barry mentioned he and Zanski had been together in Zurich doing some antiquities deal, so things were getting too close for comfort. I was going to have to come clean sooner or later about what was going on with Zanski and me. Perhaps fate was taking this in hand. If my interpretation of Henry's visit with the trustees was correct, it was about to explode.

I wished Zanski would call.

"Something the matter with your omelet?" Although he almost never looked at me these days, today Barry noticed I was pushing my food around my plate rather than into my mouth.

"I'm just not hungry. Sorry."

Xandra picked up on the theme. "She never was a picky eater before. What's on your mind, sweetie?"

"Nothing. Just distracted. I've become obsessed with the lives of everyday women in the ancient world."

Xandra was clearly unimpressed. "One would think there were other subjects far more interesting. Whatever happened to that idea you had about researching the tomb Alexander the Great built for his horse?"

"It's just on hold, Mother. I'll get back to it."

Xandra turned toward Barry. "Growing up, that girl was mad about horses. I suppose all girls that age are, although I much preferred boys," she winked prettily. "You probably remember how she even named her pony after Alexander's horse. 'Bucolic,' wasn't it?"

"Bucephalus, Mother. It means *bull's head*—for the marking on his forehead."

"Alexander, huh? How beautifully ironic." Barry commented.

"Why is that ironic?" I turned my attention to him.

"You'll know soon enough." He laughed.

Xandra jangled her bracelets. I wanted to ask Barry more, but by this time I knew he was the kind of man who took pleasure in knowing something I did not. I was not going to give him the satisfaction of my curiosity.

WHEN WE ARRIVED at the employee entrance to the museum, my friend Carlos, the daytime guard, pulled me aside. "Something has happened. Dr. Zanski was taken away about an hour ago in an Immigration Department car. He did not look happy. I thought you should know."

"I must find out what happened." My voice didn't seem to come from me at all.

"What's going on?" Barry was now standing beside me.

Blackness rapidly closed in from my peripheral vision and I was about to lose consciousness. I felt cold and numb and my legs buckled. I reached for the ground, but I could not stop my fall.

"What the fuck happened?" Barry demanded to no one in particular.

Xandra took over. "Parthi, get up."

I think she slapped me, but I couldn't be sure. Not getting much response from me, she turned to Barry. "We need to get her home. She can't just stand here passing out in a public place. Help me get her in the car."

"Not until I find out what the hell happened."

"*Now*, Barry. You can sort out the rest later," Xandra

commanded.

Barry had no choice but to take my right arm while Xandra pulled my left to steer me toward the car.

Carlos rushed to open the rear door. He said nothing.

Somehow, despite my wailing, and I think kicking, the three of them got me buckled into the backseat of the Mercedes.

I lay back against the leather headrest, limp and defeated. I could hear Barry and Xandra talking in the front. "What in the world caused that outburst?"

"There's a lot going on," Barry replied vaguely.

"I haven't seen her behave like this since her father died."

WHEN WE ARRIVED HOME I wanted to call the museum and find out what had actually happened, but Xandra stopped me. "You are in no condition to talk to anyone right now. At least calm down a bit first."

Then I was in our bedroom, under the covers, although I don't remember how I got there. Xandra was standing over me. "Here, take these. They'll help you sleep." Xandra's bracelets jangled with authority. I'd noticed over the years they spoke a language of their own.

I swallowed them, followed by a few sips of water. Probably Valium. Xandra always had a supply at the ready.

"Barry had to rush off someplace. Business, I suppose."

It didn't matter. What mattered was that some horrible twist of fate had taken the only person I loved away from me. I hadn't even been able to say goodbye.

I'd been at the Warner long enough to know how these things

worked. These people either protected their own or threw them to the wolves, whichever best suited the museum's agenda. In this case, whatever Zanski had been worried about must have been serious enough for the trustees to take the drastic and final step of deportation. In my heart I knew this was final.

Xandra was fussing with the window curtains.

"Could you leave me alone, Mother? I want to sleep."

"Good idea. I'll be downstairs if you need anything."

Then she was gone, trailing the scent of Joy behind her. How ironic.

I lay there, eyes open but not focused. *Where do I go from here? What is left for me now that Zanski is gone?*

My vision cleared and I noticed that Xandra had left the bottle of Valium on the bedside table.

PART TWO

THIRTY YEARS LATER

Warner Museum
Beverly Hills, California
The present

CHAPTER 22

Grenville Hopkins was in a good mood. It had taken a lot of patience, and a bit of luck, but here he was at last, sitting pretty in the curator's seat at the Warner. Although he was for the moment merely acting curator of antiquities, the soon-to-be criminal conviction of Henry Templeton, Grenville's former colleague and current Warner curator, would leave the job wide open. And Grenville had been pretty much assured of the permanent position by the chairman of the board of trustees, who just happened to also be a trustee of the Hopkins Foundation.

Grenville had put the long wait for this position to good use. He'd collected and published the papers of his dead father, the much-quoted archaeologist Benjamin Hopkins, and had spent the previous years touring the world and lecturing on the subject. Listening to Grenville, one would actually believe he had admired Benjamin. That was the greatest of Grenville's gifts: suspension of disbelief.

He'd followed up securing his father's legacy by creating and raising money for the foundation that carried on his name and work. Needless to mention, this also kept Grenville himself at the forefront of the archaeological world.

And that gave him access to new finds.

This last was the purpose of the entire process. After Benjamin's death, Grenville's mother had asked him to go through his father's things that had been sent from the excavation site. Among them was a box containing his excavation journals. An interesting sidebar to delving into Benjamin's excavation records was the last journal entry, made just hours before his death. In bold pencil script the archaeologist had recorded finding the greatest treasure since Tutankhamun: the Mask of Alexander the Great.

It had been thirty years since Grenville had read those words, and thirty years that he had been searching in secret for the treasure. It had never appeared on the antiquities market, but he knew it was still out there somewhere, waiting to be rediscovered.

When it did turn up, the Warner would be the first to find out. And now, as that museum's curator, Grenville was in the catbird seat to pounce on it first.

His thoughts were interrupted by a knock on the door, followed by the entry of none other than Henry Templeton, his out-of-favor predecessor. Henry had recently been indicted by the Italian government for buying antiquities on behalf of the Warner that had been looted from Etruscan tombs. When this came to light the museum director and board of trustees reacted with mock horror and placed Henry on paid leave.

"Henry, old man, good to see you! What brings you here?"

Henry Templeton had changed little in the years following his original association with Grenville. His hair, although now almost entirely grey, was still thick and curly. His manner of dress hadn't changed much either: his shirt starched and trousers smartly creased. Obviously no one had told him about the current California dress code.

"Hope this is a good time to catch you. You've been so wonderful stepping in for me that I thought it only decent you should be the first to know." Henry's eyes sparkled in an unusual manner for a condemned man.

"First to know what?"

"Italy is dropping all the charges. My uncle made a deal with the Italian government, and the whole case is going away. You and I both know it was totally political from the get-go anyway."

"Whoa! That's pretty incredible. Who is this uncle of yours, anyway?"

"I thought you might have known. My mother is Italian, and one of her brothers is a cardinal pretty high up in the Vatican."

There had been gossip around Boston that Henry's Italian mother had family ties to the Mafia, but this Vatican connection shed a new light on his background.

"How did it actually happen?"

"A deal, of course. The Warner will be persuaded to make the Italians an offer they cannot refuse, probably cash and return of some of the objects they claim we stole, and everyone goes home happy. Especially me. My uncle will see to it that I am no longer the scapegoat." Henry paused a moment. "That's why I'm here. I'll be exonerated and reinstated." He reached his hand toward Grenville. "You've been so great about filling in for me that I wanted you to be the first to know. And to thank you."

"Then the museum doesn't know about this deal yet?"

"No. I just talked with my uncle before I came here, and he told me his people are meeting with the Warner people later this week. So just don't spill the beans. Act like you're surprised—but I thought you might want a heads up to make your own plans." Henry finished the sentence awkwardly, as though suddenly aware that his own good fortune might not affect Grenville the same way.

"My lips are sealed, old man, and by the way, congrats! We need to celebrate. What would you say to a bottle of Dom?"

"Who says no to the best champagne on the planet?"

"Then I'll be at your place about seven. You supply the glasses. Everything else is on me."

Indeed it will be.

The wheels in Grenville's head had been spinning at Mach 2 since Henry had mentioned being reinstated at the Warner. He would have to move fast.

Roman Villa Gallery, Warner Museum
Beverly Hills, California
The same time

CHAPTER 23

CHRISTOS LAVENTIS CAREFULLY RUBBED the finger smudges from a glass case that protected a small statue of a naked cherub in the newly set up "Roman Villa" gallery. All in all, this was not a terrible life that he had carved out here in Los Angeles. It was just that it was not the life that had been ordained for him.

When Powderly's cash gave out, the golden-eyed man had been forced to reconnect with Grenville Hopkins, his former lover from the Valley of the Kings. The association had proved beneficial for both men, although love, at least on Christos' side, had no part in the equation.

Grenville had maintained the image of a family man by marrying first one, then another lady whom his dowager mother approved of as "the right sort." Those marriages, and subsequent displays of sadness at their ends, served as the perfect cover for the son's less mainstream sexual appetites.

And those appetites were in large part fulfilled by Christos, whom Grenville kept as a sidepiece, marriage after marriage.

For Christos, despite the repugnance he felt at having to endure just-out-of-prison sex, his other needs were met. And this current job Grenville had set up for him as part-time guard at the Warner was the perfect vantage point to track his quarry, the mask.

During the years following his move to California, the Mask Hunter had continued the quest for the elusive artifact. As time went on, his hopes of success grew weaker. Yet he persisted.

It was certainly odd that such a valuable piece of art would not have surfaced by now. Christos had last seen the mask when Zanski and Epstein went through customs. He was subjected to a barrage of questions about why he was coming to the US, and by the time he emerged, the two men were nowhere to be seen.

But if the Warner had it, and he was quite sure they did not, it would have been on display. Was it possible the crafty Russian had managed to smuggle it out of the country with him when he was deported? One possibility, and Christos shuddered at the thought, was that Zanski had sold it to a private collector, in which case it might remain hidden forever. He willed that not to be the case.

In Egypt, Christos' father was growing old and impatient to have the mask restored to Alexander's mummy before he himself crossed into the land of the dead. Yet, try as he might, turning over every stone he thought might lead him to his quarry, Christos invariably came up empty-handed. He developed hypervigilance by day and imagined terrors by night.

Zanski was killed in a car crash a year after leaving California, making Christos' mission to find the mask seem even more hopeless.

Then three months ago, events began to break in the right way for the golden-eyed man. One evening at dinner, Grenville casually mentioned that a man named Barry Epstein, a former business partner of Zanski's, had just returned from a trip to

Russia. Christos asked why this was important and Grenville responded that he made it his business to keep track of shady antiquities procurers, present and past. "One never knows what will turn up."

Christos knew well who Epstein was: the young American whom he had seen with Zanski that day in Zurich in 1985. The day he had lost track of the mask. Epstein's trip to Russia had to have something to do with that.

Alexander's protector decided he had to find out what Epstein knew, and whether he had the mask. It was risky, but he had to confront the man and frighten him into telling what he knew.

Familiarizing himself with Epstein's house, he had noticed that the man did not use his garage but parked his car directly in front of the building. An underground parking lot would have been better for an ambush, but Christos would work with what he had.

Luckily, Epstein's habits were rather regular: he seemed to leave the house, presumably for dinner, about seven, returning somewhere between eleven and two in the morning.

Christos made a habit of driving past Epstein's house to check on the presence of the car. The night he chose for the confrontation was a moonless one, lit only by the sparse streetlights.

He waited out of sight on the landscaped lawn, smoking, being careful not to leave cigarette butts. He stamped his feet for circulation and breathed in and out carefully to calm himself. He was acutely aware of the Glock 9mm in his jacket pocket. He had bought the pistol when he first arrived in LA for his own protection. He remembered how amazed he had been that just about anyone could buy a gun in this country. Basically with no questions asked.

He knew it would defeat his purpose to kill Epstein, but he had to make him fear for his life enough to provide the information Christos needed. The gun would do the trick. But what if the man screamed? Christos could only hope he did not.

At 1:35 a.m. Epstein's car pulled to the curb and stopped. Christos waited to hear the chirp of the electronic lock before he donned a stocking mask and eased himself from the bushes, blocking Epstein as he walked toward his entrance steps. The Glock was pointed at Epstein's chest.

"One word and you die," said Christos, his voice muffled by his mask.

Christos sat Epstein down on the grass and eased himself down beside him, still pointing the gun. Even though he could not see Epstein well in the darkness, he could smell his quarry's fear.

"Listen to me," he continued. "If you tell me where the mask is, I will not hurt you. If you scream, I will have to kill you. Do you understand?"

Epstein nodded, and Christos could tell from his body language that the man was a coward and would comply.

"What do you want?" Epstein asked, as if he didn't know. Here it was. What he had been fearing. The person who had left the images was now in front of him.

"The mask."

"I don't have it."

"But you know where it is?"

"Not exactly, but I know who does. I'll tell you if you just let me go. Please."

"How can I believe you?" Christos could smell the sweat oozing from Epstein's pores.

"You've got to. It's all I have. I haven't actually seen the damn thing since 1985." Fear was making Barry Epstein blubber.

"Just tell me who has it."

"Parthi, my former wife."

"Tell me where I can find this woman and I will let you go."

"Not exactly sure. Her full name is, or was, Parthenia Guthrie, and her mother lived in Colorado. I haven't seen or heard from her in years. That's all I got."

In reply, Christos placed his hands on Epstein's throat in a warning gesture. "I think you know you would be a fool to do anything but forget about this visit. Now go in peace."

Christos rose from the ground and melted from Barry Epstein's sight. His next step was to watch this man very closely.

Warner Museum
Beverly Hills, California
The same time

CHAPTER 24

Grenville Hopkins had no time to waste. He needed to stop Henry before he told someone else about his happy reversal of fortune, or before the meeting between the Italians and the Warner took place and Henry's criminal conviction went away. Either would put Grenville where he did not want to be, outside the Warner inner circle.

Originally healthy, the Hopkins Trust had steadily dwindled, thanks to Benjamin's pricey excavations, his widow's support of countless charities, and Grenville's own poor choices in spouses. All in all, if he was going to continue his lifestyle, the younger Hopkins had to become creative.

While he was waiting for the mask to surface, and surface it was bound to sooner or later, other measures were in order. Old Zanski had done a pretty good trade back in the eighties, shaking down dealers who wanted to make sales to the Warner, and it had struck Grenville that it would be logical to revive this easy source of extra income. But he needed this office, the cache of curator, to make it happen.

Henry had to go. Grenville would have preferred more time to think this through, but he was, after all, a Hopkins, and he would make do. By a stroke of luck there had been a *60 Minutes* segment on suicide via helium only a week before.

Grenville was humming as he closed his office door minutes later.

His first stop was the museum's restoration lab, where he borrowed a white coat without asking, but with the certainty he would have it back in the morning.

A quick stop at the hardware store for a coil of clear plastic tubing, then it was on to Joe's Party Central. He chose Joe's because it was off the beaten path, at least the Beverly Hills path, with the least likelihood that he would run into anyone he knew. As if any of his sort would even be likely to cross the threshold of such a place. Oh well, it was always a good idea to play it safe.

Grenville paid for his purchases, a canister of helium and a packet of red, yellow, and blue balloons, with cash, barely noticing the red-haired clerk who rang up the sale.

"Sure you don't want to rent the helium tank? Most people do."

"No, just want to buy it."

"Your call. Just trying to save you a few bucks."

Grenville ignored the comment. He pocketed the change the young man held out and quickly exited the store.

At the public library, he had downloaded and printed the suicide manual *Final Exit*, the Oregon-published manual for painless suicide. It lay on the seat beside him, next to a bottle of Dom Perignon in its chilled carrier.

Grenville parked around the corner from Henry's Miracle Mile apartment building on Wilshire Boulevard, donned the lab coat, tucked *Final Exit* into the pocket, and looped the tubing over his arm, covered by a cleaners' bag. Carrying the canister in his left hand and the champagne in his right, he quickly walked the two blocks to Henry's building.

Pricey neighborhood. More than a curator's salary could buy. The press had picked up on that, using it as proof that Henry had been dealing antiquities on the dirty side. They were proved wrong when a title search showed the apartment was owned by the Templeton Shipping Company. But fake news tends to stick.

HENRY TEMPLETON'S EYES WIDENED slightly when he opened his front door to his visitor.

"Special delivery for Henry Templeton."

"Gren, it's a bit early for a full-on celebration, and why the get-up?"

Henry ran his eyes over the lab coat and fixed on the canister. The latter was emblazoned with brightly colored balloons and the words *Joe's Party Central.*

"Just my feeble attempt at theatrics, old man. Anyway, I thought we could have a bit of fun. How long since you've had a party with balloons?" Grenville pulled a packet of red, blue, and yellow rubber inflatables from his pocket.

"You mean we're actually going to blow those things up?"

"Maybe later. But first let's sample this bubbly. Hope I didn't shake it too much on the way up."

Shaking his head, but smiling, Henry produced two glasses.

Grenville carefully removed the bottle's cork. "Ah, don't you just love that sound?" He filled both glasses. "Oopsie, looks like I've spilled some."

Indeed there was a trickle of champagne dripping from the coffee table to the marble floor.

"I'll get a towel. Don't worry about it." Henry disappeared into the kitchen.

Grenville took that opportunity to empty the contents of five Valium capsules into Henry's glass.

"NOW, TELL ME MORE about this stroke of glorious fate that has delivered you from the clutches of an Italian prison."

"Simple. Too many valuable antiquities have been leaving Italy and showing up on this side of the pond, and the Italians got fed up. They just happened to pick on the wrong curator."

"Yes, who knew you had so much pull in the right places?"

Henry yawned. "I must not be used to drinking. I can feel this stuff going straight to my head."

"I'm a bit giddy myself. But, hell, let's finish the bottle." Grenville emptied its contents into their glasses. "Bottoms up!" They clinked glasses.

This was the first time Grenville had been in Henry's apartment. He looked around. Not lavish, but tasteful. Monkish really, decorated in tones of grey punctuated only by a pot of white Phalaenopsis orchids on the coffee table. No antiquities—not much in the way of art at all.

Henry yawned again. "Sorry, my friend, but I am distinctly tipsy. Better lie down before I topple."

"Here, let me give you a hand." Grenville steadied his companion as they walked to the bedroom. The Valium was doing its work nicely.

When his host was stretched on the bed, Grenville began to unlace his shoes. "Let's get you all cozy now."

Henry did not reply. He was already asleep.

It didn't take long to complete the rest of the "suicide" preparations. Wiping his fingerprints clean and donning gloves, Grenville positioned the helium tank on the bedside table and attached one end of the plastic tubing to its gas outlet. He tied the other end into a hole he had made in the cleaners' bag, checking to see that it was airtight. Then, gently, so as not to disturb Henry, he lowered the bag around the sleeping man's head and secured it around his neck with the man's belt. A nice touch, he thought. Last of all, he took Henry's right hand and pressed his fingers against the tank.

Finally, Grenville pressed the lever that released the gas from the tank. The slight hiss was comforting. After a few puffs Henry would be unconscious, death following soon after.

Grenville waited until he was sure Henry had stopped breathing, then placed *Final Exit* on the night table beside the canister. With everything in order, Grenville left the light on but closed the bedroom door as he retraced his steps to wash the wine glasses.

Minutes later, lab coat neatly folded over the empty champagne bottle, Grenville was back on Wilshire Boulevard heading toward his car. He was whistling.

Boulder, Colorado
Two days later

CHAPTER 25

This has been a year of change. I weathered a second divorce, and my mother died, leaving me this large and somewhat intimidating house just outside of Boulder. I wasn't sure what I was going to do with it—or with my life.

Adding to the malaise was my morbid fascination with the latest Warner Museum saga unfolding day by day via the *Denver Post*.

I had been sure I was finished with the Warner specifically and archaeology in general years ago, but here I was, devouring every word of the lurid details of Henry Templeton's suicide.

I had known Henry back in the eighties when we were both Warner interns, but I hadn't followed his career. Of course I knew he had rather mysteriously replaced my former lover, Roman Zanski, as antiquities curator, but I had pretty much pushed that out of my mind.

It would have been hard for anyone, even one who had no connections with the museum, to ignore the drama that seemed to unfold daily. Originally it was reports of a "punitive action" taken by the Italian government against the Warner for the alleged trafficking in antiquities stolen from dig sites. Henry Templeton was cited as the principal offender.

How could he have been so stupid, repeating Zanski's moves step by step? It boggled the mind.

The latest, which had come out in today's paper, was an even bigger shocker. Henry's suicide. I certainly had made the right call to stay miles away from that profession.

I thought I'd finished reading the paper, but at second glance something caught my eye. A sidebar story dealing with Warner misdeeds, past and present. Not strange. The press was always hungry to topple a giant.

But there was more. At the conclusion there was mention of Zanski and his misdeeds that were still being uncovered so many years after his death. I felt like I had been shot. I had pushed all thoughts of him out of my mind, but I guess I hadn't pushed hard enough. He was still there. And I hated myself for that feeling. Hated myself for my weakness in giving even one thought to the man who had been a traitor not only to his profession but to me as well.

A month or so after I was released from the hospital following my suicide attempt, I was back in Boulder, living with my mother. One day in a supermarket checkout line a tabloid headline caught my eye. At first I thought I was hallucinating and that the drugs had permanently damaged my brain. Then I forced myself to look again and the headline was still there:

SHADY FORMER WARNER CURATOR LANDS ON HIS FEET

The headline was accompanied by a photo of the man I thought was my love, arm in arm with a voluptuous blonde.

I can still remember the words written beneath the photo, or most of them at least:

SHADY FORMER WARNER CURATOR
LANDS ON HIS FEET

> Roman Zanski, the prestigious Warner Museum antiquities curator who left his position in March amid a flurry of speculation that he had profited from stolen artifacts, has apparently moved on to blonder pastures. The dashing Russian, newly divorced, is shown here strolling the streets of Paris with his fiancée, Texas oil heiress Gisele Scott. Where will he turn up next?

Had I not still been on heavy meds, who knows what I would have done? But from that day forward, with the help of more counseling and a lot of willpower, I managed to keep him from my thoughts. That is, until today.

The years since that stab to my then-young heart had been ones of healing. I divorced Barry, and soon after remarried and moved to a horse ranch in Nevada. Unfortunately, I had chosen the wrong man yet again.

My mother's illness and subsequent death in Boulder two years ago provided an easy transition from a marriage that should never have been. I moved into her house to help organize the around-the-clock nursing staff she required toward the end, and while I was sorting her life's worth of treasures, a love of interior design was born.

Friends began asking me to rearrange their spaces and find them special pieces. This made the shift from my old life on the ranch smooth, and even pleasant. I loved the prospect of sourcing and acquiring valuable and exclusive furniture and art. I was beginning a new chapter.

Los Angeles, California
Two weeks later

CHAPTER 26

On the days that Scotty Jones worked at Joe's Party Central, he wore long sleeves to cover the tats that marched up and down his arms. The boss, Joe himself, a strict born-again Christian, believed all body art was the mark of the Devil. But in Scotty's way of thinking, there was always an upside to everything, and in this case, it was obvious: who else but a total fool or a religious nut like Joe would give an ex-con like himself, fresh from the slammer, a job behind a cash register? But Joe had, and so far, Scotty had kept his nose clean and his tattoos out of sight.

The job didn't pay much, but what Scotty took home at the end of the week was enough for his rented flophouse room, with some left over for food and a few beers. No drugs. Not for the time being at least. Not while he was on parole, not while he was on the prowl for the next con. He didn't know where it might come from, but that was the beauty of his profession: the unpredictability, the possibility that at any moment the big score might pop up. A mark could be anywhere, and he would not miss any opportunity. Scotty had no doubt that if he had been born an animal, he would have been a coyote: smart, sleek, forever alert, hungry sometimes, but always ready to prey on the unsuspecting.

Scotty had done two years' hard time for relieving an aging former actress of most of her ready cash. It was not like he'd left her starving or anything, and she'd gotten her money's worth. Scotty fancied himself quite the stud, and he smiled as the memory swam to the surface of his thoughts. The whole thing had been a blast—that is, until he got greedy and signed the lady's name to one too many checks. Ah, live and learn. He would be more careful next time. A coyote never took more than one chicken at a time. Scotty could learn from that.

This was a slow morning at Party Central. This business was like that, either no one in the store or a dozen customers wanting everything all at once. Scotty sighed from boredom and nodded to Sam, the stock boy. "I'm going on break. Watch the register for me."

"Will do," Sam mumbled, not looking up from the boxes of balloons he was arranging on a middle shelf.

Scotty stretched and walked slowly to the curtained-off space at the back of the store that served as the break room. He poured himself the last of the tepid brown liquid in the Mr. Coffee carafe and sat down at the only table in the room. "Shit, this stuff tastes worse than shit," he mumbled to himself, spitting a mouthful of coffee back into the cup.

Without much thought, he picked up a section of the *Los Angeles Times* that was lying on the table. It happened to be the Arts and Culture section, and the top page caught his eye. There was something about the photograph of the smiling man illustrating its lead story, "Grenville Hopkins promoted to head curator," that struck him. Then he knew what it was. "What the fuck? This is the dude who bought the helium tank from me!"

Scotty remained seated on the hard metal chair for a few more minutes while he allowed the significance of the photo to sink in. One of the tools of a con artist's trade was a memory for faces, and Scotty possessed this talent in spades. As he looked again and again at the newspaper photo he became more certain that the face staring back at him was the same man who had bought the canister of helium from him the day before it became the vehicle of a suicide that made the front pages.

That had been a couple of weeks ago. When the police had interviewed him a day or so later, Scotty remembered thinking back to the day the posh dude had come into the store to pick up balloons and a canister of gas that he said were going to be decorations for his kid's birthday party. He didn't know quite why, but something about the guy just felt off. Then, when the cops pulled out the picture of the dead guy, Scotty knew for sure there was something fishy afoot. The dude in the photo didn't look anything like the guy he'd sold the gas to. But hell, it was none of his business, and more importantly, nothing in it for him, so why mention it? If there was one thing Scotty had learned during those two years on the inside, it was that no good ever comes of sticking your nose into other people's shit unless there was a payoff.

And what he was now looking at was that payoff. A supposed suicide plus a promotion soon after—the pieces fit together. Scotty licked his lips as he walked to the front of the store and took up his station behind the cash register.

He waited until closing time, when all of the customers had left and the two other employees were heading for the door, before he began to put his plan into action.

"I'm going to stay and count up the cash before Joe gets

here," Scotty smiled.

"Brown-nosing again, huh?" Moe, the good-natured window-dresser, joked as he put on his jacket. "See you *mañana*." And he was gone.

Scotty was alone and with just enough time to close out the register and make the call he'd been itching to make all afternoon.

The dude in the *Times* article was a big shot, and most likely one with some bucks. Scotty hadn't played the blackmail game before, but how hard could it be? No harder than banging old broads and wasting days perfecting their signatures, he surmised. The only trick now was to set up the meeting with the guy before Joe walked in the door.

Scotty was in luck. The number was listed. His hands shook a little as he punched the numbers into the store phone. He was prepared to hang up if a machine answered, but his luck held. The mark himself picked up on the second ring.

"This is Party Central," Scotty announced himself.

There was that moment of silence on the other end of the line, the expected intake of breath before the man replied. "What is this about?"

Scotty affected a confident snicker that he didn't quite feel. "I think you know. Let's cut to the chase. Check your caller ID and you'll see I'm calling from the place you bought the gas."

There was another silence as Scotty imagined the wheels turning in the head of the man on the other end of the line. Then the reply, "How do I know you're not recording this conversation?"

"You don't, buddy. So why don't we get together and talk face to face, and I'll even let you check me for a wire," Scotty laughed. "And while you're at it, bring something with you, say fifty thousand, in small bills—you know the drill."

"I'll need a bit of time to get my hands on that kind of cash."

"OK then. How much time do you think you're gonna need?" Even though he tried to make his voice gruff, Scotty was afraid it was a few octaves too high. He was probably right about that because the mark was calmer than expected. The man's tone was businesslike as he replied, more like he was arranging a social engagement than a blackmail payoff. "I have meetings tomorrow that I can't cancel, even for this. But I do want to sort this out with you."

Scotty let out the breath he'd been holding. The toff—Scotty had picked up that word from a BBC show he'd seen during his many hours of prison TV—was hooked for sure.

The man continued, "Here's what I can do: I'll meet you when I'm free. Say six o'clock?"

That was perfect. Scotty was working the early shift the next day, which would free him up by five thirty. Plenty of time to get somewhere to meet his mark by six.

"I think we'd both be more comfortable meeting somewhere other than your store," the composed voice continued. "Perhaps we could do this over a bite to eat?"

This is going to be easier than I expected. This guy is scared as shit and trying to act like this is no big deal. Maybe I should have asked for more? Oh well, too late for that. This time anyway. "There's a pretty good Mexican place on South Central on the corner of 6th. Can you find that?"

"OK, I'll find it." He was silent for a moment, writing the information down, Scotty imagined. "I don't think I'd remember you. Sorry about that. How will I recognize you?"

Scotty laughed. "But I remember *you*. And I got your picture right here in the paper. Nice shot of you at the Warner. Anyway, you can't miss me. I got red hair. Natural."

"This should be easy then," the man replied, still smooth and cool. "See you at six."

Scotty noticed his hands were still shaking as he put the phone down.

ON THE OTHER SIDE of Los Angeles, Grenville frowned as he replaced the phone on its stand. This was an inconvenience he had not expected. But perhaps he should have. Oh well, if this loose end had to turn up, better to get it out of the way now rather than later.

Meeting with this lowlife from the party store wouldn't be his favorite way of spending tomorrow's cocktail hour, but there was no way around it. Sending someone else would just create another possibility for problems.

There had been no choice but to eliminate Henry. Poor sod. It was his tough luck to have an Italian uncle with enough pull to wipe away the smuggling charges. So the cookie crumbles.

Now Grenville sat at the desk that had once been Henry's, determined not to let some two-bit blackmailer mess with his plans.

Dealing with this latest wrinkle would not be a picnic, but one must do what one must in order to succeed. His father had taught him that. Smiling to himself, he locked his office door, determined to fortify himself with a good dinner before facing tomorrow's unpleasantness.

THE NEXT MORNING, Grenville decided his day would be better spent in preparation for the evening's activity than going into the office. Making those preparations might not fit into a predictable time frame, and he wanted to make sure everything went just right.

His first stop was a Salvation Army store, where he selected a nondescript overcoat, two sizes too large, and a baseball cap without a logo.

Carrying his purchases to the checkout counter with gloved hands, he was conscious of holding his breath during the transaction, thus hoping to deter any of the myriad real and imagined germs from entering his nostrils.

Once out in the street, in the relatively fresh air if indeed any air in Los Angeles could be considered fresh, he exhaled at last. *On to the next task.*

The girl behind the counter at One Hour Cleaning and Sanitizing took the coat and cap without comment, dumped them into a bin to her right, and handed him a receipt with 2PM printed in oversize letters.

Fifty-five minutes to hang around for the clothes, then who knew how long to find the drugs he would need—so, all in all, it had been a good idea to leave plenty of time to get everything done before the balloon-store employee left work. His father's mandate to "hurry up and wait" replayed though his ears. He smiled, wondering how horrified old Benjamin would be if he knew to what use his son was putting that lesson.

At two minutes to two he retraced his steps and retrieved the clothing that seemed only slightly less revolting after whatever it was it had been treated with.

"Showtime," he murmured to himself as he scooted behind the building, where he quickly donned the coat and then the cap, which he put on backwards, and finally tossed the plastic bag into a convenient dumpster.

Then he was back on the street, heading in the direction of Gladys Park, one of the lesser-known landmarks of Los Angeles' Skid Row. He'd heard this was a likely place to find drugs. The whole place was reported to be full of dealers.

Grenville's customary patrician swagger was gone, replaced by a shuffle that blended him well into his surroundings. It didn't take long to spot the kind of people he was looking for: two Hispanics somewhere in their late teens to early twenties leaning against a sagging fence, passing a joint between them. He shuffled over to them.

"Hey man, got a fix?"

After some quality street banter on Grenville's part, he effected a shaky hand, offering a handful of bills he'd carefully crumpled earlier in the day. In exchange he received a syringe.

"This ain't gonna do it for me. I'm gonna need more." The younger of the two young men, the one with the pockmarks, shook his head.

"No, man, you don't need more, and unless yer planning t'check out, ya better be careful with that one ya got. We was fixin' to split it, so you got a double dose in there."

As Grenville turned to leave, one of the young men called after him. "Hey man, go easy on that stuff. If you do the whole thing at once, it could be bye-bye."

With his back toward the two, the older man smiled and continued to walk down 7th Street.

THE DEAL HAD GONE SMOOTHLY and more quickly than Grenville had dared to hope. He still had almost three hours to kill before the balloon man's shift was over. Sightseeing in the area wasn't much of an option, and he had no appetite or desire to even drink a cup of coffee in any of the nearby questionable-looking fast food restaurants he shuffled past on his way toward Party Central. He decided to find a place to sit and just wait. He hated wasting time, so decided to treat this as an exercise in discipline.

He found an empty bench a block from Party Central and sat down. He was edgy, wanting to get this whole thing behind him so he could return to his house in Brentwood and take a bath. As he sat, he kept thinking about the lethal syringe in his pocket, hoping it actually was what the punks had promised: strong smack.

Yesterday, after the call from the balloon man left him no course of action but to eliminate the problem, the man who was now slumped on a grubby bench in downtown Los Angeles had thought of using a nice clean shot of potassium chloride that would stop the heart more reliably than heroin. The catch was that one needed an in with either an MD or a veterinarian to get the stuff. And how to produce a plausible reason why he had a need for a substance whose primary use, outside of surgery, was to euthanize condemned criminals and either mortally ill or unlucky animals? No, heroin was the only option. At least as far as he knew. He was a curator, not a chemical expert.

This was totally Henry's fault. If he hadn't been so selfish about wanting his precious name cleared, none of this would be necessary.

At last it was four forty-five. Grenville rose from the bench, stiff from sitting so long, and shuffled off to a place where he could wait for his mark to emerge.

INSIDE JOE'S PARTY CENTRAL, Scotty looked at the clock for the tenth time in the last five minutes. It never seemed to move. Funny about time, he thought. It never seemed to go forward when you wanted it to. Some big brains somewhere must be able to explain that. Four forty-five. Fifteen minutes until quitting time. The boss wasn't around, so maybe he could take a chance and duck out early. Moe could lock up. Yah, why not? If he got caught, he could always say some emergency had come up or something like that. He was getting antsy just hanging out here behind the counter marking time until the meeting with the toff.

At 4:50 Scotty's patience gave out. He walked to the back of the store where Moe was reading a pulp fiction thriller. "Hey, man. Clock out for me and close up. Nothin's happenin' here anyway, and I got me a big business appointment. If it goes down the way I'm thinkin', things will be changin' fer me in a big way."

Moe didn't bother to look up. Just nodded and kept on reading.

Scotty was almost skipping as he left the store. He figured he'd walk around a bit and run through the upcoming meeting at the Mexican restaurant. Out of the corner of his eye, he noticed a bum leaning up against a scraggly tree. Scotty was in a good mood. If the bum tried to hit him up for a handout, he decided he'd give him a buck or two. After all, he was about to become a man of means, so why not help a down-and-outer? However, the man slouched against the tree seemed not to notice Scotty at all. His loss, the redhead thought.

Scotty had plenty of time. But instead of walking around to kill an hour, he decided to go directly to the cantina, drink a few beers to calm his nerves, and wait for the toff to appear. There was a route avoiding the tougher part of LA that lay between the store and the restaurant, but Scotty figured there was no reason to take it. After all, he'd done time on the inside, and his street smarts were pretty well honed. He walked this way often.

As he walked, he sensed a shuffling man following him, speeding up. Scotty's street antennae picked up the change in pace without his even turning around. Probably nothing, but to be on the safe side he decided to turn at the next corner and see if the guy followed. The man did follow. The golden red hairs on the back of Scotty's neck began to react in alarm. You could never tell what kind of nutcase was on the street in this neighborhood. Luckily, he knew the territory well. There was an abandoned warehouse a few blocks up that was currently being used as a crack house. Scotty headed in that direction.

Probably nothin' to worry about, Scotty told himself. *I'm jumpy, that's all.*

He glanced behind him and saw the lumpy figure stop, sway a bit, and then fall to his knees. Scotty laughed to himself. *Just a strung-out junkie.* Nothing to be worried about. But to be on the safe side he decided to duck into the crack house until the odd fellow passed.

The entrance, if one could call it that, was accessed via a cut-out area of the chain-link fence intended to protect the building. Scotty slipped through it and then entered the building where a side door was suspended by only one hinge.

Inside, his eyes became accustomed to the darkness fairly quickly, and he was able to make out several figures, most of them men, all but one huddled on the floor under blankets. Scotty could not make out if they were alive or dead, and he didn't much care.

He'd wait it out here for ten minutes or so, and then he'd be on his way to the cantina and fifty thousand dollars.

Outside, the overcoated man smiled. *Rat in a trap. All I have to do is wait.* He glanced around and saw a two-by-four lying on the ground. "How convenient. This will do nicely." He picked it up, moved into position, and waited.

Ten minutes later, as if on schedule, his quarry emerged. He did not see the figure behind the door until it was too late. He briefly saw stars as the two-by-four crashed onto his skull. Then everything went blank.

GRENVILLE BENT OVER his victim long enough to determine he was unconscious. Then he carefully removed the syringe from his pocket and injected its contents directly into the jugular vein. "That should do the trick," he smiled.

The next morning there would be one more overdosed junkie found on Skid Row.

Los Angeles, California
Two days later

CHAPTER 27

The Mask Hunter was restless. He could feel something in the air, but he wasn't sure what it was.

He had grown accustomed to the frenetic energy of the American city he now called home, a society of diverse nationalities where he blended in easily. In many ways his life was more exciting than the one he had left in Egypt so long ago, yet he was constantly aware of his unfulfilled mission to bring the Mask of Alexander back to its rightful owner.

Ever since Barry Epstein had returned from Russia and confessed that there was a woman who might hold the key to the mask's location, Christos had made a habit of clocking Epstein's movements to see if they might lead him to this woman. It wasn't always easy, since he himself worked odd shifts at the museum, but he did the best he could. He was confident that the purity of his intentions would lend him spiritual assistance.

On this particular day, a morning when both the smog and heat were high, he stationed himself, as usual, across the street from Epstein's Malibu beach house, knowing that his nondescript car would blend in well with those of the morning surfers.

Fortune smiled. He had barely removed the lid from his coffee when he saw his quarry emerge from his front door. He was dressed in California chic: blue jeans, what looked from that distance to be an expensive shirt, open at the collar, and Gucci loafers without socks. He carried a small leather duffle. The duffle meant this was more than a morning Starbucks run.

Obviously our little visit has stirred him up.

The Mask Hunter slid his coffee into the cup holder and started the car. After so many hours wasted following Epstein to places that had no relationship to the mask, he was reluctant to get his hopes up this time. Nonetheless, he wondered if this time might be different as he followed the sleek Maserati through the morning traffic in the direction of the Los Angeles Airport. If Epstein's destination was Las Vegas, he decided he would not follow. He'd been down that road before, wasting time watching the middle-aged libertine feeding cash into slot machines and plastic-breasted women.

He followed Epstein into the parking area that served the domestic terminal, parked his own car a discreet few spaces away, and walked briskly behind his quarry as though he were just another commuter late for his flight.

Once inside the terminal, the Mask Hunter watched as Epstein headed toward a departure gate marked "Denver." That was in Colorado, he believed. *Interesting.*

Two and a half hours later, both Epstein and the Mask Hunter arrived in Denver. The latter was mesmerized by the mountains and would have liked to act the tourist for once. But that was out of the question. He was on duty. He sighed and followed Epstein to the Hertz desk, making sure to stay far enough behind him so as not to call attention to himself.

Once in his own rental car, the Mask Hunter made sure to stay far enough behind Epstein's so that the man would not be aware of his presence. There wasn't much traffic, so it was not difficult to keep the car ahead in sight, even from a distance.

About a half hour from the airport, Epstein's car pulled into an impressive circular driveway that led to an equally impressive shingle-covered house. Christos caught his breath. It was magnificent, a house built into the very rock itself. The thought crossed his mind that this was a house fitting for a Pharaoh. Perhaps this was where Zanski had hidden the mask. Christos' heart beat wildly, and his hands shook as he parked more or less out of sight on the street about a hundred yards away.

He watched as Epstein lifted the iron knocker on the massive oak door and rapped twice. Not exactly to the Mask Hunter's surprise, the door was opened by a woman. Women always figured somewhere in Epstein's activities. From his vantage point he could not make out this one's features, but he could tell she was dark-haired (Epstein's usual), slim, and taller than average.

Then the door closed, and the Mask Hunter considered his options: if he ventured closer, he might be able to look through the window and find out more about this woman and the reason for Epstein's visit. But then, there might also be a dog or something else unpleasant. This kind of house indicated some sort of guardian, and being exposed now would ruin everything. Better to just wait and see.

Epstein had not taken his bag inside with him, so this would probably be a short visit.

The Mask Hunter's museum shift was about to begin. Grenville would not be pleased if Christos failed to arrive for duty. Hoping the lie he was about to tell would be believable, he pressed Grenville's number on his cell phone.

The call was answered on the first ring. "Where the hell *are* you? You were supposed to be here ten minutes ago."

"I just don't feel well. I think I ate something. Could you please make sure the supervisor knows? I would come, but I don't trust myself to be away from the toilet . . ."

His words had the desired effect. "Don't tell me any more. I'll get someone to cover for you. And stay the hell away from me until you're well. The last thing I need is some damn bug you picked up God knows where."

The call ended, as he had anticipated, not on a pleasant note, but things could be worse. It would be worth facing the American's petulance when he returned to LA, because now he was free to concentrate on his mission. He waited, eyes focused on the great oak door.

Boulder, Colorado
The same time

CHAPTER 28

THE MAN STANDING IN THE DOORWAY was Barry Epstein, my former husband, whom I had not seen since the long-ago morning when we signed the divorce papers ending our four-year marriage. But here he was now, hardly waiting for me to open the door, about to push into my living room, muddy feet and all. He did not greet me with a hug, a hello, or even a nod in my direction. He simply began talking in what sounded like midsentence.

"He was murdered, and I'm next," were his opening words.

Barry was leaner and more muscular than I remembered but had lost none of his signature brashness. I was not sure whom or what he was talking about, so I just stood there.

"I suppose you want to come in?" After a few seconds, that was about all I could think of to say.

He stepped in, threw his jacket on a chair, and sat down, looking at me as though he expected something.

"I'm talking about Henry Templeton."

All of a sudden, a lightbulb went off in my head. Of course! Barry was probably still connected with the Warner and its dirty dealings.

I didn't even know why I'd taken Barry's call yesterday, but I had, and I learned that he had kept track of me over the years. He even knew about my second divorce. After a somewhat awkward conversation, I agreed to see him today.

But back to Henry: he and I had been interns together at the Warner a long time ago. I hadn't much liked him, and his opinion of me, if indeed he had one at all, would most likely have been a raised eyebrow, the genteel equivalent of a snort. It was no secret that in those days I had the reputation of being something of a lightweight in the scholarly arena. I was a girl in man's domain. I was very young and not very wise.

As my mother never tired of saying, "Parthi, you're spinning your wheels in the wrong direction. No matter how smart you are and how dedicated, they will never let you in. You'd better get married." A painful judgment that made me cringe to this day.

I had been watching Barry since he entered the room. He did seem frightened, looking first at me, then out the window, and taking his hands in and out of his pockets.

"What makes you think he was murdered?" I asked.

"For one thing, I got this a while back. Didn't think much of it at the time but . . ." He held out an image of the funerary mask of Tutankhamun, the one covered in gold that decorates the covers of almost every book and pamphlet dealing with Ancient Egypt. This one had been crudely torn from a tourist brochure.

I looked at it and then at him. "So what's this got to do with anything?" The image looked pretty tame to me.

"I haven't told you the clincher. You'd better sit down for this one. Two days ago I got a visit from some creep in a stocking mask, pointing a gun at me."

"Wow, what did he want?"

"This might sound like a stretch, but it's possible that whoever did Henry in thinks I have something. Something they want. Something BIG."

"What are you talking about? Henry killed himself. It was in all the papers."

Barry snorted. "Damned lazy LAPD. Close a case fast. That's what they're all about. Suicide saves them the work of hunting for a killer. A lot safer too." He hesitated a moment, then continued, "There's also the possibility that somebody at the Warner put pressure on the police chief . . ." His voice trailed off.

"Henry would never have been able to stand the pressure of going to jail. Let's face it, his world had collapsed, and he fell on his sword like, in his mind, a brave Roman."

"Convenient, but just not true."

"How can you be so sure?"

I watched as Barry mopped his forehead with the monogrammed cuff of his shirt. "OK, it's a long story. I think I need a drink."

When I knew him, Barry never touched alcohol, so this surprised me. "Do you mean a drink drink, or just something wet?"

"Whatever you got, preferably strong."

"I don't have much in the way of alcohol. Would some wine do?"

"Yeah, yeah, whatever. I just need to calm down."

That was not like Barry. The man I had known was fazed by nothing, not even being caught and serving time in Lompoc for tax fraud.

I brought a bottle of cabernet and a glass and set them down on the small table beside Barry's chair. "OK, so tell me what's going on."

He poured a full glass, drained it in one or two swallows, then refilled it. "OK, this all goes back aways. Back to when you and I were married, and you were doing a research project for that internship at the Warner. I was doing some business on the side with that professor of yours, Zanski."

"I know all that," I interrupted. "You were the money man in the deals that brought the whole place down in the antiquities scandal."

"Guilty," Barry smiled, evidently remembering what to him must have been the good old days. "Schott would locate the stuff in Europe, sometimes pilfered from tombs, sometimes made to order in little off-the-beaten-path workshops, and I would broker the deals. Then, voila! The Warner would have a new treasure."

"OK, OK, I told you, I know all that. It made me sick then, and it still does now. Why do you think I left you, left the Warner, left everything I thought I believed in?"

He ignored that, staring into space. "Anyway, there was one last deal in the works before they nabbed Zanski and shipped him back to Russia. And that's what they think I have."

I was getting impatient. "Who and what are you talking about?"

"The 'what' is easy: the Death Mask of Alexander, but the 'who' I am not so sure about."

"What? Not *the* Alexander? How could that be?" This was over the top, even for Barry.

Tutankhamun, the Pharaoh who died at eighteen leaving a sumptuous tomb of treasures, was relatively unaccomplished as a monarch, but Alexander the Great was the stuff of legend. Anything from his tomb would be priceless, and a funerary mask would be off the charts in artistic and dollar value.

And for me, his very name hurled me into the past and a time when my dreams were centered upon finding the tomb he had reportedly constructed for his beloved horse. I was mesmerized by Barry's revelation.

For a moment Barry stopped looking scared and smiled at me in the old smug way I remembered only too well.

My next question was the obvious, although my heart was thumping. "How do you know it even exists?"

"I've seen it." He was back to squirming again. "It was that last deal. The one I was working on just before Zanski got clipped. I had a bad feeling about it. Knew from the beginning it would come to no good. But even *I* never dreamed I'd be running for my fucking life."

"But how could an object as important as the mask you're telling me about have stayed under the radar for so many years, and why come to the surface now?"

Barry let out a noisy puff of air. "Good question. I don't have a clue, but it's got to have something to do with Henry and the smuggling he was doing." He was quiet for several seconds, then continued, "And his death."

"Why would Henry have been any part of that mask deal? He was still an intern like me in 1985. Much too far down on the food chain to even know much about any big purchases, much less being involved in something as earth-shattering as Alexander's mask. You said yourself it was you, Schott, and Zanski who put the deal together."

"Technically, yes. But remember, sweetie pie, no big antiquities sale goes through in Europe without the good old Mafia taking their cut. So it was the three of us, plus those boys who were doing the deal . . ."

"So," I interrupted. "I still want to know where Henry comes in."

"He was the nephew of a thug by the name of Emilio Brazzi. Scum, even by my standards, but he just happened to be the Mafia rep who was with Schott when he showed us the mask that day in Zurich."

That was a stunner. "And I'm supposed to believe this family association was a factor in Henry's demise?"

"Not sure. But blood is thicker than water, and what matters is the fact that Brazzi had access to the mask, Henry had access to him, Henry's dead, and all of a sudden I start getting fan mail and a visit from a thug with a gun."

"That's a bit of a reach. But let's assume you're right, and whoever thinks you have the mask is now pressuring you because of some connection to Henry's death. How do all the pieces fit together, starting with the unlikelihood of a preppy East Coast guy with a name like 'Henry Templeton III' being related to Emilio Brazzi, non-preppy Mafia member?"

"I thought you might have known," Barry began. "Henry never talked about it, of course, but his mother was a refugee from Southern Italy named Giulia Brazzi who came to the States after World War II, got a job as a maid with a blue-blooded Boston family, married the oldest son, and there you have it. Her brother Emilio stayed behind in the Old Country, but she still kept up contact with him after she became Mrs. Henry Templeton Jr. Eventually brother Emilio landed under Schott's wing, supposedly as an 'apprentice,' but, dollars to doughnuts, he was Schott's

Italian connection to the underground antiquities trade."

"So we don't even know for sure how much contact Henry had with his uncle, do we, and if in fact they did any illegal business together?"

Barry shook his head. "But we don't know that they didn't, either."

"How do the rest of the pieces fall into place? How are you still involved?"

"Remember, I'm the last one alive of the Big Three, outside of Brazzi of course, who would make it the Big Four, who's actually seen the damn mask, and I can only guess that Henry had some connection with the wrong people as well."

"More pieces, please." The more I concentrated on the pragmatic, the less my mind questioned the reason I was being pulled back into a world I had left safely behind so long ago.

"OK, OK. As I see it, it's all about the connections here." Barry had obviously spent time sorting the situation out in his mind.

"Zanski and Schott are dead, and we know from his indictment that Henry was pulling the same scams as Zanski, so maybe the mask was what Henry was brokering when he got caught. When he took over as curator at the Warner, he did business with Schott, which points to a likely connection with his uncle Emilio. That court case in Rome proved that he just kept on with the same old–same old scams that Zanski had been pulling. Hard to say exactly how, really, but I just know this is all tied together, and I figure in there too, because I'm on the hook for something I don't have."

"It still boggles my mind that Henry would be so stupid."

"Look, baby, that's the museum world. Odds are, he didn't

act on his own. Getting the best stuff for the Warner was what he was hired to do. Like Zanski, the big boys didn't care how he got the goodies, only that he got them."

"How do they get away with it?"

"Who's to stop them? The average working joe on the street doesn't give a rat's ass about some piece of old clay or stone in some museum they've probably never even gone into. They've got bigger problems, like feeding the kids and paying taxes. So as long as the big museum boys keep their noses clean with the IRS, who's to stop them? Only the people they've robbed, the Italian and Greek governments mostly. But the old boys have that one covered too. If they get caught, they throw the offended party a bone, or in this case, a curator, and everyone else goes home happy. Except of course the curator. With Zanski the penalty was deportation, and for Henry a date with a Roman judge. All the big museums run that way. It's not just the Warner. It's the Met and all the rest. Run by a few guys on the top. And I do mean guys in the literal sense. It's an Old Boys' Club and don't you ever forget it. They think because they're in the art business they're above the law. It's a dirtier operation than any I've ever been into. But they dress better. That goes a long way, I guess."

"OK, I get all that. Still men, and mostly white men, at that. I was hoping there was less misogyny than in my day, but I guess it's not the case. But where do I fit into this puzzle? You and I haven't seen each other for years. So why fly out here from LA and bare your soul to me? What's going on?"

He looked at me for a minute, then down at the floor. "I knew all along what was going on with you and Zanski. I'm not a total fool. The Warner was the biggest fish buying our stuff at the time, so I sucked it up for two years while Zanski screwed my wife at the same time he was sticking his so-called educated nose up at me. But that's all past, and I really don't give a shit about it anymore, so let's just pick up where we are today. I'm really just trying to save my ass. But I do need to know: was there ever any pillow talk between you and Zanski about the mask?"

I could feel my cheeks flush and my pulse quicken. I thought Zanski and I had been so careful. How had Barry found out about the affair, and why had he never brought it up before this? Not even during the divorce?

I felt the old panic coming back, the panic that had driven me to wake up one morning a day or so after Zanski had been deported, in a hospital room God knows where, dizzy from sedation and the pills I'd taken, and crying for my daddy. Now, like then, the room began to spin. Barry must have noticed because he put his arms around me and held me close.

"I'm sorry, baby. I didn't come here to torture you, even if you do deserve it. Just help me, please."

Even though we had both cheated during our marriage, I didn't feel good about it, so I owed him that at least. The room came back into focus as Barry caressed my hair.

"I wish I could, but you've got to believe me, Zanski never said one word to me about any mask. Ever. And I didn't even know he was in such a mess with the law until they said he was deported."

"Was that what drove you over the edge?"

"Perhaps. I just don't know. I only remember I had to get away from you, from thinking about him, from anything that reminded me of archaeology. I was sure even the figurines I was cataloging were robbed from sanctuaries someplace. I ran, and

I got away. That is, until you called yesterday."

"I was surprised you didn't hang up on me. Why?"

"A lot of things, but I guess guilt mostly was in there somewhere. I figured you must have a pretty good reason to call after such a long time, and I owed it to you to at least listen, but I never once thought it could be anything like this."

"Would it have made a difference if you had?"

"I'm not sure. I just don't know if I'm strong enough to reopen this book."

"Fair enough."

By this time my breathing felt normal, and there was no more pain in my chest. I returned to a less painful topic. "If Henry was in fact murdered, and those same guys are after you, how exactly do you think I can do anything about that?"

"For starters, help me find out who they are."

"And how would I do that? I've been away from that world for years. I wouldn't even know where to begin."

"That's just why you are so perfect for this: you've been out of the picture so long, no one I want you to sniff out will even suspect you're back on the academic scene again, given your, er . . ." He hesitated a moment—probably searching for a word that was gentler than the reality—"abrupt departure, and especially not in cahoots with me, because, remember, we're divorced, and not expected to be on any kind of friendly terms."

I turned my attention back to Barry, "And just who are these people you want me 'sniffing out'?"

"Start with the people at the Warner. Past and present. Then, I guess it would be a good idea to find out what Henry was working on before his death . . . and we'll go from there."

Any involvement, even this conversation, was a ticket back

to the past. Chances were, given the amount of time that had elapsed since my flight from the Warner, it was unlikely many people who knew of or about me would still be there. Yet going back to the museum was still a terrifying prospect. If Barry had known about me and Zanski, perhaps other people did too. I could feel the shame and nausea rising in my stomach.

Barry was looking at me with both hope and questions in his eyes. "What's the matter, baby? Ghosts? I can tell you not one of them is half as scary as whoever is after us."

I didn't answer.

"What was it with Zanski, anyway? What did you see in a weird old guy like that? Not to be insulting, but if you wanted an excuse to dump me, I think you could have done better. After all, what we had was probably a starter marriage anyway. Most first marriages are, and we, especially you, were just kids."

"That's cynical, but possibly true. Anyway, it took me years of therapy to realize the obvious: the daddy thing. When you're four and your father shoots himself with a .416 Rigby, it leaves a scar. Zanski offered me the safety of the academic world and the excitement it lacked."

"I know it must have been tough for you as a kid to have a parent who'd offed himself, but I'd hoped you'd gotten past that."

I shook my head. "One never gets past something like that."

"Well, get over it now. Plenty of people have been through worse and they manage to lead pretty decent lives. Look at it this way: at least your old man was on the wrong end of that elephant gun and not you."

"Why are you so cold?"

"Just pragmatic, baby."

Leaving the memories of my father, and the room with its

equal parts of spattered blood and bits of what had once been the person I most trusted, I returned to thoughts of Zanski.

"Zanski was fun, dammit."

"OK, I'll bite. What did he have that I didn't?"

"He was magical. He wasn't just a teacher or a scholar. He made the ancient world come alive. It was as if you were there, in Greece or Rome, and he was leading you through it. Museum objects are so off-limits, not to be touched or even breathed on—but with him all those taboos were irrelevant. I got to sit on an ancient throne, touch any marble statue I wanted, and drink out of Greek wine cups. Those are only for starters."

Barry seemed to be underimpressed. "Yeah, I think you mentioned that. Lunacy. The combination of wine and the lead paint on those cups could have given you a nice case of lead poisoning. No wonder your mother had you locked up."

That stung. The time at Broadview was something I hated being reminded of. "Leave it, Barry. Why don't you just tell me the real reason you're here. If you're really so scared about the mask thing, you could just hire somebody to find out who's stalking you."

"I thought Zanski might have told you something."

"And . . . ?"

"Before I answer that, I need to know one more thing. Probably none of my business, but it's bothered me all these years. When did you start banging Zanski?"

"OK, Barry, I'm not proud of this, but I don't see any point in not telling you. The attraction first took hold on that trip the three of us took to Greece a year or so after you and I were married. We were visiting a new excavation at . . ." I paused a moment, thinking back to that moonlit night almost thirty-five years ago. "Corinth, I think it was. Anyway, you had made some comment about how much the tomb finds would bring on the antiquities market, and it annoyed me. You seemed so crass and materialistic. We started to fight, and you stomped off and refused to go to dinner."

"So it was my fault?"

I didn't answer.

"Go on."

"Zanski and I ended up going to dinner without you. He'd rented a ridiculously large Mercedes, there was a full moon over the Acrocorinth, and, let's face it, Barry, I was twenty, and in my mind escaping a boor of a husband . . ."

"Sounds like a typical setup for a Dracula evening," was Barry's sardonic comment. "Did he bite your neck?"

I ignored him and continued, "Since you want to know, I'll tell you. Nothing happened that night, but when we got back home, we were no longer just professor and student."

"Enough," Barry interrupted. "TMI."

"Well, you asked." It was time to change the subject. "You were saying you thought Zanski told me something about the mask," I reminded him.

"Well . . . I got a letter from one of Zanski's daughters a few months ago. Said she'd been going through some papers in her father's old house and found a letter addressed to me. I naturally asked her to just pop it in the mail. She wrote back that she was trying to piece together Zanski's life for a biography she was writing and wondered if I would visit her in Moscow and go through his papers with her, since we had done so much business together and the Warner had refused to cooperate. No wonder."

"And you went?"

"Yup. I thought it was worth a shot to see if there were any clues about where the mask went. Maybe I could find it and get my money back . . ."

"Who blew the whistle on Zanski, anyway?"

"Didn't you know? It was Henry. Made a deal with the trustees to give them enough dirt on his boss to take the heat off themselves. Henry gave the trustees Zanski, and they gave him Zanski's job."

"That's a surprise. I would never have thought Henry had that kind of grit in him."

"Stranger things have happened. Maybe the Italian genes."

"You still haven't told me what this has to do with me."

"Well, the daughter gave me free access to more than his papers. His personal stuff as well, like his whole attic full of just about everything. I thought maybe, just maybe, he'd stashed the mask there—unless of course he was even crazier than everybody thought, and planned to channel Alexander by being buried with it." He stopped his narrative for a second and laughed at his own cleverness, then continued, "So I figured, hell, it was worth a try. The guy owed me from way back, anyway, so why not give him a chance to make it up at the end?"

"How noble of you."

"You don't have to get sarcastic. Anyway, I searched the whole place. Nada. Then I opened the letter and voila! The clue I was looking for."

I held my breath. "And what did it say?"

Barry laughed again. "Here's where you come into the picture, sweetheart. Now, mind you, the guy was always a drama junkie, so I should not have been surprised."

"Just tell me what the letter said."

Barry chuckled. "'If you are reading this, I am more than likely dead. You will be looking for the mask. However, my friend, you will have to go to our Parthenia for that.'"

He shook his head, "Crazy old coot put the screws to me one more time."

"Is that all the letter said?"

"Yep. Short and not so sweet."

"Just a minute!" The news had sent me reeling. "I told you, I never saw or even knew the thing existed. Please tell me you don't think I have it."

He shook his head. "Beats me, but now, considering what I'm 100 percent sure happened to Henry, it's no longer just a matter of finding the mask and finishing the deal with the Warner . . ."

"You wouldn't think they'd touch it after all the scandal."

"Oh, yes, they would. In a heartbeat. Those guys are a breed apart. They run the richest museum in the world. They're power junkies. I guess I know because I'm one myself," he laughed. "Anyway, don't be naïve. They've gone through two major wrist slappings, and now the probable murder of one of their own, and still, despite all the damning publicity, or maybe because of it, swarms of people still stand in line to see their latest find. They would jump at the chance to get that mask, pay through the nose, of course, and find a way to make themselves heroes in the bargain. I wouldn't get any credit, you can be sure. Dealers are really second-class citizens in their book, but I would be paid."

"All that turns my stomach, and I never intend to go back."

"That ship has sailed, baby. You're in this thing, like it or not.

Do you think for a minute that I'm the only person Zanski told that you had the mask? My bet is that whoever is after me, they will come a-knockin' at this hand-hewn door next."

"Why would they do that?"

"There's something I left out." Barry's face changed color a bit and his eyes dropped to his shoes. "That guy who came to visit me, the guy with a gun. He meant business. I had to give him something or get shot. I told him you had the mask. I didn't mean to, Parthi—I didn't mean to throw you under the bus. It's just who I am, I guess," he finished, almost in a whimper.

It took a minute for the whole thing to sink in. How could my lover and supposed mentor have implicated me as some sort of accomplice in the mask deal?

And even worse, Barry, snake that he was, had pointed the finger at me as well.

"Is this some sort of revenge for the divorce? You were the one who wanted out, not me. If anything, this should be the other way around."

But it never was with Barry.

He could have been followed here. If Barry had been threatened with a gun, what would happen to me?

"Tell me everything I need to know to get us out of this horror show."

"I like the way you use the word *us*."

I ignored the inference. "Let's go back to the time you and Zanski brought the mask to Los Angeles. What happened when you got there?"

"The last time I saw the mask was when he got out of my car with it just after we got back from Switzerland. The next day he got deported, as you well know, and the mask went missing."

"Do you think he managed to take it to Russia with him?"

"Possibly, although they whisked him to the airport pretty fast, and I don't think he would have had much chance to pack a toothbrush, much less something like that. But here's another thought," he continued. "I don't know 100 percent if he even brought it to the States. All I actually saw was the duffle he was carrying. Anything could have been inside. He was no dummy, and he might have suspected something nasty was about to go down. So he might have had a Plan B—a way to sell the mask to someone else."

"You mean someone in Europe?"

"Could be. Or Dubai, or Denver, or almost anywhere the money was good."

"Interesting. Speaking of money, I gather you could use that money back?"

"Yep. Badly."

"Gambling again?"

"Guilty."

"This is a mess. Do you know anything else? For example, where did the mask come from in the first place? Does this mean that someone has actually found Alexander's tomb?"

"Wish I could tell you. I tried to press Schott about it, but then I went to jail myself for the tax thing, as you may recall, and that put me out of commission. When I got out, I was on probation for five more years, so that sort of cut into my ability to deal with the darker side."

"Do you mean the smugglers?"

"Who else? The feds suspected I might still have a finger in the antiquities trade, so to make damn sure I didn't go back to my old tricks, they watched me like a flock of hawks. That's what they're doing with our tax money, harassing businessmen like me and letting the killers go free."

"Should I be sorry for you?"

"You really hate me, don't you?"

"Even if I did, which I don't, this is no time to think about that. Where do you think the mask came from originally?"

"Anyone could have dug up the mask anywhere, but the two likeliest places are Macedonia or somewhere in Egypt. Macedonia is a bit less of a bet because their antiquities boys keep a closer watch on looters. But on the other hand, Alexander being buried back in the land of his ancestors is a distinct possibility. I just don't know."

I was feeling overwhelmed. "This mess gets worse and worse. My gut tells me to push you out that door and pretend we never had this conversation."

He shrugged. "You could do that, I suppose. But since I already told the guy about you, and maybe a hint about where to find you, that would not be a wise choice."

I took a deep breath. Yesterday I was on a new path forward, free from a marriage to a controlling man, in a new place and with a budding new career. Today I was about to fight for my life, and through no fault of my own. It was up to me to save myself from this horror both Barry and Zanski had thrown me into.

The room was spinning again, and I could feel the numbness in the back of my legs. I just didn't know what to do. What if I broke down again?

"I need to think. Can we talk tomorrow?"

"Fair enough. I'll get a room in town for the night and call you in the morning. Be sure and lock your doors."

Boulder, Colorado
Minutes later

CHAPTER 29

Eventually Epstein emerged, alone. He looked carefully in all directions before he got into his car and drove away. The Mask Hunter was tempted to follow, but instinct told him to stay and learn more about the dark-haired woman.

He almost missed her as she emerged from the back door about fifteen minutes later. Luckily, he had decided it was safe enough to leave his vehicle and move closer to the house. That gave him the vantage point he needed to watch her as she walked toward a large garage at the rear of the property. She was older than he had first thought. Perhaps close to his own age, but still very beautiful. Her long, dark hair fell in soft masses around her face and bounced as she walked. He'd seen a lot of European and American women, beautiful ones, but there was something about this one that was different. He knew he should not be thinking such thoughts, but in spite of that, he gave himself over to the briefest fantasy of reaching his fingers underneath the loose sweater she was wearing and caressing her nipples until they became erect.

She took a key and entered the garage. He noticed she did not lock the door behind her. The windows of the building were small and obscured by dust. If the Mask Hunter wanted to observe what the woman was doing, he would have to follow her inside.

After five minutes of agonized deliberation, he approached the door and cautiously turned the handle. It made a scraping noise as he pushed it open. He froze. What was he doing? If she in fact was keeping the mask here, he could not take it from her and leave her alive. But he could not bear the thought of harming this vulnerable-looking woman if there was any other way to accomplish his mission.

Soundlessly, he backed out of the door and retreated to the bushes.

Boulder, Colorado
The same time

CHAPTER 30

After Barry left, a thought occurred to me. Zanski had written me a couple of letters after he went back to Russia so many years ago. I was hurt by his betrayal in taking up with another woman, and so quickly, that I had not answered them, but I had kept them—I guess because I was not ready to let go. If my memory was correct, I had stored them in the apartment above the garage in the same box with my dissertation notes while I was living at my mother's house after my breakdown.

Although not specifically a hoarder, my mother had been one of those people who never threw anything away. Chances were that the box was still there, gathering dust along with the rest of my young memories. Before she died she had reminded me that I had "stuff" to go through up there, but I hadn't had the inclination to do anything about it.

I'd dressed up a bit for Barry's visit: a cream silk blouse and tapered black pants. Much too fancy for a foray among mice and cobwebs. Had I wanted to impress him? I hoped not.

I changed into my standard gardening outfit: blue jeans that had seen better days and a cashmere sweater that had clearly provided sustenance for many a family of moths.

The garage door was a bit warped, but it opened with a good push. I pocketed the key and walked toward the stairs. Like the rest of the interior, they were pretty much dust covered. Clearly no one had been up to the apartment in some time.

The apartment itself could only be described as "basic." Intended for a groom or chauffeur, it was built, like the house, in the day when servants were presumed to have no lives outside of their domestic duties, and thus were in no need of any great creature comforts. It was essentially a single room with two alcoves: one served as a kitchen and the other as a bathroom/dressing room/closet. I headed for the latter. It was piled fairly densely with random horse tack, a couple of tennis racquets with broken strings, and the box.

I pulled it out from underneath the rest of the paraphernalia and carried it into the main room. After examining the La-Z-Boy recliner for other occupants, I sat down and lifted off the cardboard cover.

I had only just begun to plow through the file folders crammed with class notes when I felt something was wrong. Like I was being watched. I tried to shake the feeling off. Barry's jitters were obviously rubbing off on me.

I got up and looked out the window. Nothing there. No sound, no movement. I went back to my folders. The two letters I was searching for were easy to find. Addressed to me in care of my mother and written in Zanski's distinctive hand. I trembled a bit as I opened the first one. It was like those blue eyes were watching me as I read the single short page that was little more than a note:

> *Little One, this bleak landscape reminds me of how much I miss you. But fear not, this stupid bureaucratic red (appropriate color, yes?) tape will all be sorted out soon and I will be back with you.*
>
> *Until then, I love you.*
>
> *Z*

No mention of what the wife and kiddies would think of that. Also, no mention of any mask. I opened the second letter, a bit longer than the first:

Little One,

I have not heard from you, and it troubles me greatly. I hope that filthy propaganda about me and another woman did not reach your eyes. If it did, please believe in us and not those lies. I also am not even sure where you are. Please write and tell me you are well and if and when you will be returning to your studies. As you know, that interests me greatly.

I love you.

Z

My mind drifted a bit, remembering Zanski: his amazing white hair and kisses more passionate than one would have expected from a man his age.

I was brought back to the dreary room by a slight noise downstairs. Stupidly I had left the garage door unlocked, even after Barry's warning to be careful. Heart a-thump, I tiptoed to the landing and peeked down. Nothing. I must have been imagining things. No matter, the mood was broken, so I piled the letters and the folders hastily back into the box and beat a hasty retreat down the stairs and outside, looking cautiously in all directions.

Safely back in the house, I replayed Zanski's few words in my mind. He had mentioned nothing about any mask, nor did he even hint at anything like it.

I paced a bit, looking repeatedly out the window. It was no good. I had to get out of there. I was probably imagining things, but even so, I needed to talk to someone. I decided on my psychiatrist.

DR. HERMAN SCHWARTZ, a Vienna-trained psychotherapist specializing in panic disorders, had been living and practicing in Boulder since the 1990s. I had been seeing him since moving back here last year when my mother was ill.

Only the discreet office directory posted on the converted Victorian house in the center of town revealed that the building was anything other than a historical landmark. The residential ambiance continued inside, with velvet-covered chairs and tables draped with Turkoman rugs. More of the same rugs covered the dark oak floors.

Two hours after I had called him, Dr. Schwartz met me at the door and led me into his office. Because of my history of mental instability, Dr. Schwartz always made room to see me even without an appointment.

"Let's begin with a few relaxing exercises before we start the session. Please sit in this chair and plant both feet in front of you." The psychiatrist pulled one of the red velvet chairs opposite his own.

"Now close your eyes and take a deep breath in through your nose, then hold it for four counts, then exhale for six. Place your hand on your abdomen to make sure you are drawing the breath into your stomach and not your chest."

He watched as I inhaled slowly. "Good. Now hold for five seconds and exhale through your mouth."

I'd been through this exercise before and knew it would calm my rapidly beating heart.

When I was calm enough, Dr. Schwartz's voice changed

from a soothing purr to his normal tone. “All right, Parthenia, what’s going on?”

I told him about Barry’s visit and the fear I was feeling. I told him about my impulse to flee.

“You’ve been running, Parthenia, since you were a little girl, and it hasn’t done you much good. It looks to me like your past is searching you out. This time it seems you cannot run. You must be strong enough to face this.”

“Dr. Schwartz, I’ve been coming here every week for almost a year. I’ve learned a lot about myself. I’ve learned how we create what happens to us . . .”

“Not so fast, Parthenia. You need to think a minute here. Yes, you have in part created this situation, but that path was in motion long before Barry came to your house today.”

“You mean, when I got involved with Zanski?”

“Yes, and before that, when your father, like Zanski, left you in such a brutal and abrupt way. This is all like a great ball of yarn we have to unravel.”

“Chickens coming home to roost?”

“One might say so.” A smile crossed Dr. Schwartz’s face. “But these chickens are a lot more dangerous than ordinary barnyard fowl.”

“You think the threats to Barry and me are real?”

He shook his head. “I just do not know. What I do know is that it never hurts to be cautious.” He stopped a moment, then continued, “You still haven’t yet told me if you have any idea what you plan to do.”

“Dr. Schwartz, I’m boxed in. It’s like there’s a cattle prod at my back shoving me into a killing chute.”

“A bit dramatic, your description, but I must admit, somewhat apt." He looked at his watch. It was after seven. "Why don't you go home now, sleep on this, and call me in the morning?"

Going home was just what I did not want to do. The idea of my dark, empty house was terrifying. What if Barry was not lying and there were dangerous people watching us?

After leaving Dr. Schwartz's office I sat in my car without starting the engine, mulling over my options. Going home was not one of them. Arriving on my BFF Sandra Peters' doorstep asking her to take me in for the night would require an explanation I wasn't ready to give. That left Barry and the Red Lion, where he mentioned he was spending the night. Not a perfect choice, but being alone felt scarier than the danger of being around Barry. I had his cell number from his call yesterday.

He picked up on the third ring. "Parthi?"

My name must have come up on his screen.

"What's up?"

There was noise in the background—maybe he was in the hotel bar. I hesitated, not sure how to explain myself, then blurted out, "I'm afraid to go home after what you told me, so I was thinking of taking a room at the Lion . . ."

"Great idea! I was just about to have dinner. Want to join me?"

I hadn't planned on being social. Not exactly. I'd suggested the Red Lion to Barry because it was somewhat removed from town, about a mile from my house, and populated more by locals than out-of-towners—not the easiest place for a shadowy assassin to strike. I did have to eat, and Barry was at least someone I did not have to fake a calm exterior for, so I agreed. "I'll meet you in the lobby in ten minutes."

"I SEE YOU DIDN'T DRESS FOR THE OCCASION." Barry scanned my ratty-looking jeans and holey sweater when he greeted me on the steps of the hotel. He looked like he had showered and changed since our afternoon meeting. "Some lipstick wouldn't hurt."

"So don't eat with me. I'm here only because this seems safer than my house, thanks to you and Zanski."

"OK, OK, you'd look fine in anything. I was just trying to be cute. My mistake."

I considered telling Barry about my foray into the attic and Zanski's notes, then decided against it. The exercise had given no new information, so what was the point? Or was I still clinging to that last shred of intimacy with my former lover, reluctant to open his words to anyone else? I couldn't be sure.

"Just give me a minute to check in."

He looked at my smallish handbag. "Is that your luggage?"

"I just didn't want to go back to the house. I had that feeling in my spine."

"Go back? You mean you were out somewhere in that outfit?"

"Only to my shrink."

"You must have been in quite a hurry."

I didn't reply, so Barry changed the subject. "How about after you register, we eat, and I drive over with you to grab a few things?"

"Thanks. I'd appreciate that." After what Barry had presumably told the shadowy assassin, any sane woman would have steered clear of him. But I was desperate.

Once we were seated at a quiet table at the back of the dining room, menus in hand, an awkward silence fell between us.

I was the first to speak, and I got right to it. "I want to know what the likelihood is that Alexander was buried with the kind of mask you saw."

"Hmm." Barry folded his menu and looked at me. "I could go for a steak. What about you?"

My own menu was still untouched. "I guess salmon. Dinner originally seemed like a good idea, but I'm not really hungry."

"None of that no-eating stuff. A budding girl detective needs to keep up her strength."

Once we ordered, Barry gave me his full attention. "So how much do you know about Alexander?"

"I'm not clear on every detail," I began. "Remember, it's been a long time since I studied this stuff. Alexander died in Babylon but was buried a lot farther away, Alexandria I think."

"And this means . . .?"

"Not a great dinner conversation, but in the fourth century it would take a while to transport a body that distance. And in a hot climate . . ."

Barry jumped on my thought before I had finished.

"Let's eat fast and pick up my laptop."

"You got it."

We spent the rest of the meal in relative silence, each of us picturing in our heads what the next steps might be. I wasn't sure about Barry, but I felt a bit of my anxiety replaced by a spark of excitement.

Back at my house after dinner, Barry waited while I threw what I would need for the next day into an overnight bag, looking out my bedroom window as I did so, expecting who knew what.

"Could you unplug the laptop and take the cable with it?" I called down the stairs as I added my makeup bag to my sparse luggage and zipped it up.

"Sure thing. Anything else?"

"Not that I can think of."

"That was fast," he smiled as I joined him in the living room less than five minutes later. "Got everything?"

"Probably not, but I need to get out of here. I just want this whole thing over."

"In your dreams. It ain't even begun."

Red Lion Inn
Boulder, Colorado
Later that evening

CHAPTER 31

The fire in the small room off the lobby at the Red Lion was burning in full force when Barry and I sat down in two overstuffed chairs, my laptop on a small table between us.

"So where were we?" Barry began. "And how did Alexander die, anyway? And better yet, how did he live?"

"Well, he was not even quite thirty-three, so he didn't die of old age."

"What did him in?"

"As far as I can remember, nobody quite knows for sure. People have speculated about poison, diphtheria, even West Nile virus. Or it could just have been hard living catching up with him."

"Yeah, I heard he was fond of the grape." Barry took a sip from the cabernet he'd brought from the bar, closed his eyes, and swished it around in his mouth.

"He also had a busy love life. Wives, male and female lovers, supposedly even a eunuch."

"Holy shit! I can't even imagine what anybody would do with a eunuch."

"Don't try. Zanski used to say that the Greeks were so much

more advanced in their ideas of sex and morality than we, as he called us, 'bourgeois moderns.' "

"Yeah, yeah, sounds like him, but get to the point. Was the guy, Alexander, not Zanski, gay or not?"

"He, Zanski, not Alexander, said there was no concept of 'gay' or 'straight' in ancient Greece. Most men had sex with men, but married women."

"People do that today. So?"

"His point was that this was expected behavior."

"OK then, for his time he was just a normal guy."

"That's about it. Nothing he did in the sexual arena raised an eyebrow. What was abnormal about him, godlike to most of his world, was how much of it he conquered and how fast.'

"Aha, and now we get back to why he rated so much folderol when he died."

"Exactly. It's been more than thirty years since I've thought about Alexander the Great or anything else ancient, so let's check the facts before we jump to conclusions about that mask."

I Googled "death of Alexander the Great" and immediately found what I was looking for. When I turned the screen in Barry's direction, it took him only a few seconds to find the sentence that had caught my attention.

"They quote Plutarch, not a shabby reference. Alexander's body was handled by Egyptian embalmers." Barry read on, paraphrasing as he went. "The body was supposedly transported in some sort of cart from Babylon to Alexandria. It seemed to have taken two years to get there. And in the heat of the Middle East? They definitely would have had to have done something to preserve it."

"Exactly. And that something must have been the mummification mentioned by Plutarch. And besides linen wrappings, masks are the most common asset of an Egyptian mummy."

"Why was that?"

"The soul used the mask as a vehicle for eating and breathing."

Barry was still reading. "Looks like that mummy or whatever bounced around quite a bit, first to Memphis, the original capital of Egypt, then on to at least two separate tombs in Alexandria, Alexander's city, before suddenly dropping out of sight around a thousand years later. Seems like, even dead, our guy was always on the move."

I nodded. "So it looks like there's a good chance such a mask did exist at one time. But is it the same one you saw?"

"Beats me, baby. But I'd say there's a more than even chance."

I noticed the boyish look on Barry's face as he contemplated the import of what he had just said. There was a light in his eyes, and his upper lip curled into a quirky grin—a true Peter Pan gone awry.

He looked at me over the laptop screen. "It's kind of hard to wrap my head around a Greek military hero ending up as a mummy. What was going on with him, anyway?"

"A lot, I think."

"Do tell." Barry was looking at me expectantly.

"Well, let's start with how Alexander lived. He didn't just conquer other countries. It was almost as if they conquered him."

"Why do you say that?"

"It's well known that Alexander took on the clothing, customs, and religions of the cultures he conquered . . ."

Barry interrupted me. "I remember reading that he did that

for diplomatic reasons. Made his new rule less offensive to the natives."

I nodded. "Yes, that's part of it. But my theory is there was something more."

"I'm all ears, professor."

"I think it had a lot to do with family dysfunction."

"What?" Barry was shaking his head.

"For starters, it's pretty much a known fact that there was no love lost between Alexander and his father, and it has always seemed obvious to me, if to no one else, that he went off to find a new identity."

Barry laughed. "Maybe, but what does that have to do with his ending up as a mummy?"

I read him something I'd seen a few minutes back—a Roman scholar named Quintus Rufus claimed that Alexander wanted to be buried in the temple of his real father, the god Zeus-Ammon, at Siwa Oasis in Egypt, and not next to Philip of Macedon in Greece.

Barry looked up at me with an expression I couldn't quite read. "Wasn't Philip of Macedon the guy most people credit with being Alexander's bio-dad?"

"Yep. This could be a total Roman fabrication, written years later, about Alexander's final wishes, but it's the best intel we have so far. It's pretty well known that Alexander's family myth was that he was descended from Zeus, making him a god . . ."

"People actually bought that shit?"

"Incredible, isn't it, that people believed that? And that, in an age without social media or even newspapers, his life history could have been so well known?"

"He must have had a great PR team," Barry commented.

"Odd you should say that. In fact his PR had a lot to do with his success—and his reputation today. But if the propaganda is true, and let's assume for the moment it is, it's evidence that Alexander, at the end, identified in a big way with Egypt, much more so than Greece." I paused a moment. "So we have not only the practical body preservation pointing toward mummification but Alexander's mindset as well."

Just then my cell phone buzzed. I looked at the screen. It was Sandra, my good friend and current interior design client. I took the call, mouthing to Barry that this would not take long. He nodded and turned his attention back to the computer screen.

"So how much should we bid on the desk?" Sandra's voice was breathy, as though she had just been running.

I had totally forgotten that I promised to research the value of her dream Art Deco desk, which was being auctioned in Los Angeles on Saturday. "Um. Not sure, S., a lot will depend on who is bidding against us."

"Woo, a real test of strategy," she giggled.

"Just to give you a ballpark, I haven't checked any recent comps, but I think we should be able to nab it for $30,000—that is, if none of the big collectors are interested. No way to be absolutely certain, but let's keep fingers crossed."

"Hey, guess what?" Sandra's voice took on an even more excited tone. This was obviously a rhetorical question because she did not wait for my answer. "It turns out I can go with you after all. To the auction, I mean. John's going on some sort of river-rafting thing with the boys. We'll have an absolute blast."

"Fabulous!" I tried to sound enthusiastic, but my mind was wandering back to the fourth century. It occurred to me that this could work out well for both her desk and my first stab at finding out something about that mask. As long as I was in this mess, I knew I had to solve it.

I turned on speakerphone and gestured to Barry to listen. "How about we stay at the Beverly Wilshire and walk to Sotheby's—and everything else on Rodeo Drive?"

Sandra squealed, "Yay! I'll book it. When shall we leave?"

"Let's see," I mentally calculated how much time I would need to fulfill my desk-procuring obligation and have enough left over to find out what I could about Henry, his demise, and the mask. I continued, "This is Tuesday. The auction is Saturday, and we need to be there in time for the preview the day before, so I'd say we want to leave here on Thursday."

"That doesn't give us a whole lot of time to get ready, but I'm game if you are. Let's plan to stay over a couple of days after the auction. Give us time to play. If I'm going to the Big City, I want to do it right."

"Meaning?"

"I want to hit that high-class pawn shop where all the fab jewelry turns up, for one thing. And for something a bit more intellectual, I was hoping you would give me an inside tour of that fancy Warner Museum."

Barry, listening across from me, perked up at the mention of the Warner, giving me a nod and a thumbs-up.

"I haven't even been inside the Warner since I was a student, and it's all been redone since then, so I would not be much of a tour guide."

"I don't care that much about the actual stuff in the place. I want you to tell me about the old days—and the scandals, and what's your take on that Henry Templeton person in the news."

I had to reach over and block a whoop that was about to escape from Barry's mouth. "I don't know anything more than what we all read in the papers," I lied, then I steered the conversation in a more comfortable direction. "I have a good feeling about your desk."

"Oh, do you really? It would look so good in my library. And," she added, "even if you don't have any inside scoops on the Warner, it will be fun going there with you anyway."

She obviously didn't want to let the subject drop.

A few feminine squeals later, our plans were set: Sandra would book the hotel and the flights, and I would make the auction arrangements and work out a strategy to outwit any other buyers.

As she and I discussed the details of the trip to LA, Barry, impatient, was making the universal "cut" gesture, sliding his index finger across his throat. I, too, was relieved to be able to end the call at last.

"Well, even though your friend does not sound like a great mind, she does think alike. That auction will be a perfect cover for your snooping in LA."

"I was just thinking that."

He stood up and yawned, "Been a long day. I'm turning in. Need anything?"

I shook my head, suddenly tired as well. "Breakfast?"

"Sure. Sleep tight."

I sat for a moment after Barry left the room, staring into the waning fire.

Boulder, Colorado
The next morning

CHAPTER 32

Although I kept an eye in my rearview mirror on the drive back to the house, that was really only pro forma. The morning sunlight did a good job of routing the feeling of someone following me. Mostly.

Nevertheless, when I pulled up in my driveway, I parked as near as I could to the front door. Then I looked in all directions not once but twice before I got out.

My key fit smoothly into the front door lock, and, opening the door, I looked at the house—really looked at it.

Something about Barry's visit had reopened the past, and the chance it offered to face those old demons once and for all gave me a surprising sense of exhilaration. It was time.

So what if some Mafia person or whatever was about to pounce on me to get an object I didn't have? Since I had no idea at all about the mask, they would think I was holding out and pull off my fingernails and a tooth or two before dressing me in cement shoes. But even that did not frighten me as much as the life I now realized I was leading: hiding out in the house I had inherited from my mother, going through the motions of living without being truly alive, and waiting for the next bout of panic to strike.

Was being an interior designer what I really wanted to do with the rest of my life? As I looked out the living room window at the massive rock into which part of the house was built, and named after, I realized that many of the world's risk takers, the adrenaline junkies, are really just depressed people trying desperately to feel something, anything except the apathy that traps them.

I had always thought of Barry as the rash one, but that did not seem so true at the moment. The prospect of real danger, the kind we were facing, had no appeal for him. But it did for me.

My morbid inner soliloquy was interrupted by my cell phone buzzing. Ironically, it was Barry.

"Hey." He began the conversation as usual without the nicety of *hello*. "I just got another love note, or love picture, if you will, tucked into the windshield of the rental car. Whoever it is that's after us is pretty close. In Boulder. Following me. It creeps me out, to state the obvious. Don't want to scare you, but are you home yet?"

I felt an immediate stab of dread. "Just got here. I did keep an eye in the rearview when I was driving. Did you see at all what this person looked like, the one who confronted you?"

"Well, it was dark, but I could see he was pretty tall—taller than me, anyway. As I told you, he was wearing a stocking over his head, so I couldn't see the hair or eyes or anything." Barry was five feet nine.

"What about his voice?"

"Pretty muffled, but maybe Middle Eastern? Can't be sure. You're pretty calm for a lady alone in a house with a lot of places a marauder can hide."

"Thanks for reminding me of that. Anyway, did you call the police?"

"And tell them what? That somebody left a cutout of a Hellenistic coin on my car? Since when is that illegal?"

"Didn't you even report that you were held at gunpoint?"

Barry was silent for a minute, then answered in a somewhat sheepish voice. "Well, he warned me not to . . ."

About what I could expect from Barry. I changed the subject.

"I just thought of something I forgot to ask you before, but was the first photo, the Tutankhamun mask, sent through the mail?"

"Yes, plain cheap envelope with an Atlanta postmark."

"What do you think that means? Do you know anybody in Atlanta?"

"It means just about zip, Sherlock. Anybody could have slipped a few bucks to some random guy getting on a plane to Atlanta so he would drop the envelope in a mailbox when he landed. Done all the time. Don't you read crime novels like you used to?"

"I just wasn't thinking. I guess I'm still not ready to wrap my head around the fact that all this is real." I changed the subject. "You know I'll be in LA the day after tomorrow. That auction thing, but Sandra will be only too happy to see me spending time with my first husband. She's such a romantic. Anyway, that will give you and me time to figure something out."

"OK, but what should I do in the meantime, lock myself in my house with a gun?" Barry's voice was whiney.

Of course he wanted reassurance, but I couldn't resist giving him the opposite. "You could, but it probably wouldn't do much good. If they want to, and of course they do, whoever is after us, or, more correctly the mask, will get to us anyway."

"I did contact a bodyguard service, so when I land in LA a six-foot German named Gunnar and I will be cozy roomies." He paused. "I just need to get on and off this plane in one piece . . ."

I could hear the loudspeaker in the distance, calling what must be his flight.

"They probably will leave you alone in the airport and on the plane. Too much security around for them to take the chance."

Barry sounded dubious. "If you say so."

"Hiring that bodyguard is a great idea! That should take your mind off the jitters for the time being. I need some sort of protection too, since you have painted a bull's-eye on my back. I'm going back to the Red Lion until I leave for LA. See you either Thursday night or Friday morning."

We signed off, but my own jitters did not.

I SAT DOWN. Then all of a sudden I began to think about things differently. I realized that what had begun with Barry's visit yesterday was the answer to the problem that had been bothering me for so many years. I needed to do more with my life than mope about dead fathers and lost lovers. I'd left the Warner so long ago not because of Zanski but because of what he represented: greed and dishonesty and careers built on robbing the dead. That's what it boiled down to. How misguided I had been to ever have thought that life glamorous. But now I had a second chance. I would find that mask and return it to its rightful owner: the man it had been buried with.

I exhaled and got up. I had a clear path at last.

Sandra and I were leaving for Los Angeles in the morning, so I knew I had to devote some time to packing, but that could wait. I was no longer a silly middle-aged woman flailing around on the planet. I had a purpose. I was a mask hunter. As a horse-crazy teenager I had been obsessed with Alexander and his horse Bucephalus, galloping across the fields on his namesake, imagining I was conquering the world. Alexander had led me to study archaeology, and now it was Alexander again who was leading me back into it. But how different it was this time! This was real.

Flight 2862 to LAX
Denver, Colorado
The next day

CHAPTER 33

The flight from Denver to LAX took roughly two hours, during which Sandra never stopped talking, so I had no time for thoughts of Alexander.

"What's our strategy for getting the best price on the desk?"

As far as the auction was concerned, I wasn't sure whether or not I wanted it known that my client represented major money.

"Most buyers want to keep a low profile in the hope that the other bidders will overlook a major piece like your desk, but nothing's a sure thing at an auction."

"Meaning?"

"We'll really have to see when we get there who's likely to bid against us. But in this case it may not hurt to let the competition know you can outbid anyone in the room."

Sandra laughed, flattered but feigning modesty. "Let's hope that's true. If I see any Saudis in the room eyeing the desk, I may head for the hills."

"No matter what, it will be exciting."

My words were encouraging, but I was only going through the motions. Overnight, Alexander and his mask had relegated the upcoming auction of one of the finest pieces of furniture created in the twentieth century to a bland footnote.

Not so for Sandra, who had the auction catalogue on her lap open to the photo of the Jean-Michel Frank desk that was the object of our quest. She was reading the accompanying blurb.

"Says here Frank just about single-handedly created the minimalist aesthetic."

"Yes," I replied. "The wood and workmanship of that desk carry the whole thing. Wait until you run your hands over it."

Sandra sighed. "I can't wait. I love the fact that the lines are so straight and simple, but it's still so luxurious."

I nodded. "Frank was a genius. Did you also know he was a distant cousin of Anne Frank?"

"No, how fascinating."

"He was so brilliant, but so tortured," I continued. "Jumped out of a window in New York while he was relatively young." I stopped a minute. "I think you know about my father . . ."

"Yes," Sandra replied. "I am so sorry. I hope asking you to get this desk for me hasn't opened old wounds."

"Not at all," I assured her. "I live with those wounds every day, anyway."

"Oh, you poor thing! Let's have fun in LA and help you forget the sadness."

After landing at LAX we had no trouble finding the limo Sandra had hired, but once inside the car the pace of our trip slowed. It seemed as if we were stuck in traffic for an eternity as the long black vehicle inched its way down Wilshire to the hotel. The 405 freeway had been bad enough, but this was insanity.

Another reason I had left the city.

Once in the elegantly understated third-floor suite at the Beverly Wilshire, looking out over some of the most expensive real estate in the world, I told Sandra a tiny white lie about a headache and settled down for a welcome hour of alone time before I was due to meet her downstairs. We planned to have tea first, then a walk over to Sotheby's, which I had found out would conveniently be open until 7 p.m. for previews of the auction.

I sat by the window with a cold Perrier at my elbow, one of the countless amenities provided by the management. I shuffled the papers I had brought with me until I found what I was looking for.

At first reading I had discounted it as one of the more absurd of the quests for Alexander's tomb, but after looking it over, it made some sense. Twenty years ago, a waiter in Alexandria claimed he had located the tomb and would sell that location to the highest bidder. He was supposed to have amassed more information than most scholars. If he had also combed the city for bits and pieces of what once might have been parts of the tomb, he might indeed have been on to something. I was intrigued. If I were looking for a missing tomb, I would look for it not as a whole building but as pieces of one. And, if my logic was correct, those pieces would be part of, or near, existing houses or retaining walls. Since the poor in Alexandria, in antiquity as well as today, had only limited means to transport heavy objects such as stone, it was likely the fragments were, even now, not far from the tomb site.

I constructed a bull's-eye with radii of about ten miles in each direction of any suspiciously opulent marble elements in otherwise humble structures. But why was I wasting time with this when I was not supposed to be searching for the tomb site or any of its building blocks? Little by little, it began to dawn on me that I was still tethered to archaeology. My challenge was to find a mask, two feet long at most. That was a task even sketchier than picking up scattered blocks of marble.

Beverly Hills Hotel
Beverly Hills, California
The next day

CHAPTER 34

Barry and I met for lunch at his old watering hole, the Polo Lounge of the Beverly Hills Hotel. As I remembered, rubbing elbows with head honchos of the film world who all knew his name had always been his idea of the right place to be. He hadn't changed. The moment we sat down, he flashed a crisp Ben Franklin at the waiter, directing him to deliver a bottle of Dom to a table in the corner. I didn't look, but I guessed the recipient must have been either Stallone, a pal of his, or a nameless starlet he hoped to bed. No, he definitely had not changed.

"Put it on my tab, Raul," he directed the tuxedo-clad server.

Raul nodded, pocketing the bill. "Right away, Mr. Epstein."

I pretended not to notice. "I've done some more research on this Alexander mummy thing, but that doesn't help us find it."

"True. Right now we're at a dead end."

"What about some of your old contacts? You know, the Mafia guys?"

"Are you kidding me? How do we know they aren't the ones after me?" He shook his head as if he were talking to a backward child. "There should be some way your scholarly brain can come up with something better than that."

Barry had never completed much formal education, and

during our marriage he had invariably expressed an ambivalence, if not downright scorn, toward my academic path. "You may have the school smarts, but I've got the brains and the money to prove it," he had constantly taunted. "You might know about antiquities, but I know how to buy and sell them, and that's what puts the gas in your Mercedes."

In retrospect, our union had had no chance of survival, with or without Zanski.

"OK, I get your point." I changed the subject. "Let's have a look at the latest missive. Did you bring it with you?"

He opened his wallet and took out a folded black-and-white advertisement that looked like it had been torn from an auction catalogue, although there was no way of knowing which auction or how long ago it had been printed. I thought I detected a slight trembling of his hand as he pushed it across the table to me. Maybe I imagined it. I studied the image but could see nothing in it that revealed a clue about its sender. The silver coin featured a common depiction of the great man with the face in profile, the deep-set eye and flowing locks creating the illusion of a superbly handsome man, while the ram's horn headdress, symbolic of the uber-god Ammon, proclaimed to all that this was no mere mortal.

"So what do you think?"

"Basically not a lot more than I did before. He, or maybe it's a she, is for sure trying to spook you, but to what end? Drop the mask and run? Or is somebody just trying to intimidate you for some other reason? Who hates you these days?"

Barry shrugged his shoulders. "Haven't a clue, don't know, don't care. But whatever it is, I don't like it." He turned his face toward the corner of the room, indicating a blond muscle-builder type who I gathered must be Gunnar. "This guy better know his stuff."

"He looks up to the job," I reassured him. "OK, then, let's see where we go from here. I'm tied up most of the day tomorrow catering to Sandra, but we can get together in the late afternoon if you want. In the meantime, let's both make up lists of who might be involved in this—both from 1985 and now. I really think we should start with the Henry angle. After all, he has to have figured in this somehow. And if he did not commit suicide . . ."

"Someone knows who did him in," he finished for me.

Polo Lounge, Beverly Hills Hotel
Beverly Hills, California
The same time

CHAPTER 35

The Mask Hunter sat at a small table in the far corner of the Polo Lounge. He would have preferred sitting at the bar where he would have a more direct view of Epstein and his female companion, but he decided it was wiser to choose a spot where he was less likely to be noticed.

Visually at least, he was a far different man than the one who had left the Valley of the Kings so many years ago. There were perks to being Grenville's kept man. Instead of the lumpy homespun suit, he now wore a pair of slim-fitting Italian slacks that showed his waist had not thickened over the years. His white linen shirt was open at the collar, and his shoes, Italian like his slacks, were the kind that caressed his feet as he walked. When he thought no one was looking, he rubbed his palm against the soft weave of the shirtsleeve. There was nothing quite like the feel of handwoven linen. To wear it elevated one from the masses, prisoners in their starched tents, or, worse yet, victims of drip-dry. His own shirt, without being overly tight, skimmed his chest like an elegant skin. It reminded him of the garments the Pharaohs wore, covering the body, yet revealing the muscles beneath. He wore the clothes with ease, belying the fact that by day he was still engaged in menial, if not exactly physical, labor.

Although he was older, the years had been kind. His hair bore no telltale signs of grey, and the golden eyes were as fierce as ever.

When the waiter came, he ordered a gin and tonic. He would have much preferred the sweet comfort of a Coke, but he had learned early on that one does not drink such drinks in places like this.

Christos instantly recognized that the dark-haired woman with Epstein was the same one he had followed to her garage in Boulder. Dressed in city clothes she was even more beautiful. She was also far more elegant than the women he was used to seeing Epstein bring to this bar. The body language was different as well. She and Epstein seemed engaged in conversation without the tension of an impending seduction.

Three days ago in Boulder, after this woman had driven away from her house, he broke into her garage. He had taken nothing—not that there was anything to take. Some old sports equipment and horse tack badly in need of oiling, but nothing of much interest or value. Except the cardboard box. But it contained no mask. For a minute, when he looked inside and saw reams of notes on Hellenistic artifacts and even two letters from the Russian, he was sure he was on to something. It took him some time to read all the notes and the letters carefully because his command of written English was good, but not good enough to understand all the technical terms. He noted that they were written in a feminine hand, presumably the woman's. He was impressed with her descriptions of the smallish figurines that seemed to be the main theme of the notes. If she knew so much about the period when the mask was created, it stood to reason she also knew something about the mask as well. He was getting closer.

Turning his attention back to Epstein and his companion, he tried to decipher what they might be discussing. He was too far away to catch any of the conversation, but this meeting must have something to do with the mask. Otherwise why would a man like Epstein waste his time with a woman who was almost his own age? Christos would just have to be patient and wait and watch.

In the meantime, the waiter reappeared with his gin and tonic and a small plate of olives. The golden-eyed man nodded to the waiter and absent-mindedly sampled one of the green olives. It was soft and spicy. He smiled to himself, wondering what his father would think if he could see him at this moment, elegantly dressed and having an alcoholic drink in one of the most famous bars in one of the most famous cities of the world.

The man knew his father would be far from pleased. He had wasted so many years and yet not fulfilled his mission to bring Alexander's mask back to its owner. But it had not been for lack of trying.

So much had happened since the day he had arrived in Los Angeles, trailing the mask and the Russian who carried it.

He had continued to endure Grenville's physical and verbal insults not only for the security the man provided but because, as in Egypt, he represented a possible link to the mask. Christos kept reminding himself that his mission in life was to serve the god Alexander, and if this was the way, so be it.

The golden-eyed man sipped his drink without enjoyment and watched Epstein and the dark-haired woman intently.

Sotheby's Auction House
Beverly Hills, California
The next day

CHAPTER 36

Deepak Chopra explains *synchronicity* as a chain of events that occur in a perfect pattern. These events come about when we are at one with our inner selves and allow the divine pattern to manifest itself. He uses as an example the chain of events that led to the completion of one of his projects. Chopra knew he needed music, and a certain kind of music that set to song the words of the poet Rumi. Just as he was thinking about what he needed, one of the few musicians in the world who could fill that bill telephoned him. And the rest followed from there.

Two events happened during the next few days that proved the wisdom of Chopra. The first was at the Sotheby's auction. Sandra and I arrived early, collected our paddles, and found seats in the middle of the room. That seemed kind of right—not in the front row, which would have looked too eager, nor in the back, which was a much too obvious stab at invisibility. No, where we were was just perfect.

"You can look around at who's here if you want," I commented. "Just don't overtly stare at anybody."

"I was brought up better than that!" she giggled, delicately maneuvering her auction paddle like a fan in front of her face.

By now the room was filling up, and a well-dressed couple entered our aisle, hesitated a moment, obviously waiting for us to move over and give them our choice center seats. Although the move meant that we were no longer in a direct line of view of the podium, staring them down did not seem worth it, so, albeit reluctantly, Sandra and I pushed ourselves two seats over.

The new seats put Sandra at least, who was on my right, in view of a different section of the room. A moment later she nudged me in the ribs, "Oh my god, I didn't expect to see a soul I knew here, and right over there is Grenville Hopkins, John's old fraternity buddy. Excuse me a sec. I need to say hello."

Without an afterthought she thrust her paddle at me. She swooped elegantly over the toes of the well-shod couple and darted two rows up the aisle.

I got up and followed her in total disbelief, and to the obvious annoyance of the elegant couple, who by now probably wished they had chosen another place to sit. When I reached the spot at the side of the room where Sandra and her companion were standing, the perfunctory hug having been completed, they were on to the "small world" part of the exchange. My arrival changed that.

"Good gravy! Parthi! What are you doing here?"

I hadn't seen Grenville since I'd left the Warner so many years ago, and although recognizable, he had aged some. One would not say he had gone to fat, but there was the suggestion of a paunch visible beneath the blue oxford shirt he'd tucked into a pair of khakis. The elegant yet casual effect was completed with a pair of tasseled suede loafers that must have cost as much as some people paid in monthly rent. As he readjusted the cashmere sweater knotted over his shoulders, I could not help noticing the overly large gold signet ring on his left pinkie.

Overall, he carried himself with the same air of entitlement I remembered from the days he, Henry, and I had been students of Roman Zanski. Since there had been only the three of us, one might think we spent time together. Nothing could have been farther from the truth. My sense was that each of us kept a wary distance from the other two, watching to make sure our territory was well protected. Little wonder I was glad to no longer be involved in such petty rivalry.

I was conscious that both Grenville and Sandra were looking at me, waiting for some sort of answer to Gren's query.

"Sorry," I stammered, "I was so surprised to run into you that I seem to have forgotten my manners! How have you been, Gren, it's good to see you."

"How do you two know each other?" Sandra liked to put people into their assigned boxes.

"We were Warner interns together," Grenville answered for both of us. "It was a memorable time, to say the least."

"So you both were at the Warner when all that scandal erupted? Were you students of, what was his name, the one who did all the smuggling and bought all the fakes?"

"Roman Zanski. Yes, we were. It's quite a story."

We were interrupted by an imperious voice from the loudspeaker, strongly recommending that everyone take their seats. The auction was about to get started.

"Look," Grenville said, "the lot I'm interested in is way at the end. What about you girls? Do we have time to gab in the hallway for a few minutes and catch up?"

Since the desk would not be on the podium for at least a half hour, we had time to spare. What luck! Grenville Hopkins was at the top of my list of people to see in LA, and until three minutes ago I'd had not a glimmer of an idea how to go about contacting him. Now, here he was, served up neatly, giving me the perfect entrée into renewing our past. Thank you, Deepak!

"OK, let's start from the beginning," Grenville began when the three of us were huddled into a small alcove close enough to the auction door to be aware of what was going on inside, but far enough away to chat without too much distraction. "How do you two girls know each other?"

When we had established how we were connected—Grenville and Sandra via her husband John, and she and I in an old friend–designer/client relationship—the conversation shifted to what we were all doing here at this particular moment. I might not have been so forthcoming that our quarry was the Art Deco desk, but Sandra seemed to see no problem baring her hand to Grenville. He raised one eyebrow, I guessed in approval, and chatted on about why he himself was here.

"The old pile is pretty empty these days . . ."

I had always hated his staged Anglophile expressions.

". . . Now that Stephanie is gone, with almost everything, including my parents' monogrammed napkins, I thought I might treat myself to something to sit on."

I gathered Stephanie was the most recent wife. That he should be casually picking up house furnishings at one of the priciest auction houses in the world was no surprise. No Hopkins had deigned to set a well-tailored bottom on anything less than a period antique for the past two hundred or so years. That included campaign chairs and Georgian silver Grenville's flamboyant father allegedly brought to his not-so-humble excavations in Egypt. It was because of that illustrious father's fame that Grenville had been given access to the museum world in a big way—however, the family money did not hurt.

Rumor had it that the Hopkins fortune originated just after the American Civil War, when old Josiah Hopkins arrived in what was left of Atlanta with his carpet bag. No one seemed to know where he came from, but when he left to go to Chicago several years later, that same carpet bag had been loaded with gold. From there, the family fortunes increased steadily, and eventually the golden boy of the clan was born: Grenville's father Benjamin, who, after graduating from Harvard at the age of sixteen, took off for Egypt. There, defying all odds, within a matter of a few short years he unearthed four spectacular royal tombs in the Valley of the Kings.

Overnight, Hopkins Sr. became the darling of the Royal Geographic Society, where he first reported his findings, always judiciously giving due kudos to his Egyptian colleagues. From there he continued on to make a name for himself lecturing, publishing, and sitting on the boards of three of the largest museums in the world, one of which was the Warner.

Then in 1985, while Grenville, who had graduated from Harvard the year before (I always suspected as a legacy), was a Warner intern, Benjamin had died in Egypt, presumably from food poisoning. But his name and fame lived on.

I remember Zanski telling me that when he retired, he was going to name Grenville as his successor as curator of antiquities.

"He's just about perfect for the job, a stupid man to fill a stupid job for a bunch of stupid trustees," he'd said to me in a resigned tone. In Zanski's opinion, all rich people by their very nature were corrupt. But had he even suspected that in Grenville he had a true Iscariot on board?

Grenville of course was quite delighted to be next in line for the plum job in the antiquities world. He had alluded to the fact casually when our paths crossed either in class or at the museum, presumably to keep me from getting any ideas that I myself might rise from my current lowly status as a graduate student to a person of power. In actual fact, the job wasn't anything I was remotely interested in. My love lay with research and excavation rather than the social requirements of the curatorial life. Or had I just adjusted my expectations to what I thought was possible? Archaeology was a tough playing field for a woman. Grenville probably had no inkling of that, self-involved as he was, more interested in shining up to the trustees than contemplating the status of his fellow students.

I tuned back into the present and the conversation going on between Grenville and Sandra.

"I haven't had much chance to pump Parthi for info about Henry Templeton," Sandra was saying. "What with the library she's doing for me, and her divorce and her new house . . ."

Grenville turned to me, "So you're back on the market too? Join the club. We need to get together while you're in town—you too, Sandra love—and hash out old times."

I smiled with what was intended to be a promise of intimacies to come. "Love to! When?"

"How about tonight? Since you girls are staying at the Beverly Wilshire, how about I turn up there about sevenish and buy you some grub?"

Nothing could have suited me more. Despite having been edged out of the top job at the Warner by Henry twenty-eight years ago, Grenville would have been in a position to know what had been going on behind the scenes at the Warner just before Henry's death and directly after. And, mole that he believed himself to be, Grenville, if anyone, would have ferreted out any possible rumors about the mask. What he said next was icing on the cake.

"I guess you both heard that I'm acting curator at the Warner while the trustees go through their search for Henry's replacement. Off the record, I think I stand a pretty good chance myself, but they of course have to maintain professionalism and go through their due diligence."

Sandra and I both widened our eyes, and she added a flattering gasp. There must have been an announcement of his appointment in the papers, but neither she nor I seemed to have picked up on it.

However, I could not overlook the obvious: Henry's death gave Grenville another shot at the job he had been waiting for for decades. Was that reason enough for him to have committed murder? And if he had, did that mean he also knew something about the mask? I would have to be careful in dealing with him, but without a doubt, Grenville Hopkins was somebody I needed to spend time with.

THE AUCTION WENT EVEN BETTER THAN PLANNED. By the time the desk came up, the room had thinned considerably, and there did not even seem to be much action in the front of the room where two smartly dressed young things were manning the telephones, relaying the offers of unseen bidders who could have been in London or the next room.

"Are we all in at $22,000?" asked the British-accented auctioneer, looking in our direction where Sandra's paddle shook slightly in her hand. No sound came from the room. I looked around as discreetly as possible, but there seemed to be no opposition to our last bid. "All done, then, at $22,000. Thank you, Madam," he nodded toward Sandra, who at last exhaled.

"We got it! I just can't believe it's mine!" she gushed into my right ear.

"Congratulations, Sandra, you got a great buy. Let's pay now so we can get out of here before there's a line at checkout. That is, unless there is something else you want to bid on."

"Nope. That's it for today. Can you pay and arrange to have it shipped? I want to hit a few shops on Rodeo before they close."

"Absolutely. Have fun. I'll see you back at the hotel. Don't forget, we're meeting Gren at seven."

"I wouldn't miss that for the world. I never did get a chance to pump him about Henry. It will be so much fun to hear about the whole thing from a current insider, don't you think?"

"That is just what I was thinking. See you at seven."

Beverly Hills, California
Later that day

CHAPTER 37

"Cool," was Barry's remark when I called to tell him I would not be meeting him that evening, and why.

"Yeah," he added, "I forgot to tell you that old Grenville's the Warner's head honcho in antiquities these days now that Henry's no longer with us. Wonder how long that will last? I hope long enough for you to find out if he knows anything, or if there is any record of that mask in his files. Although, knowing Zanski, and Henry too, I'll just bet there are no traces."

How right he was. His words took me back to an afternoon, probably sometime in early 1985, when I was seated in Zanski's office, pages of my dissertation teetering on top of the untidy stack of paraphernalia that adorned his desk.

"You'd better get this out of the way fast. Just submit it the way it is. No one on your committee knows anything about the subject, anyway, so if I say it's good, they will pass you." As he spoke, he'd gestured toward my painstakingly researched attempt at scholarship that sprawled in front of him in a disorganized clump of loose pages.

I remember looking at him in disbelief. He could not possibly be referring to the current chaos the dissertation looked to be in. I had submitted it to him neatly organized, but far from complete.

“What do you mean?” I had asked, in retrospect naïvely. “All the data for the pieces from the North African shrines aren’t even properly catalogued yet.”

His reply gave me what now, years later, proved to be a window to his psyche.

“My dear, I am the chief authority on your project. As I just told you, the other committee members wouldn’t know a votive from an amphora handle. You can pretty much write what you want.”

How could this be? How could the great scholar advocate fabrication of scientific data?

“Look, the degree is what is important. Once you have it, you can go on and really learn about your subject. This dissertation thing is only a formality.” He punctuated his words with a dismissive wave of his hand that threatened to topple the whole pile. “Most probably, nobody’s ever going to read it anyway. Also,” and with this he fixed his clear pale-blue eyes on my bewildered face, “I may not be here much longer, and I want to see you with a bona fide degree safely in your hand before I go.”

I knew Zanski was nearing retirement age, but he didn’t look sick, or even particularly old, so I didn’t place great significance on these last words. However, in the ensuing years, they had played over and over in my head. Zanski had indeed planned his exit from the Warner, and for some time. The question remained: had the Mask of Alexander been intended as his final commission-generating acquisition for the Warner? Or had he planned to go completely rogue and cut the museum out of the deal?

Beverly Wilshire Hotel bar
Beverly Hill, California
That evening

CHAPTER 38

The bar at the Beverly Wilshire was just beginning to fill up when Sandra and I arrived at 6:58. She had changed from the yellow Valentino blazer and skinny jeans she had worn to the auction into a flouncy black Stella McCartney dress with a shortish skirt. I had also dressed for the occasion. Hoping it would not escape Grenville's eye, I had chosen an Armani pencil dress, also black, and four-inch Louboutin heels designed to seduce any straight man. I was not attracted to Grenville, but I wanted him attracted to me. That is, if I did not fall on my face in the ridiculous shoes.

"I hope this dress isn't too much," Sandra whispered as we crossed the room to the small table in the far corner where Grenville sat.

"Of course not. This is Beverly Hills," I whispered back.

At the sight of us, he rose gallantly, bowed from the waist, and smiled first at Sandra and then at me. I was aware that Sandra and I had caught the attention of most of the people, predominantly men, who were sprinkled around the room at tables much like the one we headed for. Not bad for a couple of old ladies.

"I am the envy of every man in this room," he began, "with

not one, but two of the most stunning ladies in Beverly Hills."

Sandra and I both blushed. We sat down, but not too quickly, in the seats he held out for us, she on his left, me on his right. He raised his chin slightly in a patrician summons to the waiter, who came quickly to the table.

"They do a fantastic margarita here, if you're interested in that sort of thing."

"I'll stick with Perrier," I volunteered. "Alcohol at night keeps me awake."

"I never knew that," said Sandra. "It puts me to sleep, and that would be a good thing tonight, since I'm so wound up from the auction and my new desk, and the fun of being here. I'm like a kid in a candy store. I don't get away from the Rockies nearly often enough."

"In that case, a celebration is in order. You must try this great Montrachet." Grenville gestured toward his own barely touched glass and the bottle beside him chilling in an ice bucket. "I highly recommend it."

"Great, I'll do that."

"One Perrier and one more glass for the 1999 Ramonet Montrachet."

The waiter nodded and trotted off. In Beverly Hills, a $6,000 bottle of chardonnay must not be an unusual order.

Is he trying to impress us or does he do this every day? I wondered.

Grenville turned toward Sandra. "I had no idea you were such a fan of Deco. That Frank desk slipped right past everyone in the room but you."

Sandra blushed in appreciation. "I'm just a baby beginner, but that desk spoke to me."

Grenville nodded. "I might have taken a crack at it myself if you hadn't wanted it."

It was at that point that the second synchronistic Deepak Chopra moment occurred.

Sandra opened the Judith Leiber clutch she had placed on her side of the table and took out an oblong velvet box, which she handed to me.

"I was going to wait for the perfect moment to give you this, but I just can't wait, and if I'm thinking about it, it will spoil our visit with Gren." She turned toward him, "I found this for Parthi this afternoon as a tiny thank you for getting me my desk."

I opened the box and stared at the gold necklace that was cushioned inside.

"Sorry, I didn't have time to get it wrapped."

It did not need any wrapping. I was holding a piece of jewelry that would have been spectacular in any circumstance, even if its featured element had not been a silver coin of Alexander the Great. It was almost exactly like the coin depicted in the ad Barry had shown me last night. I couldn't take my eyes off it.

This coin, probably struck in the years following Alexander's death, showed the hero's face in profile to the right, the ram's horn nestled among the copious ringlets that cascaded down his neck. The image was beautifully detailed, emphasizing the romantic upward gaze of the subject. The coin was set in thick, probably 22-karat, gold studded with a diamond at the top and a small sapphire at the bottom. The link chain supporting it was formed of more of the same heavy gold. I could tell, even without the box, that it was clearly Bulgari workmanship.

"I don't know what to say," was all I could manage. "But thank you, thank you! It is really beautiful. But where did you ever find it?"

"I happened to be walking down Rodeo, and there it was in the window of an estate jewelry store. I got a bargain—not that I wouldn't have paid anything to get you the right thing," she hastened to add.

I handed the box across the table to Gren.

"My, my, this is quite wonderful," he commented, turning over the piece slowly in his hand, caressing the relief sculpture of the coin. I was watching him closely, trying to see if I could detect anything that would indicate he was connecting the image to the mask I was seeking. As could have been expected, his expression told me nothing.

"Did you both see the eyes, actually the eye, in this coin?" Sandra asked.

"Yes, those deep-set, soulful eyes are the trademark of Alexander," Gren replied, somewhat patronizingly, I thought.

"Of course, I learned that from Yossi today."

Apparently she was already on a first-name basis with the flamboyant Israeli who had made estate jewelry chic. "But this portrait coin is even more fascinating from a medical point of view."

That was not the usual comment Sandra made when assessing a piece of jewelry. Both Gren and I pricked up our ears, wondering what she would say next.

"John has recently been adding elements of Chinese medicine into his practice." She was obviously referring to her husband.

When both Gren and I looked puzzled, she smiled and explained, "You know, Chinese medicine is where medical practitioners look at the face and tell you what diseases a person has. Well, anyway, he was telling some dinner guests one night about how one can tell if there is a kidney problem by looking at the eyes. Deep-set like these"—she gently removed the necklace from Gren's hand and pointed with her forefinger at the exaggerated hollow of Alexander's eye socket—"are indications something serious is going on. Dehydration or downright kidney failure." She concluded her assessment with the obvious satisfaction of a finishing-school product enlightening two pompous academicians.

We were both stunned. Gren was the first to comment, "I don't know if you know, Sandra, that Alexander's death at only thirty-three has always been a huge mystery in the archaeological world. You just might have solved it. I can see the headlines now, *Socialite discovers cause of the death of Alexander the Great*."

"John and the Chinese really deserve the credit, if any is being handed out. I am only the messenger." Her husband was a well-known nephrologist, having made a name for himself in the field of high-risk transplants.

"Still, you connected the dots, and that's everything in solving any mystery," I insisted.

Come to think of it, the possibility of weak kidneys in Alexander's case explained a lot. Exhausted as he was from constant campaigning, irregular water supplies, and having relied on wine for most of his liquid intake, his kidneys could easily have been so compromised that they simply failed. No mystery, no poison, not even a particular bug.

Fascinating as this was, it was not leading me closer to the mask. Yet all this reference to Alexander must mean something. Deepak would take it seriously, have me listen for the message beneath.

"I can't wait to have you show John the necklace," she continued. "It will be fun to see what he says about Alexander's early death."

I fidgeted a moment before answering. My plans, especially now that I had made contact with Gren, were to stay in LA until I discovered something about the mask.

"I think I might stay here a while. I have another client who wants me to track down a few things, and this is the best hunting ground."

"No problem, sweetie. After it arrives, I'll just leave the desk packed until you get there. But any idea when that will be?"

"Not exactly, but if I need to stay more than a week or two, I'll arrange to fly back and get your library set up in between sales here."

As I had hoped, Gren picked up on the fact that I would be in the city longer, and alone. "I hope you'll have some time to let me show you the changes at the Warner."

"Could I be included?" Sandra asked

"Absolutely! When do you go back?"

"My flight is Monday afternoon."

"That gives us the rest of the weekend. Let's shoot for a museum visit tomorrow."

"Does that work for you, Parthi?" Sandra looked toward me.

"Perfect."

Gren's cell phone, sitting on the table, vibrated. He looked at it, annoyed. "I hate this thing."

Then he glanced down at the screen and frowned, "It's the museum. If anyone from there is calling this late, it must be something that needs attention. I need to take this. Excuse me."

He quickly left the room.

He returned no more than three minutes later, mopping his brow—a bit dramatically, I thought, as the room was air-conditioned. "Something's come up. I have to go back to the museum. I'll call you in the morning."

Whatever had happened at the Warner was obviously not good.

Sandra and I ate dinner alone, and although the food was divine, something of the earlier exuberant mood was dimmed by Gren's abrupt and somewhat ominous departure.

Grenville's house, Mandeville Canyon
Los Angeles, California
Later that night

CHAPTER 39

"What the hell were you doing in my office?" Grenville grabbed Christos by the shirt collar and began to shake him.

The golden-eyed man did not answer.

Grenville pushed him against the wall. "Answer me! After all I've done for you for years: food, clothes, a goddamned green card. But obviously all that wasn't enough. You have to go snooping in my office when I'm not there. Why?" He gave Christos no time to answer. "All you had to do was ask and I would have told you what was in my filing cabinet or wherever you were looking."

He released his hold on Christos and just stared at him.

Christos spoke at last. "It was because of her."

Christos had debated about saying anything to Grenville. After all, he had been so careful for so long to keep his lover in the dark. But he was getting desperate enough to try any lead.

"Who the fuck are you talking about?"

"I don't know her name. The dark-haired woman. She and Barry Epstein are up to something. And I think you are in it also."

Grenville looked bewildered. "What's Epstein got to do with

this? And how do you know him?"

"I don't have to explain it to you."

"Oh yes you do, my friend. I covered for you with museum security. But I can just as easily go back and tell them I recognize you on the surveillance tape, and wham! You'll be back in that Egyptian dust bowl before you can mount a camel. So talk."

"Perhaps it is time. May we sit like civilized people?"

"OK. But this had better be good."

"We have been together for many years, but there are things I have not told you."

"Tell me now."

"Before he died, your father uncovered an object that is sacred to our culture. The Mask of Alexander the Great. I have been seeking it ever since."

"You and everybody else." Grenville sat closer to his companion. "Perhaps we can help each other. Tell me what you know."

Neither man trusted the other.

"I know that the Russian Zanski and Epstein brought the mask to Los Angeles in 1985. Three days ago Epstein went to Colorado to see the dark-haired woman, and then you met her tonight . . ."

There was a spike in Grenville's interest. "What about Epstein and the dark-haired woman?"

"I followed him. And he went to her house."

"What? And all this without my knowledge? Why were you keeping it from me?"

"I don't really know. I am sorry. I guess I thought you might want to take the mask yourself and not return it to Egypt where it belongs."

"You assume too much. We can sort out where the mask should go after we find it. Epstein and the dark-haired woman—her name is Parthenia, by the way—used to be married, so that visit might have to do with a possible reconciliation."

"I don't think so. Epstein was with Zanski when he brought the mask to Los Angeles. I have been hoping it would show up here . . ." He hesitated a moment. "And there is something more . . ."

"Go on."

"Epstein took that trip to Colorado directly after I might have prodded him a little."

"I'm all ears."

"I put a picture of Tutankhamun's mask on his car. I wanted to spook him. And then I did something more."

"Go on."

"I might have frightened him a bit. With a gun."

Grenville laughed. "You little rascal, come here." He put his arm around Christos and pulled his head down to his lap. "We can solve this mystery together. No more secrets."

HOURS LATER, lying beside Grenville, the Mask Hunter could not sleep. Now, more than ever, he was worried about having taken the American into his confidence.

Beverly Wilshire Hotel
Beverly Hills, California
The following morning

CHAPTER 40

Gren called early the next morning. "Damndest thing. When security called last night, I imagined the worst. The Museum either vandalized or robbed, or blown up, but when I got there it turned out that there was in fact a break-in, but not where one might expect. In my office, which used to be Henry's. I don't keep anything there, not even lunch money."

"What do you think they might have been after?"

"Who knows?"

I had a strong suspicion. I was pretty sure that since he was filling Henry's shoes as curator, chances were that he occupied Henry's office as well. It seemed likely that whoever was after Barry suspected Henry's connection to the mask and was searching for information.

"Was there anything missing or disturbed?"

"Not that I could see. The security camera picked up something, but it was too blurry to make out if it was even a person, much less someone we can identify. The alarm must have frightened him off, and he got out of the building through the fire exit."

"It does sound like someone looking for information, rather than robbing the place. What do you suppose it was?"

"Knowing Henry, it could have been anything, but I suspect there was nothing. Underneath that posh facade the guy was as slippery as an eel."

And yes, he had a point. I had known Henry too. Although it certainly was not kind to think ill of the dead, I had liked Henry even less than I liked Gren. Although during most of our mutual tenure at the Warner he had remained respectfully in the background, I had never trusted him. Worse than that, his overly serious attitude had always made me feel as though I was just a bit of fluff, and it was he who was the true scholar. His one nod to any frivolity was the endless parade of chocolate chip cookies he produced (home-baked, presumably by his housekeeper) that were eagerly awaited by the staff every Monday morning.

And I had been right about him. Zanski's chair was scarcely cold before Henry occupied it, acing Gren out in a silent coup with the trustees. How he managed that was something no one had ever figured out. Unless, as it now seemed, he had known something, or had something that the museum director, or the trustees, or both, did not want brought to light.

I needed to get into Gren's office also, because from the guard's account, the intruder had not been in there long enough to find and remove what he or she was looking for. But how to convince Gren to let me rummage through Henry's, now his, filing cabinets? In cases like this, sex usually worked. It was not something I would normally think of doing, but then, I was not normally in a position like this.

"You sound like you had quite a night. I have to admit I was selfishly disappointed when you had to leave so fast last night. I was looking forward to spending more time with you."

I didn't want to be too obvious, but I hoped he would interpret this as code for my finding him attractive.

Right on cue he replied, "Me too. Now that we're both divorced, and at least temporarily in the same city, we ought to use this opportunity to get to know each other better. I confess I always found you attractive, but years ago was just not the time to do anything about it."

"I know. I'm glad about this second chance too."

"Anyway, I guess we'll be seeing each other tomorrow. Things are pretty quiet here. Adam," he referred to the museum director by his first name, "decided that since nothing was taken, we should keep this little incident in-house. I guess he was thinking about the impact more negative press might have on his job. The fact that Henry followed right in Zanski's footsteps buying hot loot for the museum has left the whole place reeling. How could he not have learned a lesson? He was right here, we all were, when Zanski's deals were outed. What made him think he could get away with it?"

Indeed, that was a mystery. A year ago, when news of Henry's indictment for procuring looted antiquities for the Warner hit the news, shouts of disbelief echoed throughout the art world. During his more than twenty years' tenure as head of the Warner's world-famous antiquities department he had appeared to the outside world as the epitome of moral rectitude. Grim, efficient, and proper, he had exuded a respectability that was, now in retrospect, misleading. However, irrefutable proof of his guilt had surfaced in the form of incriminating correspondence between him and the dealer Peter Schott, the same unscrupulous antiquities dealer who had brought the Warner down the first time. Schott, Barry always maintained, could sniff out the most succulent morsel on the hot antiquities market, but he was no one that any respectable buyer, much less a world-class museum, should be doing business with. Everyone knew that if Schott was peddling it, it was surely hot.

I thought for a minute, wondering how much I should share with Gren. I began cautiously, "You know, I read in all those newspaper articles that came out after his death that Henry always maintained he took the fall for someone higher up, and he was only doing his job. What do you think about that?"

"Well, I know from my own experience with him that he was a snake. I never did learn how he managed that end run over me and got himself appointed curator. But, and this is of course a big *but*, when that news came out about him being caught with his hand in the cookie jar, the whole thing began to make sense. To me at least. He owed somebody for getting him the job, and the payback was those dirty deals. I haven't a clue which side his benefactor was on, somebody high up in the museum, or else someone putting pressure on that same somebody for whatever reason—or possibly a wild card entirely. Just about anybody who could gain from having Henry in their pocket to help them get their hands on some Warner money would qualify. If he wasn't entirely out of the antiquities game, your former husband would be a likely suspect."

That was an angle I had not explored. What if Barry was still a player in the smuggling trade, and he had involved me either to appear innocent, or because the deal was going sour? He could have made up the letter from Zanski—after all, I had not seen it—to manipulate me into helping him find the missing mask and complete the dirty deal. I knew from our past history together that his mind had a tendency to move in that direction.

Then there was Gren himself. Resenting Henry as much as he obviously did put a big bull's-eye on his forehead, in the matter of his death at least. He was, after all, currently occupying his office and had a good chance of remaining there. But given his obvious lack of financial motivation due to the Hopkins legacy, it was unlikely he had anything to do with hassling Barry about the mask. Nor could I even imagine him skulking about putting crude cutouts on car windshields. Yet neither of these gentlemen was to be completely trusted. I needed to be smart about how much information I shared with anyone.

My answer was noncommittal. "He went to jail once; that should have taught him a lesson."

"Ah, but money, large amounts of it, does strange things to people."

I nodded.

He stated the obvious. "Not to brag, but that's one problem I don't have. People like me can do the right thing much more easily than someone who has to count pennies to keep the kiddies in school. I did notice, rather, I think it was one of the wives who noticed, Old Henry was no slouch in the spending department. Of course, it could have been family money, but word on the street was that old man Templeton was pretty tight with a buck."

"He did need to convey a certain image in his position." Who knew why I chose to defend Henry, but I did.

"Well, of course. But perhaps his relationship with his Mafioso uncle Brazzi had something to do with those fine feathers as well. As I recall, Brazzi fancied himself quite a peacock. Easy to imagine he wanted the same image for his nephew. Must have been good for business in every way."

"I'm surprised you notice things like that. Anyway, we'll probably never know for sure what went on with them," I mused.

"Nope, guess not. Anyway, I'm looking forward to ushering you ladies through the museum. Ten o'clock OK?"

"Perfect, I'll tell Sandra and we'll meet you at the entrance."

"I'll leave your names with the guards. See you then."

The Warner Museum
Beverly Hills, California
The following day

CHAPTER 41

The Warner had undergone more than a few changes since I had last been there so many years ago. Originally housed in the former mansion of its founder, Thaddeus Warner, the institution had been infused with copious amounts of money upon the founder's death. Now having expanded to include the four neighboring properties, it was reputed to be one of the richest—if not the richest—museums in the world.

The overall impression, while still that of an Italianate mansion, was a lot sleeker. In addition to somewhat emulating the feel of an ancient building, the main structure was now surrounded by lush gardens and sported an amphitheater. Those gardens, which I remembered as being pretty much an afterthought, now seemed to be attracting almost as many visitors as the interior galleries. A stroke of genius on the part of the Warner trustees to have created so much green space in the center of the city.

The revamping of the museum was even more evident the moment we approached the entrance. Instead of entering through the garage and then stepping into an elevator, we now followed a pleasantly winding elevated walkway, paved like a Roman road and lined with what looked to be very costly hand-made columns.

Sandra stopped and bent over to catch the fragrance from a late-blooming old-fashioned rose, one of many lining the walkway. "Ah, heaven."

"Yes, it is," I agreed, surveying the garden in all directions, each part like a framed painting.

Gren was walking with us. "This is one of my favorite changes. Remember the old entrance that was like going into a garage-attached tract house?" he laughed.

"And just what do you know about tract houses?" I asked, matching his bantering tone.

"One does hear of such things," he teased.

Inside the museum I looked around for vestiges of the old Warner. My eye traveled to a side corridor at the end of which was an object I remembered from my youth. It was the white marble bathing figure that Zanski had dubbed "The Petting Venus."

It had been his first stop when touring visitors through the museum. "Nobody can resist putting his hands on a smooth piece of marble," he had reasoned. "So I stop them here and let them feel this one, so they won't be tempted to ruin an ancient treasure with greasy hands."

The Venus in question, although modeled on a Greek original, dated to the nineteenth century, expendable modernity in Zanski's opinion.

I noticed the Venus was now repurposed into a kind of votive. Visitors were encouraged to write a wish on a piece of paper and then attach it to a board behind the goddess in the hope that she would grant what they asked for. The whole idea was so much like what the ancients did when visiting a shrine in antiquity that I smiled, remembering my goddess figures from so long ago.

Zanski would have approved of this change, at least.

Sandra noticed me looking at the statue. "Oh, what fun! Let's write a wish." She walked over to the table and picked up a piece of the paper.

"Come on," she encouraged. "I've already gotten my wish with the desk. It's your turn."

A wish could not hurt. I wrote an *A* on the paper she had handed me, folded it in half, then in half again, and finally a third time, making it as small as possible, then I carried it to the wall behind Venus and pinned it behind a previous offering in the hopes of not attracting anyone's attention, especially Gren's.

By that time, he had joined us.

"I see you girls are getting into the spirit of the ancient world."

He turned to Sandra. "I suppose Parthi has told you that ancient wish figures dedicated to a god or goddess were her forte when she was here at the museum. Henry concentrated on vases and I on sculpture. Parthi's votives—small finds, archaeologists call them—don't attract such wide attention, but they are important just the same," he added.

I couldn't tell whether he intended to be gracious or condescending.

"But let me pull you away from this and show you some real art."

He led us along the often-photographed colonnade and ushered us into the interior of the museum. Like the exterior, the aesthetic of the galleries was far different from what I remembered.

Gren began to pontificate. "This new chronological approach is much more direct than the old thematic exhibits. More art historical, one might say."

I could imagine Zanski eyeing the museum's new arrangement and snorting, "Pedantic, bourgeois."

Actually, I too preferred the old way. It felt closer to the souls of the ancient peoples rather than just admiring their creations.

But I kept my mouth closed. Almost. "Don't you think there is something to be said for teaching people how the ancients thought? I mean, don't you think we could use a few reminders of what it means to be a hero and how to look at a woman as a goddess?"

"Well, I suppose so, but the audiences seem to love this new presentation," was his perfunctory reply.

We walked along the polished marble floors of the Archaic and Classical exhibits. Sandra came right to the point. "Which of these are the pieces Henry smuggled?" she asked.

"None of these, I am happy to report. All of his ill-gotten goods have been pulled from display and duly returned to their countries of origin. Everything you see here is 100 percent legal. I base my reputation as a curator on that."

He continued, "Parthi will remember the Athena."

Gren was referring to the heroic-scale marble statue of a female swathed in flowing drapery; it had for years been the subject of scholarly debate about whether it was genuine or a forgery. "And you as well, Sandra. It got quite a bit of publicity in its day."

He gestured around the gallery dramatically. "Nowhere to be seen." He leaned closer to us. "In the basement. Everyone knows the thing is as phony as a three-dollar bill, but they're not coming right out and admitting anything."

Sandra looked perplexed. "I never realized there are so many politics involved in museums."

"Sadly, my dear, yes."

She returned to the subject that interested her more. "So they wiped away all evidence of Henry's sins?" she asked innocently.

"Yes, but that Athena was a sin well before Henry's time." Gren winked at me. "That was Zanski's baby."

Then he switched gears and spewed forth what sounded like rehearsed propaganda.

"As much as we can stand here and revile Henry for what he did, we also have to thank him for what we are seeing. He worked hard to make this vision of the new Warner a reality. We shouldn't forget that."

Sandra looked a bit disappointed to hear anything but dirt about the dead curator, yet she persisted, "How did he do it? Smuggling the stuff, I mean." She was obviously thoroughly involved with the subject and not about to let it go.

"You mean, how does an object go from being robbed from a tomb to finding a home in a prestigious museum?" Gren asked.

"Yes, aren't there ways to check if a piece has been illegally excavated?"

I weighed in on this. "Of course, but Henry got around that the way everybody does: it's pretty much standard practice among people of questionable ethics to search out some respectable but impoverished European family and have them swear in writing that this or that piece has been in their family for centuries."

"It's that simple?"

Grenville reentered the conversation. "Yup, unfortunately Parthi is correct. Takes a bit of clever paperwork, of course, but very doable. Nobody really believes the subterfuge, but the phony documentation is enough to give a museum the green light to buy. Especially when they're salivating over a piece that every other museum and collector in the world would trade their firstborns for. With that kind of pressure on their ethics, museums will jump at any straw that allows them to support the fantasy that it's a legally procured piece."

"Amazing that it's so easy."

"Yup again. In the art world, provenance is everything. Let's go into the Hellenistic Gallery and I'll show you a case in point," he continued.

He ushered us into the next gallery as if he were herding schoolchildren. He stopped in front of a heartbreakingly beautiful bronze sculpture of the god Apollo.

"Isn't it marvelous to see our beautiful boy out of intensive care?"

Sandra looked puzzled. Gren draped his arm casually around her shoulders and explained.

"He came to us from the sea, and being submerged for so many years, preserved by the water, one feared his demise if there was too rapid a change in atmosphere, sort of like the bends for statuary."

"Fascinating," Sandra breathed, running her eyes appreciatively along the delicately muscled figure.

"There's a sidebar to this," Gren smiled. "Back in our day," he gestured toward me, "there was quite a tussle with the Italians over this piece. As I told you, it came out of the sea, but no one can prove the exact spot it came from . . . So there, as one says, lies the rub."

"What was it doing in the sea?" Sandra asked naïvely.

"Most probably being transported to its final destination. The story is rather fascinating: two Italian fishermen claimed to have pulled it up in their nets more than the requisite two miles offshore, giving them the legal right to sell to whomever they wished without government intervention."

Sandra nodded, but she looked a bit skeptical. "Wasn't that just a bit too convenient?"

"Undoubtedly, but the courts upheld our claim, so here we have what is perhaps the finest ancient bronze in America."

Sandra looked as though she remembered something. "Of course. The story was in all the papers. Wasn't it that Russian we've been talking about who bought it?"

"You have an excellent memory, my dear. Indeed it was Zanski. Success seemed to have gone to his head or something. That Athena I just mentioned was his most outrageous dubious purchase. No one knows to this day if he knew all along it was a fake. But I have my suspicions. He went on, of course, to load the museum with more and more questionable pieces, as well as some other totally flagrant forgeries. I guess, like any criminal, he became bolder and bolder. I might have been pretty low on the museum totem pole but I was no fool—I could tell a crook when I saw one. I was pretty much on his tail the whole way. I could tell you stories . . ." Gren stopped and looked at me. "But we don't want to bore Parthi."

I could feel myself blushing. Did Gren know about Zanski and me, and was he taunting me?

The potentially awkward situation was averted by Sandra, whose attention was now focused on another spectacular object in the gallery.

"Ooh," she squealed, "it's Alexander. After buying you that necklace, Parthi, I feel he and I are old friends. I'd know him anywhere." She walked closer to the marble head.

Gren nodded. "You have excellent taste, Sandra. This is another of our most outstanding pieces."

I moved closer to Gren so I could see his expression. Did this reminder of Alexander strike any chord with him? As with the necklace last night, nothing.

Gren and Sandra had now moved on and paused in front of a glass case containing Greek funerary vases.

"Do any of these ever come on the market?" Sandra turned toward me. "Two like this would be a smash on either side of the front door in my Boulder house, don't you think?"

The thought didn't seem pleasant to me, but I didn't think either of them would understand that these pieces were intended as offerings to go with the departed, not as decorations for a living person's house, so I dodged the question. "I don't know, Sandra; collecting antiquities can be thought questionable these days."

"I suppose so, but if you're determined you can always find what you're looking for," was Gren's reply.

Listening to their conversation, I was struck by its arrogance. No one seemed to care that those vases were not their property at all but belonged to the long-dead people in whose tombs they had carefully been placed.

How could these two not see the lack of morality in collecting antiquities? And how could I reconcile the fact that I had accepted Sandra's gift of a coin that was most probably also a tomb find? But I had enough sense to keep my thoughts to myself.

SANDRA'S FLIGHT BACK TO DENVER was at four o'clock, so after the tour, the three of us grabbed a quick bite at a nearby wine bistro.

"Thank you so much, Gren." Sandra smiled as she got into the limo that was to take her first back to the hotel for her bag, then on to the airport. "Running into you was absolutely the icing on the cake of this trip. Parthi and I would have had a blast no matter what, but getting the inside scoop on the Henry Templeton skullduggery was amazing."

"I can't see that I told you that much, but thank you, anyway."

I stole a look at Gren through the cover of my Chanel sunnies but could not get a read on what he was thinking. Did he buy the party line of Henry's suicide, or, like Barry, did he suspect there had been something more sinister afoot?

As the limo pulled away, Gren took my hand. "Want to come back to my office for a chat? I want to drive you back to your hotel at some point, but since I am only acting curator, I don't want to press my luck and have Adam catch me playing hooky too long."

Did I want to? More than anything.

The office was unremarkable. A massive nineteenth-century mahogany desk dominated the large room. Two Louis XIV armchairs (somehow, I doubted they were the real thing) were placed in proximity, while behind the desk was a leather and wood campaign chair.

Gren saw my eyes on it. "A memento of Dad's first expedition into the Valley of the Kings. It seemed fitting to bring it here."

"A very special piece."

I was impressed. Rumor had it that the Hopkins father and son had not been on the best of terms at the time of the former's death. Was the chair meant as a tribute or a "see, I am successful too" statement? Gren's tone gave no clue.

I continued to look around the room. The walls, painted a soft ecru, sported some fairly respectable nineteenth-century etchings of Greek vases. Bookcases lined the rest of the vacant space.

The filing cabinets, which were my quarry, were lined up in an adjacent alcove. I walked over to them. "Ever plowed through these? "I asked innocently.

"Of course. It was the first thing I did when I moved into this office. Nothing. Henry was a lot of things, but he was not dumb. If there was anything else incriminating besides those letters the Italian authorities found, he obviously destroyed it, either before the indictment, or at least prior to offing himself."

"Whoever broke in here last night must have thought there was something to find, or why take the risk? It doesn't look like you keep much of value in here."

"My point exactly. It's a mystery."

"What else do you know about Henry's dealings?"

"Not a whole lot. As you know, he and I were never very close. I was actually surprised when the news broke about him."

"I was too. I heard you mention Brazzi earlier—isn't he that sleazy antiquities dealer Henry got his goods from?" I asked innocently.

"The worst. But you probably know more about him than I do."

I looked puzzled.

"Forgive me if I am wrong, but I was fairly sure he had had some dealings with your former husband, so I thought you would have known about them."

I could feel the red spreading across my face. I had been stupid to try and play dumb with Gren, who obviously knew all about Barry's dark antiquities deals.

"I heard bits and pieces, but mostly I tried to stay out of that part of Barry's life." My words were not untrue.

"I know it must have been difficult for you to be married to a, forgive the expression, crook. But back to Brazzi and Henry: I can imagine how it went down: Henry, nephew of said criminal dealer, lands the plum job in the Warner antiquities department, and since we both know how close blood ties run in Italian families, both he and Uncle Brazzi flourish. That is, until the Italian authorities blow the whistle and cowardly Henry falls on his sword rather than face the music."

"That's a thought. I always wondered how Henry got the job rather than you. As far as I knew, and I really knew very little, Zanski was grooming you to take over when he retired."

Gren snapped his neck so he was looking directly at me. "Where did you hear that?"

In retrospect, I should not have mentioned that. I made a lame stab at covering my blunder. "Oh, I think it was pretty much common knowledge. It was obvious Zanski didn't think much of Henry, and he seemed to spend more time with you. You were quite his golden boy."

Gren laughed. I couldn't tell whether it was in amusement or scorn. "If it was a matter of who Zanski spent time with, it would have been you and not me who was next in line for the big job."

I felt like a butterfly who had just been pinned to a cork. It must have showed, because Gren continued, "Or maybe you were out of the running because the trustees knew about you and Zanski and they couldn't trust you."

"How did you know?"

A few days ago, when Barry had told me he knew about my affair with Zanski, I had been thrown into full-blown panic. This time I was shaken, but the room was not spinning, and I felt no danger of fainting. It no longer mattered what these people thought of me. All that mattered was that I was going to do the right thing for once. Saving the mask trumped shame.

"Everybody knew. But nobody really cared. Don't worry. I'm not judging you."

He leaned down and squeezed my hand. Then he leaned closer to me, his eyes crinkled with amusement. "Just imagine what your pal Sandra would say if she knew. Ha, ha, but I won't tell her—not if you are good to me."

Gren's light tone took some of the sting out of my embarrassment.

"Was Zanski the reason you left here so fast?" he asked. "I've always wondered, and now that there are no more secrets between us, I can ask."

"Yes and no. I had sort of a nervous breakdown. Originally, I thought it was about Zanski leaving, but now I realize I just hated the whole private acquisition-of-antiquities thing. It just seems so wrong." It felt good to say for once what I was really feeling.

"Breakdown? Really? My, you are a complex little creature." He patted my hair, ignoring the fact that I had just bashed the profession he had devoted his life to.

"It's not so interesting, really. I'll tell you all about it sometime."

"Fair enough. You do intrigue me."

I changed the subject. "Do you think the trustees knew Henry was related to an illegal antiquities trader when they gave him the job here?"

"Aha! That's the question. There is a slim chance they did not because he obviously traded on his Boston ties rather than his Mafia roots, but if they did . . ." He broke off, letting me fill in the blanks.

"What's Brazzi doing now? Was he indicted too?" I asked.

"As far as I know, he escaped the net. Schott was arrested and died in an Italian prison before he could testify. Heart attack, I heard. Anyway, if he had come to trial, it's just about certain he would have hung Brazzi out to dry."

"Do you think anyone could have done him in?"

"Schott, you mean? With the Italians anything is possible, although the man was no spring chicken."

He changed the subject, "Why don't you sit here for a bit while I return a few calls? Then I'll take you back to the hotel."

"That's really not necessary. I can grab an Uber."

"No, no. This shouldn't take long."

I absentmindedly leafed through the latest *American Journal of Archaeology* as I waited for Gren to make his calls. I was half involved in an article about the complexities of Bronze Age trade when he put down the phone and swung his feet off the desk.

"Sorry, my dear, but it turns out I have to spend a few minutes with Adam before I call it a day. Why don't you wait right here while I take care of that?"

I smiled up at him. "I am quite cozy here. Take your time."

Left alone I had time to think over the past few days. I had faced the past without a panic attack. Could that mean I was cured? After so many years of agony this was too good to be true.

It didn't take long for Gren to return to the room. "I am so sorry, but it looks like this will take longer than I thought. I took the liberty of calling you a taxi just now. As much as I don't want our afternoon to end, duty calls. The cab will be here in about twenty minutes. How about I walk you out, and on the way, I'll introduce you to Adam. I don't think you've met him. Nice chap. Used to work with my father."

Gren closed, and I noticed carefully locked, the office door before we proceeded down the long hall to the corner office, which was open. He peered around the jamb, "Knock, knock. Adam, got a minute?"

The museum director was seated behind a desk even more massive than the one in Gren's office. Apart from the manila folder that lay in front of him, the desk was devoid of all paperwork. It held only a decorative blotter, a telephone, and an open laptop. He looked up, removed his glasses, and smiled at us. "Come on in."

Probably not sure if I was anyone important or not, Adam Summerhill, director of the Warner Museum, looked expectantly at Gren but said nothing, waiting for an introduction.

"This is Parthenia Guthrie. We were students together here years ago. I was just showing her how the place has changed since then, and I wanted to introduce her to you."

The director held out his hand, smiling, but, I guessed, not actually very interested in meeting someone who offered him little to gain. His handshake seemed perfunctory.

"Well, what do you think about the changes we've made since your day?" His voice, too, was more rehearsed than spontaneous, like a speech he'd given one too many times.

I answered in kind, realizing that he probably didn't much care what I had to say. I neither liked nor disliked him. As a matter of fact, I got no read on him at all. If he was the one who had been pulling Henry's strings, he was obviously a man who could conceal his motives well. I made a mental note to ask Barry what his take was on Summerhill.

The lukewarm pleasantries concluded, I excused myself, leaving Gren and the director to posture without female interference. Once in the cab, I texted Barry.

I could have called, but who knew if the cab driver wasn't some part of all this? A mole of the museum, or perhaps even the Mafia? I was probably being totally absurd, but Henry was dead, and stranger coincidences have occurred.

Within seconds my phone pinged, signaling his response. "Can you come to the house? It's 202 Palisades Park Drive."

Malibu, California
Fifteen minutes later

CHAPTER 42

Despite the LA traffic, we were at the address Barry had given me in less than fifteen minutes.

Gunnar, the bodyguard, opened the cab door for me, paid the driver, and directed me up the flight of steps that led to the front door.

"He's inside, door's open," was all he said.

The door in fact was open, not only to me but to a heart-stopping view of what appeared to be miles of the Malibu coast. I found myself in a glass-enclosed entry hall that led to the open living/dining room at its end. Not bad for someone crying poor.

Barry must have been alerted to my approach, because he was already standing when I entered.

He kissed me on both cheeks. He was wearing khakis and an open-necked Ralph Lauren polo shirt.

"Welcome to the bachelor pad."

I was surprised that there seemed to be no female in residence. Barry had never been known to live alone.

I almost said something about that, but by this time I was growing used to keeping my thoughts to myself. It was none of my business whether or not my former husband was cohabiting with anyone other than the formidable Gunnar.

"So tell me all about it," he began. "Did you sniff out anything? Were you able to pump Gren at all? Pompous ass. I wonder if he has a hand in this anywhere."

"I'm pretty positive he's not the one sending you the unwelcome mail, but Henry's death gave him another chance at the job he always wanted, so there might be something in that line of thought."

I decided against sharing the information about Gren's office being broken into. It was being kept out of the papers, and I did not want to risk compromising Gren's trust by leaking any information, however irrelevant it might be.

"What do you know about Adam Summerhill?" I asked.

"Not a whole lot. He's headed the Warner for the past ten or so years. East Coast guy. Pretty low-key."

"Do you think he could possibly be involved in this?"

"By 'this' do you mean Henry's death or our own predicament?"

"Actually, we've agreed they're connected, so both."

"Well," he scratched his chin, "that's been my thinking too. These squeaky-clean types like him can be as dirty as hell. Plus, Henry worked for him, so, yes, he could have a hand in this. So . . . where do we go next?"

"Well, I want to follow up on the connection between Henry, Schott, and Emilio Brazzi. Henry was in bed, figuratively at least, with Schott, via his relationship with Brazzi. Both of those dealers originally had access to the mask, and I can't help but believe Henry got his fingers in there somewhere."

"Hmm, I follow."

I unwound the scarf around my neck. Barry's house was much warmer than the museum had been.

"Here, let me help you with that." He reached over and took the scarf from my shoulders. In doing so his eye caught Sandra's necklace. He recoiled in actual horror, "Whoa! What is that? Are you trying to give me a coronary?"

His reaction was almost laughable.

"Can you believe Sandra bought me this basically out of the blue? I think it means good luck on our venture."

He eyed the necklace dubiously, as though it would come alive and bite him like a cobra.

"If you say so, but could you please take it off? It gives me the creeps."

"No problem." I unfastened the golden chain and slipped the necklace into my handbag, "You really are frightened about this, aren't you?"

"Would I be down on my knees to you and living with Gunnar if I weren't? I was around those Italian crooks enough during my day to know that if it's them behind this, they mean business."

"You weren't so sure who we were looking for last week. Did something happen to eliminate any other suspects?"

"No, it's just that I've had more time to think about it, and stuck here in the house most of the time, it's hard to think of much else. Anyway, it keeps banging around in my mind that if Brazzi was the front man for the sale of the mask, and he was also Henry's uncle, there has to be a connection. I mean, a curator with the means to buy what he was selling, the same one who was proved by a court of law to have filled the Warner with tainted goods . . . it's just too much of a coincidence to be anything but fact. Here, I made a list of the people who might be involved."

There were four entries on the handwritten list:

> 1. *Emilio Brazzi, Italian smuggler. Henry's uncle. Present at the meeting in Geneva in 1985 when Schott showed the mask to Zanski and me.*
> 2. *Adam Summerhill and/or one or more of the Warner trustees. Possibly about to be implicated by Henry for mandating he buy the hot stuff.*
> 3. *Persons unknown.*
> 4. *Vatican?*

They're always in this kind of thing somewhere.

"I see you do have Summerhill on the list. How likely do you really think it is that somebody on that level would stoop to murder?"

"Oh, baby, you ain't seen nothin' yet. A Harvard degree is no guarantee of honesty. Not in what I've seen in my day. I'd believe anything about anybody. Especially when there is sex or money involved."

The last entry on Barry's list read:

> 5. *Grenville Hopkins. Probably not directly responsible for the missing mask, but with a definite motive to kill Henry.*

"Hmmm. It seems odd that Henry's death would not be connected to the mask. But I do see your point about Gren. I was thinking the same thing myself."

"Were you really? Then great minds think alike. I was beginning to worry you'd succumbed to his Ivy League charms." Barry's tone was light, but I could feel his old competitiveness surfacing.

I brushed the comment off. "Let's get back to Henry."

He nodded and continued, "The likelihood of his putting that bag over his head by himself is getting more and more remote."

I shivered, remembering the media's lurid description of Henry's death scene.

"Why that form of death, do you think?" I asked.

"Why not? It's quiet, and I guess humane, if this was a murderer with a soft heart. And don't forget, sweetie pie, it's the preferred method of self-offing by the terminally ill. Nothing about it to point to murder, and especially not to Mafia execution."

"No, I've heard they prefer other means. I hate thinking about death, in any form. Could we just get back to the list?"

"Ah, always the scholar. Removed from the seamier side of life. But I got news for you. This *is* the seamier side, and like it or not, you are now up to your eyeballs in it."

I had noticed that, with the obvious omission of himself as a suspect, his list was similar to one I had made myself. It was hard, though, even for me, to believe Barry had been responsible for the planned death of a human being.

"Now that I have reestablished contact with Gren, I can see what there is to find out from him. I've invented an LA client—rather, I've let him believe my client is interested in furnishings rather than saving his own neck."

"I suppose that means your expensive suite at the Wilshire is now on my tab?"

"Of course, but I'd better let you reimburse me rather than you paying my hotel bill directly. We don't know if anyone is checking. You are good for it, aren't you?" I asked.

For reply, he reached into his pocket and pulled out a wad of bills. He peeled off five thousand dollars in crisp hundreds.

"Will that do you for a few days?"

"Nicely." Then, feeling a bit guilty about accepting money from Barry, I added, "You don't have to do this . . ."

"No, I sorta do. I did get you into this, so I'm going to man up. Now let's get back to finding out who is threatening me and why."

"Odd that no one has made a more overt move. If they are after the mask, why not just demand it? Why merely terrorize you?"

"I think they're watching to see who might be in this with me. Any Mafioso worth his marinara knows that the first thing a scared rat, that's me in this case, does is to get together with his cohorts and hatch a plan. Hi there, cohort."

My inner voice said to run out the door, screaming to any Mafia member who might be watching the place that I was innocent, that I had not even known there was such a thing as a Mask of Alexander until a few days ago. But that was the old me speaking.

I now saw this bizarre turn of events that had put me here, in a situation not many people would envy, as more of a gift than a curse.

I halted my train of thought for a minute. Did I really believe that? I shook my head at myself. My mother had been right all along. I was just not normal. I wasn't a bigger-than-life character from a Dan Brown novel. I was a fairly ordinary middle-aged woman without hefty credentials, superpowers, or even a normal sense of self-preservation. The only extraordinary thing in this entire story was that I was here, in the middle of something that was itself extraordinary. If I could find the mask and return it to its rightful owner, a denuded mummy now resting who knows where, I might be able to make up for my lackluster past.

I was conscious that Barry was looking at me, undoubtedly expecting some sort of a tirade. When none was forthcoming, he turned on the old innocent "aw, shucks" face I remembered so well.

"Look, Parthi, I never planned to put you in the hot seat, honestly I didn't."

I decided to toy with him for a minute. "So why did you do it then?"

"I was desperate, I guess. Like I told you in Boulder, I'm scared. And there's something else. If Zanski was the one who had possession of the mask before it went missing, maybe, since the two of you were so close—well, it seemed like he was being honest about having told you where it was." He shook his head. "I know you don't like this, Parthi, but I keep coming back to you."

"Me? No way. I have no idea why you can't get it through your head that this does *not* come back to me. I've told you so many times I'm sick of hearing my own voice, but just for the record I'll say it once more: I had no idea any mask even existed until you told me about it last week. Now, let's go back to you. Tell me everything you remember about that day you saw the mask in Zurich."

"Zanski and I went to a private bank vault in the Credit Suisse. Schott and Brazzi met us there. I remember I was surprised a big-time dealer like Schott would bring a nobody like Brazzi with him. I knew just about all the main Mafia guys in the business in those days, and he sure wasn't one of them."

Barry paused to make sure I was following. I nodded.

"That made me think this wasn't a regular deal, and that whoever really owned the mask wasn't showing himself. That's what made the Vatican cross my mind. Those boys have been known to turn a trick or two, and who knows what they've really got in those vaults? I thought about that again a little while ago when I read some English guy's theory that Alexander's mummy eventually made its final stop in Venice, where on account of some clever Christian sleight of hand, it was substituted for the body of St. Mark. Kind of fitting, really."

Barry paused and grinned. "Alexander would get a bang out of that if he were alive, considering how he always took up whatever religion that helped his case. Quite a guy, always pandering to the local gods, whoever they might be. Yep, St. Mark's Square is the perfect spot for his mummy. Of course," here Barry screwed up his face in mock sadness, "no one seems to be worried about what happened to poor old Mark."

"I hadn't heard about the Venice connection. What's that about?"

"Well, this guy whose name escapes me is writing books, posting internet videos, and in general stirring up the Vatican boys with his never-ending rant that one of their biggest saints ain't buried in Venice in his fancy tomb, but lo and behold, a well-known pagan is. That sort of thing makes the Catholics crazy, but . . ." and here he stopped to think for a few seconds, "if somehow poor old Mark's mummy was misplaced or ruined or something, some slick priest well might have covered his ass by putting another mummy in its place. After all, a mummy is a mummy, especially to a Christian. And, although this is a long shot, what if that replacement mummy just happened to be Alexander's?"

"This seems a bit too convenient, doesn't it?"

Barry shrugged. "Who knows?"

I returned to the former subject. "I'm missing something. How again did St. Mark get involved in all of this, and what's the story of his ending up as a mummy?"

"Apparently not everybody in Alexandria in the old days, even the Christian old days, loved either the Christians or St. Mark, so probably a bunch of pagans got liquored up one festival day and dragged poor old Markie Boy through the streets until he finally died."

Not being much of a Christian scholar, this was all news to me. I was impressed that Barry had found out so much. I had always thought he had the makings of a fine scholar if he had ever turned his mind in that direction.

"Here's the part that gets interesting: apparently somebody gathered up Mark's pieces and wrapped them up in linen, like a mummy. There must have been quite a crossover in how the Christians and pagans sent their dead off in those days. It would make sense, anyway, that those guys would want to preserve what they had left of poor old Mark, and since this whole thing took place in Egypt, and everybody there knew mummification was the way to go . . ."

"It seems like a stretch, but possible, I guess." Somehow, the whole thing was just too tidy an explanation to be true, but then, anything was possible. "Why don't they just take this mummy that's in St. Mark's tomb and do some DNA testing?"

"You know the Catholics. Paranoid at every turn. Suppose, just suppose, that whoever is in St. Mark's tomb is not Mark at all, but some pagan homo warlord? How's that going to go down with the faithful? No, they don't want to risk it. I gather there is a lot of fuss and feathers in the works now with that guy pressing his case so much in the media. But I didn't look all of this up just for fun.

"Let's say this guy has a point. For sure the faux Mark would not have been put in his tomb sporting anything as obviously non-Christian as a mask in the image of a well-known Pagan, soooo," he drew out his words for emphasis, "if the mask and mummy were still one at the time of the body switch, the mask had to go somewhere, and knowing those money-grubbing priests, either they melted it down or took it to the Vatican."

"Wow, there are a lot of *ifs* in your theory, but it makes for a great mystery."

"I've got more of a theory." Barry was on a roll. "What if the Vatican was the owner that Schott was fronting for?"

Listening to Barry, it was no mystery why he was so successful at selling just about anything. But he wasn't finished. "There's more to my theory."

"Wait a minute. The Vatican wanted to sell it? Why? I never heard of those people doing anything but hanging on to everything they have."

"Let's be creative here: suppose somebody before the current English guy had the same suspicion that it is actually Alexander who is in St. Mark's tomb, and the Catholic powers that be didn't want anything pointing to Alexander in their possession that might provide ammunition for a disinterment and DNA test."

"What would they be looking for? I didn't think DNA could pinpoint the age of bones that closely."

"Well, it might not prove that, but it certainly would prove something."

"Meaning?"

"St. Mark was a Jew and Alexander was a Greek. The test would show at least what gene pool was involved. So even though any exact identification of the body might not come to light, at least the genetic background would be known."

"I get it. Anything other than a Semitic corpse in St. Mark's tomb would spell trouble for the Vatican."

I changed the subject slightly. "So you think the Vatican was too mercenary to just melt it, so they marketed it via the Mafia. But why not just hide the mask until the heat was off? There must be tons of places in that complex to keep it out of sight."

"True," and here he paused, savoring his thought, "but herein lies the recipe for disaster. In order to ensure the mask never existed in the Vatican collection, all the records had to be wiped clean, follow me?"

I could tell we were getting into Barry's territory here. He continued, "But not every monk in the place could be trusted to keep the secret. So what if whoever was chosen to hide the goods and mop up the evidence was just a wee bit ambitious . . . or," and on this one, his eyes lit up, "what if the word came down that this whole thing was just too hot, and the mask had to be melted down or destroyed in some creative way, and whoever was supposed to do it just couldn't bring himself to do the deed, so . . ."

"That's assuming quite a lot."

"Yeah, I know, but weirder things have happened. Remember, history is made by people. It just takes one in the right place at the right time to change everything. Alexander is a case in point."

I was getting tired, and I was not about to reopen the age-old debate of whether individuals or events influence the course of history. How could I, when I was still reeling from the knowledge that Barry's shadow was now my own, and bad apples from the Vatican were equally dangerous as bad apples from the street? And in this case more so because the Vatican had better cover, and a whole lot more to lose.

Parthi's room, Beverly Wilshire Hotel
Beverly Hills, California
That night

CHAPTER 43

What is it about the night that makes us quake at every shadow and jump at any unfamiliar sound? How does a hero by day turn into a coward by night? In my case, all my daylight bravado pretty much vanished the minute I turned off the lights.

I tried to shift my thoughts to something else: why I had agreed to see Barry after so many years. What had motivated me to do that? Maybe it was because on some level I thought there still might be something between us.

I felt needy and ashamed, but at least while I was berating myself, I had a brief respite from night terror. Even with that diversion I slept very little that night.

Morning eventually came, and with it the realization that I had to think fast to get myself out of this pickle I had hopped into with eyes wide open.

"Step by step" was what I always said to myself when I had no idea where I was going, and it had always seemed to work.

I didn't have much choice in this case, anyway. So what *was* my first step?

My opportunity came from an unexpected quarter. A call from Adam Summerhill.

"Ms. Guthrie," he opened, his voice much warmer than I remembered from his office yesterday, "please forgive me for not connecting the dots yesterday. Had I known you and Gren were such close friends from years ago here at the Warner, I would have invited you then. However belated and last minute as this is, my wife and I are having a small dinner in Gren's honor this evening, and we'd love to have you join us. It's been a bit awkward these past few months with the Henry Templeton tragedy, so any sort of festivity seemed inappropriate. However, we are ever so grateful that Gren was able to step in and help us out in a tough situation. And, with that said, a welcome dinner is way overdue. Please say you can come."

"I'd be delighted. So good of you to ask."

"Nothing terribly formal. It'll be mostly staff and a few trustees. Not exactly black tie but a bit more than blue jeans." He paused for a few seconds. "Anyway, I am late for one of those never-ending bureaucratic meetings, so, if you don't mind, I'll put you on with my assistant. She can give you the directions to the house. Her name is Beverly."

"Thank you, Dr. Summerhill. I am looking forward to tonight." He had no idea how much.

Puzzled by the sudden invite, but at least with the driving directions sorted out, I had the whole day to myself.

In the elevator my phone pinged a text alert. I looked down and saw it was from Gren. "Call when you can. About tonight."

I waited an hour before calling, blaming the delay on a breakfast meeting with my imaginary Beverly Hills client.

"Sorry, I keep forgetting you are a designer now. Somebody with a real job. Anyway, Adam tells me you're on the list for the soiree tonight. Need a lift?"

"Yes, please. I have the directions and GPS and a rental car, but I'd probably get lost anyway. You're a lifesaver."

I WAS FEELING A BIT INSECURE about the coming evening.

I had not been in a crowd of museum people in years and didn't know quite what to expect. To make matters worse, I had not planned on staying on in Los Angeles, so I hadn't brought much in the way of clothes. The only suitable dress I had was the Armani I'd worn the night Sandra and I had drinks with Gren.

I had a choice: I could use the day and shop for just the right dress, or I could spend the time catching up on some of the sleep I had lost last night. It was a no-brainer. Much better to appear at the dinner with dewy skin and an old dress than in a new one that would do nothing to hide the bags under my eyes. The Armani would just have to do.

As much as I wanted to wear the Alexander necklace with it, an ornamental artifact seemed a bit too awkward in a room full of ancient art scholars and collectors. However, I had just the thing to accent the dress.

Although I had purged my mind and closet of all reminders of Barry after the divorce, the LALAoUNIS jewelry he had bought me on our honeymoon was so beautiful I had never parted with either the necklace or the earrings. Both were handcrafted from 22-karat gold in the form of stylized ram's horns, so simple they made diamonds redundant. Their pairing with the black Armani was perfect.

GREN GREETED ME IN THE LOBBY with kisses on both cheeks. He was dressed in a navy single-breasted suit and no tie, very much like something George Clooney would wear in a similar situation. Very proper on all counts.

Then he put his hands on my shoulders and held me at arms' length.

"You look smashing! I love it that you're secure enough to wear the same thing more than once. I never could understand why women have such a horror of that. After all, the great beauty Lillie Langtry made quite a name for herself for repeatedly wearing the same black dress to every posh London affair she attended."

"I'm surprised you know so much about clothes. Most men haven't a clue."

"I guess something must have rubbed off on me after three marriages."

We drove in companionable silence across Los Angeles.

The Summerhill house was a spacious Tudor in Hancock Park. In keeping with the exterior, the interior was furnished in the expected relaxed patrician taste suiting the head of a major museum.

None of the furniture was reproduction, the mellow wood of the floors was polished to perfection, and there was no sign anywhere of museum pieces borrowed for personal use. In all, just right. And quite impressive.

Gren and I merged with other guests already dotted about the high-ceilinged living room.

Here the floors were covered in mellow-toned Persian rugs, precisely arranged to create the impression of the random pattern favored by Turkish pashas. Light from the terrace glowed through the leaded panes of the large windows. A waiter in a white jacket circumambulated the room with a tray of champagne.

Adam Summerhill came toward us with his right hand extended. "Welcome, Gren. And Parthenia, if I may be so familiar. So glad you could make it." He placed his arm around my shoulder. "Come, I want you to meet Sylvia, my wife."

With that he propelled me across the room where a slim, designer-clad blonde was deep in conversation with a balding man with a distinct paunch.

"Darling, I want you to meet Parthenia Guthrie, Gren's old classmate."

"Please, everyone calls me Parthi."

"Parthi, then," he continued in the smooth fashion of a man who made these introductions on a regular basis, "this is my wife, Sylvia, and Steve Marzotti, head of our board of directors."

"Thank you so much for including me," I purred to Sylvia, before turning to the more interesting of the two, Marzotti. *Definitely an Italian name* I noted to myself before realizing how stupid that idea was, even as a passing thought. Not all Italians were Mafia, nor did the fact that an Italian man now headed the Warner board point to any sinister connection. Still, for some reason, I was interested in knowing more about Mr. Marzotti.

Men and women in Los Angeles as well as New York or Chicago or Dallas were named as trustees of symphonies, museums, and other cultural venues in what had evolved over the years into a tight symbiosis. The trustees brought power and money to the institution whose letterhead bore their names, and in turn they were given a blue chip in the social climbing game.

Rarely did these people know or care about the cultural genres they supported. Or was I merely being cynical, or echoing Zanski? Anyway, Marzotti looked to be the perfect rough-around-the-edges guy to suit the prototype.

For a moment I was not sure how to begin the conversation, but Sylvia, like the true blue-blooded hostess she was, glided us into instant communication.

"Steve is not only the chairman but quite a collector himself. In just your field, I think, Hellenistic antiquities."

Sylvia, like all well-trained politicians, had obviously done her homework on those on her guest list.

"How kind of you to make a point of knowing that, but I am long out of archaeology these days. I now spend my days, and quite happily, in the modern world of interior design. It is wonderful, though, to come back here and see what incredible changes you all have made to the Warner. I suspect you have a hand in there somewhere, Mr. Marzotti." I tried not to sound disingenuous.

I need not have worried. Marzotti was only too anxious for a chance to crow.

"The name's Steve," he smiled. "Well, not to brag, but I am pretty proud of the way things are going. Museum-wise, we're at the top of the heap, and everybody knows it. Best collection in the world. I told Adam we should fill our shelves with only the best the ancient world has to offer—legit, of course." He winked in a way that reminded me of Barry.

"I see you two have a lot to chat about, so I think I'll excuse myself," Sylvia oozed. "Some new guests have arrived and I need to say hello."

And she was off in a practiced glide toward the entrance hall, trailing a delicate whiff of Chanel No. 5 behind her.

I leaned a bit closer to Marzotti. He smelled of something manly and expensive, mixed with a hint of cigar smoke.

"I know this is totally politically incorrect, but like the rest of the world, I am dying to know—and since I am lucky enough to have your ear, can you tell me anything about what happened with Henry Templeton?"

I had blurted out what I wanted to know, but judging from the shrewd glint in his eye, I hadn't needed to. Marzotti had a pretty good idea what I was thinking about, anyway. For one, I was a woman, and to a man like him, all females were curiosity-driven, and second, Sylvia had just told him about my connection with Gren, which implied the same with Henry.

He looked like he was about to chuckle, then he caught himself and assumed the proper concerned demeanor.

"Were you close to him? We were all so sad to have to say goodbye to a member of our museum family in such a tragic way. I had no inkling, absolutely none, that anything untoward was going on, and I still can't believe those lies they printed in those pinko news rags. Why, he'd been here for years. Always so pleasant, and, as far as I could see, did a whale of a job. Always working. Built a damn fine collection for us, he did. No, I was shocked, absolutely shocked, that he should have been mixed up in anything shady. That is, if he actually was, which I very much doubt. We're a big target, you know, and people want to bring us down. Human nature, I guess. Same thing in my business. It's all about jealousy." He shook his head piously.

"I don't think I heard what business you were in, Steve."

"Oil. Olive oil, actually. I export from Italy to all over the world. You've probably read something about how we're supposed to be ripping off the public by selling mineral oil in extra-virgin bottles. They're even comparing the alleged profits to the drug market. Olive oil doctoring is supposed to be more profitable than cocaine, and without any of the risk of big jail time. Of all the insane accusations!" His face got a bit redder.

"I had heard about that scam," I replied, "and I confess I put the oil I was using to the test: popped it into the fridge to see if it hardened or not."

Steve laughed, "And what happened?"

"Actually it passed the test. But I tested only one brand, of course."

"My brand, I hope."

"Well, yes, if your brand is Simonetti."

"Oops, no, but they're a pretty honest outfit too." Steve was surprisingly gracious toward a competitor. "Of course, Simonetti is my cousin." He laughed again. "The idea that reputable companies would pull such a scam is unthinkable. Did you notice there has been no FDA recall? That proves those guys were just trying to sell newspapers and get their ugly mugs on TV."

I decided this was a good opportunity to turn the conversation back to Henry.

"You were saying that you didn't believe Henry actually bought stolen antiquities for the museum? I don't want to be contradictory, but we all read that a couple of the objects in question, a red-figure vase and a bust of Augustus, were returned to Italy. And he was indicted . . ." I made an attempt at looking like someone whom it pained to accuse a friend of wrongdoing.

"I know, I know. But I think he was tricked into thinking the whole thing was on the up and up by that Schott guy. He took advantage of Henry's integrity. Someone as honest as Henry would have trouble seeing that someone else was a crook."

I did not bring up the fact that ever since the first Warner scandal so many years ago, everyone connected with the museum world, and especially Henry, knew all about Schott, and steered a wide path around him.

"Yes, it was so very sad," I murmured.

I caught Gren's eye from the corner of my own. I had probably gotten all the information I was going to get from Steve, so to squeeze the most out of this once-in-a-lifetime opportunity to get what information I could from the horses' mouths, I needed to meet the rest of the guests.

Right on cue, Gren joined us. "Mind if I capture this beauty? There are a few other people who would love to meet her."

"Not at all, my man, I need to find Sophie, my wife. She must be thinking I deserted her entirely."

The Summerhill house, Hancock Park
Los Angeles, California
Minutes later

CHAPTER 44

"What were you two chatting about so intently?" Gren asked.

"I know it's your evening, Gren, but I can't get this thing about Henry out of my mind, and I wanted to get Marzotti's take on him."

He looked puzzled. "What are you, some sort of amateur detective? We both know that Henry was a crook. Sad to have to have to say so, but he did bring the disgrace upon himself."

Realizing that was not the politically correct tack to take, he hastily added, "I wish he hadn't killed himself. I just wish he had taken his punishment and put it behind him. Nothing is worth dying over."

"I agree, and I am so sorry to even bring up something like that here. Forgive me."

"Nothing to forgive, my dear, I just hope I can bring some dignity back to the Warner. Nobody trusts us these days, and I need to turn that around.

"On the hush-hush: Adam and I have been talking about setting up an exchange program with a couple of the smaller museums in Italy, whereby a couple of colleagues and I would go there and help them catalogue and display what they have, and their boys would come here to learn our techniques."

"Sounds brilliant. Hopefully it's not all boys. Is this your idea?"

"Well, yes, but I shouldn't take all the credit. It was the obvious next step in the museum's campaign to forge bonds with our international colleagues. Shipping objects back and forth just doesn't do the trick. If we, as an institution, are really sincere about wanting to make the world a better place for antiquities, we've got to train the people who care for them how they should be doing it.

"Big places, like the Louvre, know what they're doing and can probably teach us a thing or two, but the small regional museums are another story. And it's also places like that without a whole lot of sophistication in the care and displaying of their pieces that are the targets for the bad guys."

"And you think museums are the best places for antiquities?" I asked.

Gren looked at me like he had not heard me correctly. "Well, where else?"

"How about leaving them where they were put? In the tombs of their owners?"

Gren scratched his head like a cartoon character. "But then there would be no archaeology."

"Would that be such a bad thing?"

"Of course. Think about it. Grave robbing beats out prostitution as the world's oldest profession. If we, the good guys, don't step in and save the stuff, the bad guys will sell it to whoever can afford it, and all context of the finds will be lost, and with it, information about the past."

He had a point. But even though I might not be able to restore every antiquity in the world to its rightful owner, I was still going to do everything in my power to save this one, the Mask of Alexander.

"Why do you suppose nobody is buried with any goodies these days? People have conveniently shifted their idea of what is needed in the afterlife to spiritual rather than material possessions. Treasures encourage grave robbers—easier to rob from the dead than the living. But I think it's something else. Why waste good diamonds on dead Aunt Fanny when they could be put to much better use right here? Human nature is scum, don't you agree?" His voice was jocular, but the reality behind the words was anything but.

I returned the conversation to his new venture. "When do you start this international program?"

"Funny that you should ask. Adam plans to present our idea to the board at the meeting on Wednesday. Then, if all goes well, I will be on a plane to Rome next week to meet with the Italian minister of antiquities."

"After what happened—the Warner supposedly stealing, yet again, some of their national treasures—do you think they will even let you in the country?"

"My dear, why do you suppose the board so readily approved my appointment as acting curator? The Hopkins name tends to polish away any tarnish. My father, as you know, was pretty much the patron saint of aboveboard excavation, so, by association, I am the designated repairer of the Warner reputation in Italy."

"You're much more than that, Gren. This idea of giving them hands-on help is pretty impressive."

In spite of myself, I was actually beginning to like Gren.

So much so that my blush was totally genuine when he asked, "Hey, what are you doing next week? Don't you have any clients who are desperately in need of the latest in Italian sofas? Much cheaper at the source."

"Are you asking me to go to Italy with you, or are you offering to do some furniture shopping for me?"

"The former. I would really love your company, but if you're worried about your virtue, I can be a perfect gentleman, and you will have your own suite, of course. On me."

"That's very generous. But I do need to check with my clients here and see if that will work for them. Could I let you know tomorrow?"

"Of course. Hope you say yes."

My blood was rushing. I hoped I appeared reasonably in control, but in reality, I wanted to throw my arms around him and squeal for joy.

The sound of a bell, discreet but definite, brought me back to earth.

"It seems to be time to put the old feed bag on. I'm not sure what the seating arrangements are, but knowing Sylvia, she'll have us at separate tables, á la proper etiquette."

He had not seemed to notice how excited I was, or if he had, he undoubtedly chalked it up to the fact that I was so flattered by his invitation. And perhaps I was.

WE WERE INDEED AT SEPARATE TABLES, Gren cutting a dapper figure between Sylvia and a pleasant-looking woman I took to be Sophie, Steve's wife, and I, with a youngish man on my right and a very old one on my left. A peek at his name tag revealed the younger man to be Duncan Hayes, director of conservation.

Conservation, the science of restoring and preserving art objects, as well as mounting and displaying them, was one of the best-known and most prestigious departments at the Warner, in part because of the high-profile practice of providing free-of-charge technical support to impoverished museums worldwide. I could see how Gren's new idea of doing the same in the curatorial arena was a logical outgrowth of this successful program.

Conservation was also the place where all incoming artifact purchases first landed to be prepared for display. If the mask I was hoping to find had ever been brought into the Warner, it was likely it would first have landed in Duncan's office. However, Duncan's age made it impossible that he could have been involved in any but the most recent acquisitions. So if Zanski had brought the mask into the museum, Duncan would be of no help. But on the other hand, if Henry had secretly acquired it for the museum more recently, chances were good that Duncan knew something.

It never hurt to pry. Since etiquette dictated that I converse with my dinner partner on the right, I had the perfect opportunity to do so.

"I was always interested in conservation," I began. "I'm Parthi Guthrie, an old friend of Gren's from the dark ages of the Warner."

"Oh, nice to meet you." He looked like someone more comfortable in a laboratory than a drawing room, and conversation did not seem his strong suit.

Nonetheless, I continued in a chatty way, "Things must be totally different in the lab than they were in my day."

"Oh, did you work in conservation?" He seemed a bit more interested.

"Afraid not; Gren and I were grad students at the same time. Antiquities, with Zanski."

His interest had heated to lukewarm, "What was that like? Nobody talks about Zanski much. Those days must have been wild."

"Yes, and fun, but I was pretty much out of the loop as far as the hot objects were concerned. After all, I was a mere grad student."

It was time to edge into what I really wanted to hear about: Henry. "Henry Templeton was a student at the same time, as you may know. So sad about him."

The mention of Henry's name got a distinct reaction. "He was wonderful—made me feel really welcome when I first came here from Princeton. A lot of people thought my job should have gone to somebody from within, and I had a hard time fitting in at first. He took me under his wing. I will always be grateful to him."

That made sense. Henry, as antiquities curator, would have worked closely with the conservation department. It would have been wise for him to keep its director in his pocket. Duncan's goodwill would have come in handy should Henry have elected to bring anything sketchy into the museum.

I noticed that Duncan was looking at me with a lot more interest than when we first sat down. I waited politely for him to say something. Eventually he did.

"Look," he stuttered, absentmindedly shredding an innocent

dinner roll as he spoke, "I need to talk to somebody. Somebody not currently connected to the museum, and you knew Henry. I know you must think I'm crazy just to blurt this out, but I haven't slept much since he died. And when I do, I keep dreaming about him, like he's trying to contact me or something . . ." His voice trailed off.

I looked around. As much as I was eager to hear what Duncan had to say, even I had enough sense to be cautious. I leaned closer to him.

"I understand. Probably more than you even suspect. Look, this isn't the place to talk about anything, but are you free anytime tomorrow? I would love to hear whatever you have to say."

He looked relieved. "I don't usually take lunch, but I do have the option. Could we meet somewhere away from the museum?"

"Of course. How about my hotel? I'm staying at the Beverly Wilshire."

He shook his head, his eyes vacantly scanning the pile of crumbs he had created on his bread plate. "I don't think so. That's pretty public. How about the Tar Pits?"

I laughed. "How fitting." The irony seemed to have escaped Duncan.

Beverly Wilshire Hotel
Beverly Hills, California
The same evening

CHAPTER 45

Christos was now convinced the dark-haired woman was the key to the location of the mask. He felt that more strongly than he had ever felt anything in his life. But where was she keeping it?

The knowledge that his quarry was so close yet still eluding him gnawed at his insides. What were she and Epstein up to? The Mask Hunter had to act fast and find out before they could sell Alexander's treasure and place it forever out of his reach. His window of opportunity was getting shorter.

He'd been watching her carefully since her arrival in Los Angeles, so he had no trouble determining she was staying at the Beverly Wilshire. That was a stroke of good luck. Hotel rooms were child's play to break into.

Dressed in what he thought of as his "Beverly Hills" clothes—expensive shirt (a gift from the American), blue jeans, and Gucci loafers (another gift from the American)—the Mask Hunter entered the lobby of the Beverly Wilshire Hotel. Catching a glimpse of himself in one of the large mirrors, he smiled at the irony that what he was wearing was almost a duplicate of the outfits favored by his nemesis Barry Epstein.

Turning from the mirror, he waited until he saw the dark-haired woman leave. He immediately approached the reception desk. A man and a woman were on duty. Although the man was free, Christos waited until his female companion had finished checking in a rather noisy group of four before he approached. He always had better luck with women.

"Excuse me, miss," the Mask Hunter addressed the perky-breasted hotel clerk, "Can you tell me what room Miss Guthrie is in?"

"I think you just missed her," was the reply. "But I'll ring her room just to make sure."

The Mask Hunter watched the girl's movements carefully as she checked the hotel registry. "Let's see, Guthrie. Room 302." She was obviously mumbling to herself and did not intend for him to hear.

However, that was all the information the tall man needed. He reached across the counter and laid his fingers gently on the phone she was holding.

"On second thought, I'll just try and catch up with her at the restaurant," he lied. "No need for you to bother."

The girl gave him a puzzled look, then a shrug. People were always changing their minds.

"As you wish, sir. Have a pleasant evening." With that she turned her attention to the elderly woman who was waiting behind him. "What can I do for you, ma'am?"

Satisfied that the desk clerk was not watching him, the golden-eyed man headed for the elevator.

From here the rest would be easy. He was alone in the elevator and smiled to himself as he pressed the 3 button.

Landing on the third floor, the Mask Hunter easily spotted just the kind of domestic help that intuition told him would be a pushover to grant him access to the Guthrie woman's room.

"Excuse me, miss," he addressed the woman who was well past any hope of ever being addressed as a "miss" again. "I locked my key in my room, and I need to get in."

It was such an old ploy that he was embarrassed to use it, but it always worked. People were so gullible.

A smile and a twenty tucked discreetly into the woman's apron pocket, and he was inside.

He hesitated a moment in the doorway, feeling suddenly reluctant to intrude into the private quarters of the beautiful woman. Her fragrance was everywhere. He had never been close enough to her to smell it before, but here it was unmistakable: a light jasmine scent with a hint of citrus. He closed his eyes for a moment, lost in the fragrance.

He only indulged his senses for a few seconds. Quickly he opened his eyes and mentally shook himself. He had to search her belongings, and he needed to do it quickly.

She had been dressed for an evening out when she left, but best not to leave anything to chance and run the risk of a confrontation should she return unexpectedly.

The closet first. His nostrils were assaulted by an even stronger scent of jasmine as he riffled through the hangers. Nothing. The suitcase on the floor was empty, and the shelves above yielded nothing particularly noteworthy, although everything associated with this woman was becoming more and more interesting to him.

There was a small room safe attached to the wall at the side of the closet.

The lock gave no resistance as he forced it open, careful to leave neither fingerprints nor signs of forced entry. Inside he found a string of pearls, earrings, and other jewelry that held no interest for him. They were obviously valuable, but he was no thief.

The last item in the safe was a long velvet box. He opened it and stepped backward as though struck. There on a satin cushion was a coin of the god Alexander, encased in gold and embellished with two small jewels and suspended on a golden chain. Why did she have such a thing? Was she some sort of priestess of the Pharaoh Alexander, and perhaps not a profit-seeker at all? But how was that possible?

The Mask Hunter would have much to think about later, but now he had to complete his search of the room. He walked over to the chest of drawers, opened the topmost drawer, and ran his fingers through the silken lingerie stacked in neat piles.

He had never felt anything like this, soft and scented like her. He longed to remove one of the wisps of silk that passed for underwear and put it in his pocket, but he restrained his urge, closed the drawer, and continued on to inspect the lower two drawers. Both were empty except for a couple of T-shirts, not nearly as interesting, or disturbing, as the one above.

Quickly moving to the desk, his eyes fell upon pay dirt: pages and pages of information on Alexander, his life and his death. At the back of the sheaf of papers was a single handwritten page that he read eagerly. It was a list of names, all of whom he recognized had something to do with the mask.

Using his cell phone, he took a couple of quick shots of the document before exiting the room, making sure the door locked behind him.

This visit to the lair of the mysterious dark-haired woman had yielded two important facts: the first, that she didn't have the mask with her on this trip, and second—this one was definitely intriguing—that she, like the Mask Hunter himself, seemed to be in pursuit of the sacred object.

Knowing that he was getting closer to his quarry should have elated him, but instead it left him strangely disturbed. If the woman threatened his repossessing the mask, and it looked as though she was on that track, he might have to kill her.

La Brea Tar Pits
Los Angeles, California
The following day

CHAPTER 46

The La Brea Tar Pits, graveyard to a panoply of extinct Ice Age species, are located just off Wilshire Boulevard in the Fairfax District of Los Angeles. They were an odd phenomenon to find in the midst of a bustling modern city better known for classic Jaguar XKEs than saber-toothed tigers. The still-oozing asphalt pools are one of the favorite destinations of elementary school field trips.

I had arrived a bit early and took a minute to renew my acquaintance with the oldest area of the outdoor part of the exhibit, the re-creation of the fate of a woolly mammoth family. As I had expected, a gaggle of what looked to be six-to-seven-year-olds was marveling at this step back into a magical time.

"The Daddy's stuck in the goo," one prim little thing in a short plaid skirt commented, pointing to a partly submerged tusker that appeared to be bellowing in fear and rage from the center of the pool.

"He went in first to taste if the water was good," a small boy with black hair and an intense stare answered. "He wanted to make sure it was good for his family. He was taking care of them."

"He didn't do it very well," candidly observed another of the children.

As fascinated as I was by this astute psychological observation of Ice Age domestic life among woolly mammoths, I was even more anxious to meet with Duncan and find out what had propelled him to reach out to me.

He had suggested we meet near the Pleistocene Garden, a replanting of a small area of Los Angeles to resemble what the area would have looked like ten thousand years ago.

"We'll be less likely to run into anyone we know" had been his reasoning for choosing the spot.

It was a good choice. Cool and somewhat shaded, it was well away from most of the tourists. Duncan was right on time. He spotted me and hurried to where I was sitting on a low retaining wall.

"Hope I didn't keep you waiting," he mumbled apologetically, checking his watch.

"No, I got here early," I assured him. "I haven't been here in ages, and it was fun to look around."

"They're still digging every day. There seems to be no end to the number of fossils in these pools. I read they even found some recent murder evidence as well."

He must have seen me wince because he continued, "Gangland, I think. With all the gangs in LA I'm surprised the place isn't overflowing."

"Not a pleasant thought."

"No, and neither is the reason I asked you to meet me here. I can't stop thinking about Henry. And I also can't believe he committed suicide. We hung out fairly often. Actually, we didn't talk shop a lot. Mostly we talked about religion. We were both Catholics and never could accept how the ancients, Romans primarily, seemed to use it as a top problem-solver."

He was quiet for a moment, obviously thinking about how simple life would be if one could blame everything on the gods.

"There are still a lot of people who believe everything that happens is God's will," I pointed out.

"Yeah, lucky them. No personal responsibility."

Without any prodding, he returned to the subject of Henry. "He was more angry than despondent when he was indicted. He was out to get even and clear his name, not give up and kill himself."

That was a new piece of information that would interest Barry for sure.

"How do you know that?" I asked.

"He told me so. He was about to be cleared."

"Did he say how?"

"No. I think he was about to, but of course he died. I was in Chicago that week, consulting at the Art Institute. He called and said he'd found out something, that he didn't want to talk about it on the phone, and that he would tell me all about it when I got back."

"Those don't sound like the words of someone despondent enough to end it all."

"Absolutely not. That's why I can't stop thinking about it. Or about him. I wasn't sure what to do, who to talk to, because someone at the museum might have murdered him. Going to the police wasn't an option because the museum party line was so definitely suicide, and I had my job to consider . . . So when you turned up at that dinner last night, and I heard you had also been at the museum years ago with Henry, I thought I would take a shot in the dark that you might be someone I could trust.

Maybe there is something to this idea of divine intervention after all. You have no idea how keeping this all bottled up has been eating me up inside." He looked miserable.

"That sounds terrible. But on the practical side, how do you think I can help—and with what, exactly?

The look of misery deepened. "I don't know. I haven't even thought about that. Mostly I just wanted to talk to somebody. Somebody safe."

"I understand," I nodded, trying to decide how much, if any, of Barry's theory I should share with this man.

So I decided to play it safe. "I've been wondering also, but I'm not sure how we can go about finding anything out. Do you have any theories about the break-in at Gren's office?"

"None. But it just seems too coincidental to be ignored. Of course, no one at the museum is saying anything about it at all. A memo was sent around to all the departments the next day stressing the need for all of us to 'pull together and protect the privacy of the great institution we are all so proud to be members of.' Didn't ring true, but one thing you learn when you work at the Warner is that questioning is not good for job security. I'm just a coward, I guess, but I did—still do—also care about Henry, and want to help find his killer."

"Yes," I agreed, "we have to try."

Los Angeles, California
One half hour later

CHAPTER 47

As soon as Duncan left to go back to the Warner, I called Barry from the rental car. "I have something you need to hear."

"Well, it's about time. Shoot."

I told him about my meeting with Duncan, and how he had made it pretty clear that, in fact, Henry had not committed suicide. Telling Barry made me admit to myself, I think for the first time, that we were not just dealing with a missing artifact but with a murderer as well.

"This really scares me, Barry. Shouldn't we go to the police or something? There's a killer out there, and if we stir him up . . ."

"Yeah, I know. So let's not do anything yet."

I'd put off telling him about the trip to Rome with Gren. Perhaps now was the right time. "Look, I've been invited to go to Rome with Gren next week. Maybe I can find something out there."

"You're *what*?" Barry's voice was incredulous. "And exactly when were you planning to tell me that small factoid?"

"I just told you." I was maybe a wee bit too defensive. He picked right up on it.

"We're supposed to be partners in this caper, for better or

worse, and that means we need to clear any little side trips with each other."

"I don't remember agreeing to anything like that."

"OK, OK. But I still need to be kept in the loop, at least."

"I know, Barry. I should have told you right away. Anyway, the main reason I even considered accepting the invitation was because of the perfect cover it will give me to snoop around in Italy."

"So now you're going to take on the Mafia. All by yourself. That's smart. Really smart. I know you, and so I'm not going to waste my breath trying to talk you out of going, but do one thing for me."

"And what, pray tell, might that be?"

"Stay away from Brazzi and anyone associated with him. They're killers. If they think you have the mask and are holding out, you could be in big trouble."

"And just who would tell them I know anything about the mask? And remember, I don't."

"Yeah, but the walls have ears. Anybody could know anything. I don't like this. Maybe I should go too."

"No, Barry, you can't. Whoever 'they' are, they are harassing you already. If you show up in Rome with me, it will send a red flag for sure that you and I are up to something. And, also important, how would I explain to Gren that I am bringing my first husband along as chaperone?"

"OK, I get your point," Barry admitted. And after a few more weak attempts at dissuading me, he reluctantly acquiesced to my going to Rome.

"Just remember," he cautioned, "that the mask and the killer are connected, so be careful. And I repeat, stay away from

Brazzi."

"But I'll be with Gren, so I'll have some protection."

"Mixed situation. For all we know, he's the guy who killed Henry. After all, he's the one with the best motive."

"But you're forgetting whoever it was that Henry thought had framed him. That sounds more like Adam Summerhill or one of the trustees."

"*Rrrrr*ight. But we can't assume anything. What's with you and Gren, anyway?"

I was glad we weren't having this conversation in person so he could not see me blush. And I could feel the pink tingling in my cheeks as I answered, "Nothing romantic, if that's what you mean. But I do like him more than I used to. Now, whether that proves he is not a killer, I'm not sure."

"Just be careful."

We signed off with Barry still not convinced my trip to Rome was such a good idea.

BACK AT THE HOTEL I began to get organized for the coming flight to Rome. Ever since last night I had had the feeling that someone other than the help had been in my hotel room.

Nothing was missing, just things a bit out of place. It was probably my hypervigilant imagination. Just the maid tidying up. And considering my history of irrational panic, it was hard to separate the real from the imagined.

I turned my thoughts back to the trip. The temperature in Rome would be about the same as in Los Angeles, so most of the clothes I had brought from Boulder would be fine. But I needed more of them. One dress would hardly do for a week in Europe. Another snag was that I did not have my passport with me. It was in the small wall safe in the living room back at Rock House, along with the house deed and some other legal documents, including my divorce papers.

I could buy the extra clothes I needed here, but the passport posed a problem. I did have a cleaning staff who came into the house weekly, but no one I would trust with the combination to my safe. The thought struck me, as it had many times in the past, how alone I actually was.

During my marriage to Kirk, husband number two, I had lived his life rather than my own.

I knew other people, of course, but they had been situational friends, not intimate ones. I had not developed a support system because I hadn't needed one, but all that was different now. I made a mental note to start playing tennis again when I returned to Boulder—if, and more and more that seemed like a real question, I was still alive and able to return at all. I could also join some volunteer groups, even take a class in something. Anything that would create the potential for some new friends.

Why was I thinking about such trivia, anyway? Trying to pretend life was normal?

But I still needed my passport. About the only person I had recently spent much time with, outside of my real estate agent, psychiatrist, and divorce lawyer—none of whom had BFF potential—was Sandra Peters.

"Parthi! How great to hear from you! I was wondering how things were going in LA, and especially if Gren had carried you off to white slavery. He seemed pretty interested. Tell all!"

I laughed. It was good, for this moment at least, to be talking about romance instead of murder.

"Things are great here. You must be psychic, about Gren, I mean, because that's why I'm calling. That and the desk, of course. Has it arrived yet?" No matter what my personal concerns were, Sandra was still a paying client, and her needs had to be attended to first.

"The desk? It arrived right away. I confess I got anxious and had it unpacked. You may want to change it around when you get back, but I think it looks fab. Can't wait to show you!"

"I can't wait to see it, either! Did you put it under the window like we discussed?"

"Yes, and that chair of my grandmother's is perfect for it. I'll text you a pic. But we got sidetracked, tell me about you and Gren."

"Well, he's a hard one to figure out. He's been attentive and has asked me on this trip to Rome . . ."

"Rome?" squealed Sandra, "That's too good to be true! Are you sleeping with him yet?"

"No, nothing at all in that area. And that's something that puzzles me. He is totally attentive, but he hasn't made a move. I've been out of the dating arena for so long that I don't really know what to expect, but a kiss would be nice."

"You mean he hasn't even kissed you? That's really odd. But maybe it's just because he's so newly divorced—doesn't want to jump into anything and make another bad choice—not that you would be a bad choice, of course, but he has, after all, been married several times . . ." Sandra tended to speak in long, run-on sentences.

"That's probably it. I feel sort of the same way myself, so taking things slowly is perfect for me. And, I like his company. He's more fun, and smarter, than I remembered."

"Oh, oh, you've got it bad. I can tell by your tone of voice. And, for what it's worth, I think you two are perfect for each other."

"I have a favor to ask, Sandra. I hope it's not an imposition, but I need my passport, and it's in the safe in my house . . ."

"Say no more. I'll overnight it. Do I need a combination or something?"

"It's 7 left, 3 right, and 7 again to the left. It sticks, so you have to wiggle it a bit. And I keep a spare front door key under the flat stone beside the garage door."

"I'm on it! I think you showed me that safe one day behind your mother's portrait in the living room. Is that the one?"

"Yes, it is. Good memory. You have potential as a burglar."

Sandra laughed. "Now tell me more about the trip."

"We leave next Friday. Staying at the Hassler. Yum! Gren's treat, he says, and I get to have my own room."

"Well, unless I'm totally wrong, that won't be for long. What are you going to do there, anyway?"

"Well, Gren's going to be tied up a lot of the time with museum meetings—it's a business trip for him, so I guess I'll sightsee and shop for my LA client during the day, and spend time with him in the evening."

"Sounds like heaven. If you see anything that might work in this house, you have free rein to pick it up."

"I will. Anything in particular?"

"Everything. But I was thinking mostly about a painting for John's office. His birthday is coming up."

"I'll see what I can do. Paintings are so much about personal taste, though, so if I get something and it doesn't work, I wouldn't want you to feel obligated. I'll find another home for it."

"Great. Thanks. Hey, what about that first husband of yours? Is he still in the picture?"

"Well, I've seen him, but he's not in the picture in the sense you mean. But he has hired me to do some work, so we're in contact."

I hated the idea of any sort of lie, but technically what Barry and I were doing was a job. And it would never occur to Sandra to ask what kind of work.

"Maybe that's not such a great idea. I never knew him, of course, but from what I've heard, you're well away from him."

"I totally agree, and I am being careful."

"To return to a more important subject, how are you fixed for clothes? The weather should still be warm in Rome, but just to be safe, why don't I pack up a few cashmeres, and maybe something warm for evenings? OK if I scavenge your closets?"

"Yes! Please do! I have been so preoccupied with everything that I completely blanked on the wardrobe. I guess I was just thinking I'd pick up some things here. But your idea is so much better. And cheaper. Just throw anything you think I might need in the FedEx box. You are a lifesaver. But are you sure it won't be too much trouble?"

"Since when is helping the course of true romance trouble?"

"Well, I owe you."

We hung up, Sandra promising to have the passport in a FedEx packet that afternoon and the clothes in a separate box, and I to keep her posted on any and all progress in the Gren department. With everything going on, it was a relief to have a good friend—who had nothing to do with any of this—to depend on.

Grenville's house, Mandeville Canyon
Los Angeles, California
The same day

CHAPTER 48

Christos was fixing dinner in the kitchen when Grenville entered.

"You're going to Rome with me. Next Friday."

Christos put down the knife he was using to chop onions and turned in Grenville's direction. "When did you decide that?"

"You can be useful. Four eyes will be better than two. I have a suspicion you are right about Parthi as a mask hunter. She certainly leaped at my invitation to go to Rome with me."

"She's going too? When did you arrange that?"

"After you told me she had reconnected with Epstein, that he was with Zanski when the sale of the mask was being negotiated in Zurich, and that this mask is what they are undoubtedly looking for now. See what a good team we make?" Grenville, now standing within breathing distance of the golden-eyed man, reached over and nibbled his ear.

Christos ignored the gesture. "And you think the mask may be in Rome, and she will lead us to it?"

"Exactly, my friend—if it was here, she and Epstein would have tried to sell it already."

"How did you get her to agree to the trip?"

"Need you ask? You know I have always had a way with the ladies, much to their later chagrin, of course." Grenville's laugh was smug. "This will be a most interesting trip all around, although I may not get much sleep bouncing from room to room."

Beverly Hills, California
The following week

CHAPTER 49

The time flew by as I prepared to leave for Rome. The passport and clothes arrived on schedule, and Barry had received no more mysterious communications, so he was a lot calmer. In fact, the only troubling spot on my horizon was something Sandra said when I called to thank her for sending my things.

"Did you know the lock on your garage apartment door was broken? I noticed it when I picked up the house key. I had your gardener check inside, but nothing seemed to be disturbed, so he just fixed it."

"How about the house?" I asked.

"Nothing. No alarm tripped or anything. Anyway, I wouldn't worry about the garage. I don't even know why I mentioned it. Enjoy your trip."

Even though as a rule I can't sleep on planes, the flight to Rome was an exception. It must have had something to do with the fact that for the first time in the last two weeks, I was able to relax without imagining a marauder at the door. I was comforted by both the fact that the preflight security checks had weeded out any people who might be carrying weapons, and the fact that Gren was next to me. It would have been nice to have an uninterrupted chat with him, but my body had other plans.

My sleep was filled with dreams. They were the kind of dreams where one runs and runs and gets nowhere. In the most vivid one, I was riding my pony, Bucephalus II, across a stretch of sand that must have been a desert. Alexander the Great on his own Bucephalus was far ahead of us, and I was trying to catch up. Every time I gained any distance at all, a shadowy man swooped out of nowhere and held us back.

I was still exhausted and groggy when we landed, and all but oblivious to the sparkle of the rising sun.

Outside the plane, the city would be stirring, marked by the impatient tooting of horns that signaled the beginning of another day in the Eternal City.

Gren took my hand. "Are you all right? I gave you up for dead for a while. You were out cold. I didn't have the heart to wake you for anything to eat."

"I didn't snore, did I?" The image of myself open-mouthed, drooling, and emitting unpleasant grunts was appalling.

He laughed, "Well, just a tiny bit. But it was cute."

I shuddered. "Our first night together, and you had to see me that way. I am embarrassed. Did you sleep at all?"

"Not much. I can't believe you didn't hear that child in the row behind us. Fussed all night."

"Not a sound."

"I felt sorry for the poor little tyke. Must have had an earache or something. I almost suggested the mother pour some Scotch down his throat, but I restrained myself."

"You are a gentleman," I teased.

"You bring out the best in me. Now, on to practical things. How do you want to do this? Handle jet lag, I mean?" Gren steered me gently by the elbow through passport check and then toward the baggage claim area.

"Well, I've always heard it's best to try to suppress the urge to sleep right away and to get on the local time as soon as possible. But if you would rather rest . . ."

"No, I can manage to stay up a bit longer, at least until lunchtime. So why don't we drop the bags at the hotel and then grab some breakfast?"

AN HOUR LATER, after a jostling taxi ride along the awakening Italian streets, the Hassler bellman ushered me into the seventh-floor Villa Medici Suite, which, from the moment the door was opened, took my breath away. Gren certainly knew how to impress a woman!

I had heard that the wonderful old hotel had recently been completely renovated, but I was totally unprepared for the opulent environment that was to be my home for the coming week. Visible from the doorway was the terrace, but not just any terrace. This one took in the view of what looked to be all of Rome. The beautiful parts at least.

"Shall I put your bags here?" The bellman spoke in careful and perfect English. He gestured toward the bedroom.

"Yes, please." I returned to reality long enough to fish some coins from my handbag, hoping it was enough.

"*Grazie*, Madam, *mille grazie*. Will there be anything else?"

"No, thank you. This is such a beautiful suite. It looks like I have everything I could possibly need. In fact, I may just stay here forever."

"Ah, yes, this is a most wonderful hotel, but the beauty of Rome awaits you."

When the door closed behind him, I sank into the center of the silk-covered bed and closed my eyes. The softness was seductive. I had to force myself upright after two or three blissful minutes. Falling asleep, although I was sorely tempted after the stress of the last week and the long flight last night, was not an option. Gren would be waiting for me downstairs, and being punctual for a breakfast date was the very least I could do to show my appreciation for the posh digs and Gren's generosity in dragging me along on this trip.

I decided not to bother changing, so my only concession to primping was a quick splash of water from the marble basin, a fast pass with a hairbrush, and a smear of lip gloss. Seductive presentation would have to wait until I'd had a day or so to acclimate to the time change.

I was about to leave the room to meet Gren when the house phone rang.

"Parthi," Gren's voice was silky. "I'm just beat after that flight, so would you mind terribly if we put good intentions aside and skipped breakfast?"

"Not at all," I replied in as airy a tone as I could muster.

Actually, I was disappointed, but we had the whole week, and, anyway, Gren had made no specific promises, so I did not know what to expect from him at all. I told myself that I should just feel happy that I was in Rome, in a perfect hotel, out of danger, and with a chance, albeit ever so slight, of solving the mystery of the Mask of Alexander and getting it back to its rightful owner.

Rome, Italy
The same day

CHAPTER 50

It was a glorious autumn in Rome. The temperature was mild, while the lowering arc the sun made crossing the heavens suggested colder weather would be arriving soon. It was wonderful to be back in the city I had visited so often, first with my mother, and later, on my own.

I let myself drift through the winding streets with no destination, every now and then glancing into a shop window. Knowing I was going to meet Gren for dinner, I got back to the hotel in time for a nap and a bath. But even after almost two hours of dreamless sleep, I almost nodded off again in the deep marble tub. The rose-scented bath salts probably helped.

Promptly at eight o'clock Gren knocked at my door. He was wearing a blue blazer, an ascot knotted at his neck. I'd never had dinner with a man wearing an ascot, so this reminded me of something out of an old 1950s movie.

"I'm still a bit jet-lagged," he explained, although he certainly did not look it. "So let's eat here in the hotel. They have a pretty good kitchen, or so I have heard. Like your room?" His eyes moved around the room in approval.

"I love it! Thank you so much. I feel like a total princess here."

"And a princess you surely are. Shall we go?" He offered his left elbow and I tucked my right hand inside.

At dinner Gren explained, somewhat apologetically, that his schedule for the week was quite full of meetings with heads of various provincial museums, usually outside the city.

That pretty much added up to the fact that we would not be spending a lot of time together. I had expected as much. I was in a city I loved, in luxurious surroundings, and with plenty of free time to see if I could discover anything about the mask. But I was still puzzled. Why had he brought me with him, at no small expense, merely to essentially ignore me?

The next morning, as I trotted down the Spanish Steps toward the Via Veneto, I felt free and exhilarated.

My plan was to reacquaint myself with the city by walking as many of its streets as I could, revisiting old favorites. It was too early for the linen shop just below the Spanish Steps to be open, but I made a mental note to stop there on my way back and buy a pair of silk pajamas for Sandra as a thank-you present for shipping my passport and clothes. Pajamas were certainly not in the same league with the glorious necklace she had given me, but as a girlie girl who probably did not sleep in sweats like I did, I suspected she would love them.

My first stop was a small coffee shop nestled up against the Pantheon.

The toasty smell of the espresso wafted into the street and called my name. The early morning coffee crowd had already downed their requisite charge of energy and hurried off to their offices, so the shop was quiet. I sat at a small table facing the side street and sipped the warm and creamy concoction. I sat nursing my caffè latte for almost half an hour.

I was about to leave when I caught a glimpse—a quick one to

be sure, but a glimpse nonetheless—of a man studying me from a seat along the bar. My first reaction was fear, then I reminded myself I was in Rome, where older women like me were still ogled at. I should be flattered, not panicked.

Just the same, I was uncomfortable, quickly fishing a euro out of my bag, tucking it under my coffee cup, and hurrying out into the fall sunlight.

Once in the street, I took control of my thoughts and decided nothing was going to spoil this glorious day, surely not some random would-be Romeo.

I headed toward a street that housed antique shops. I was planning to search for Sandra's painting and see if I could find out from the shop owner where I might find dealers who sold questionable antiquities.

Barry would not approve, having made me promise to keep strictly away from anything even remotely associated with antiquities, but I was here and the temptation was just too great.

The idea of running into a stray Mafioso offering me a hot Apulian vase was fairly remote, but I did remember the grapevine between the licit and illicit dealers was pretty well entwined, so I could always hope.

As I walked, looking into windows stuffed with tempting dust-covered treasures, I could not shake off the feeling that someone was following me. It was just a feeling—I saw no one—but it was there just the same, leaving at times, then returning in the form of a slight shiver, despite the warm sunshine.

Maybe this street was too quiet. Most of the tourists who normally flocked here in large numbers during the summer were now gone. As lovely as it was not to be jostled by hurrying men and women on the prowl for a juicy bargain, the emptiness of my surroundings was a bit eerie.

I decided to head for the Forum. Even in late September, it would be a busy place.

I hated crossing the busy street that separated the ruins from the opposite curb where I was standing. After watching the blur of cars, taxis, and Vespas careening around the corner, a bit too close for my taste, I eventually gave up and hailed a cab. Nobody in her right mind would cross a Roman street in that circumstance, but I knew taking a cab literally around a corner after I had walked for miles was a bit absurd. Nonetheless, I did it, and moments later, I was deposited safely in front of the Forum.

It hadn't changed much in the ten years since I was last there: a noble pile of ruins at the center of a modern city.

When I left the hotel in the morning, the air had been chilly enough for a sweater. Now, in the full heat of the noonday sun, I found myself sweating. I hadn't thought to dress in layers and have something cooler underneath. Cursing my stupidity, I decided the next best thing to a sleeveless shell was the cool air inside the Colosseum. I picked my way over the uneven ground and entered.

The same smell of urine that I remembered from visits in the past assailed my nostrils. This had always been a popular pit stop for people too lazy to find a proper *bagno*.

The building itself, and all it symbolized, had always held a morbid fascination for me. It was a microcosm of the Roman Empire, the site that inspired the term "bread and circuses" to describe the reason for the fall of this once-great civilization.

By contrast, the architecture was a true triumph of engineering. Innovative use of concrete to create the great circular form established the norm for all buildings housing athletic spectacles past and present.

I walked down a passage that was originally a chute through which both animals and gladiators had been brought from the holding areas below into the arena on the ground level. For many, both human and animal, it would have been the last walk before facing a brutal death. I imagined the raucous and roaring crowds, the colors, the smells of sweat and fear.

Then everything went black.

Rome, Italy
The same time

CHAPTER 51

In his wanderings in search of his prize, the Mask Hunter had returned to Rome twice, visiting all the antiquities shops and shady dealers, but in vain.

The shops and the dealers were not his focus on this trip. No, this time he had a more promising target: the dark-haired woman. While he knew her name, he was reluctant to use it so as to remain detached in case the worst happened and he was forced to kill her later. Grenville agreed with him that there was a good chance she would lead them to the sacred object. Thus it was his mission to keep her in sight at all times.

Today he followed her at a discreet distance until she sat down at an outdoor café.

He ordered an espresso and sat at a nearby table pretending to be immersed in his newspaper. This gave him the opportunity of observing her at closer range than usual.

His earlier impression of the woman had been correct. She was indeed lovely, but—noting her practical tennis shoes—far from vain. There was a seriousness about her that suggested a weight on her shoulders. Definitely interesting. She lingered over her coffee. Was she expecting to meet someone here?

He noticed other men watching her and smiled. Such a lovely woman was bound to attract attention in a city like Rome.

At last she rose from the table, rather abruptly, the Mask Hunter thought, and almost rushed from the café. It was unlikely that she had noticed him, but perhaps she had sensed his presence. He would have to be very careful with this one.

Her route took her down a street lined with antique shops. She seemed to look into each window but entered none. Her trail seemed to be leading him nowhere. He sighed and kept following.

Christos continued to watch as she headed toward the Colosseum. Perhaps the rendezvous he anticipated would take place there. Puzzled, he watched her hail a cab, then ride in it only across the street. What was she doing?

He himself threaded his way carefully between the busses, cars, and Vespas and arrived on the Colosseum side of the street only slightly after she alit from the taxi.

As he followed her into the Colosseum, he was vaguely aware of the long black limousine bearing Vatican insignia that was parked along the periphery where no civilian vehicle would be allowed.

Then everything happened so quickly, he had no time to react. As if from nowhere a man appeared behind the dark-haired woman, striking her with an object Christos could not make out. Then, holding a handkerchief over her face, the man half-pulled, half-carried her into the waiting Vatican car.

The Vatican
Rome, Italy
An hour later

CHAPTER 52

I woke up in the softest bed I have ever experienced.

Well-schooled in the art of luxurious linens, I could tell this was undoubtedly more than top of the line. The sheet that covered me must have had a thousand-plus thread count, and the down-filled pillow, a welcome haven for my very achy head, felt like a cloud.

As my eyes adjusted to the dim light, I could not be sure what time of day or night it was because the floor-to-ceiling windows were covered with heavy red cut velvet. The furniture was ornate, oversize and gilded. It appeared to be Renaissance and not reproduction. The ceiling was coffered, with a circular space in the center devoted to what looked in the dim light to be a Baroque fresco depicting swirling angels and clouds.

A gilded Italian Renaissance armchair, upholstered in the same cut velvet as the curtains, held a small figure clad also in red. I must have stirred, because he suddenly came to life and rose from his seat.

"How are you feeling, my dear? You know, sitting there watching you, I was smiling about the fact that this is the first time there has been a woman in that bed, in this century at least." He spoke English with a precise but thick Italian accent.

"Where am I? And why have you brought me here?"

"I will answer your questions in time. You are in the bedroom of my private apartment in the Vatican. I am Cardinal Alphonso Brazzi. My nephew, Emilio, brought you here at my request, but certainly not in the manner that I expected. I am so sorry if he harmed you in any way. However, I needed to speak to you on a matter of the greatest urgency. And," he continued after a light pause, "of the greatest secrecy."

He looked down at me with what seemed to be concern. "Tell me, are you well enough to talk, or would you like some coffee, or perhaps something stronger first?"

Brazzi? Did the man just say his name was Brazzi, and his nephew was called Emilio? That snapped me to attention.

If Barry's Mafioso was related to a high-ranking Vatican official, this could be the connection to the mask I was looking for. My heart was beating so loudly I was afraid the cardinal could hear it.

I tried to remain calm and not reveal what I was thinking.

"Water, please. I'm dizzy from whatever put me out, and my throat is dry."

The cardinal shook his head and clucked like a concerned grandfather. He repeated his former apology. "I am so sorry for any discomfort you may have endured in your journey here."

"If you wanted to talk to me, why didn't you just telephone and invite me instead of hitting me on the head, probably chloroforming me to boot, and dragging me here?"

"We were afraid if you had advance notice of this meeting, you might inform someone else—your colleague, Dr. Hopkins, for example—and then the confidentiality of what we will speak of would be compromised.

"My nephew planned to ask you to accompany him when he followed you to the Colosseum, but he sensed you would be wary of him and refuse to go. Tell me, if he had asked you politely to go with him and meet his uncle, would you have agreed?"

So Brazzi must have also been the man watching me in the café.

"Probably not," I grudgingly admitted, "but what can be so important that you, obviously a pillar of the Church, would risk being found with a woman in your bed?"

As it had a few minutes earlier, that prospect provoked merriment in the venerable cleric.

"The image delights me." His words were accompanied by what could only be described as a titter more suited to a ladies' tea table than a Vatican apartment.

I noticed that when the cardinal laughed, the parchment-like skin around his eyes creased considerably. He looked very benevolent, considering he was a kidnapper, or at least the relative of a kidnapper.

He crossed the room and poured water from a silver pitcher into a Baccarat tumbler. He handed it to me.

"Can you sit up, my dear? Here, let me get you another pillow."

He walked with a surprisingly agile step toward an oversize armoire in the opposite corner of the room.

When he opened it, the smell of incense wafted toward me. He removed a king-size pillow, obviously made of down, like the ones already on the bed, and brought it to me, tucking it behind the one that already cradled my head. He clucked again, then pulled a smaller gilded chair close to the bed and sat down.

"There we are. Drink your water, and then we will chat."

I drank the entire glassful in greedy gulps. When I handed him the glass, he asked politely, "Another?"

"No, thank you."

"Very well then," he sighed, placed the glass on a small mahogany table beside the bed, and then, like a man with the weight of the world on his shoulders, cleared his throat and began.

"It has come to my attention that you are here in Rome seeking information about a certain mask, an ancient mask."

A shiver went down my back, but I remained quiet while he continued, "That mask is of great interest to us here in the Vatican. That interest has arisen entirely as a matter of coincidence, but nonetheless it is at this moment a fact, and one I must deal with, although it is not a happy task. I am about to tell you something, but that information must not leave this room."

"Then why tell me at all?"

"Because, my dear, other people besides you are looking for this object, and should it turn up here in Rome, it would not be a good thing for the image of the Church. And you seem to hold the key to its current whereabouts."

Why did everyone assume I had the inside track on the mask? Until two weeks ago I had not even known such an object existed. There was no way I could have any information that would interest anyone, let alone merit stalking me for it, as the Brazzi family, both clerical and criminal, certainly was. I told him as much.

He replied with a slow shake of the head, combined with a quintessentially Italian upturning of the hands.

"Who knows where the information came from? Think,

my dear. I understand you worked very closely with Professor Zanski when you were a student. Did he confide anything to you?"

"Absolutely not. We never discussed anything much except my dissertation, which he was the main advisor for, and the study collection he was building for all the students who were part of the antiquities program. The first I heard of his dealing in the underground market was when it came out in the newspapers. Plus, if he had mentioned this mask to me, it is not something I would likely have forgotten."

"Understandable, of course, and I believe you, but please try and think of anything he might have said that would give information about the mask—something you may not have previously recognized as important?"

"I have thought of practically nothing but that mask since I heard about it two weeks ago, and believe me, nothing has come to my mind. I was such a naïve student at the time that I hung on Zanski's every word, so I can tell you with absolute certainty, there was nothing. And if this 'problem' you now have is about your nephew and his legal and moral problem, I can't help you. He is already a well-known felon. I don't believe one more smuggled object could tarnish his reputation further."

He shook his head, "Although the life path that my brother's son follows hurts my heart, that is not the reason for this vexing situation.

"I will begin from the start: after World War II my brother's family was suffering from the poverty caused by that disaster. The family split apart: my niece Guilia emigrated to America, and her brother, my nephew Emilio, remained in the old country trying to scratch out a living. He fell in with the wrong people, who paid him to dig up artifacts on our family's land. Gradually he rose in the organization and eventually became the apprentice of a well-known dealer, whom I think you know or at least know of: a man named Schott. As luck would have it, he was eventually involved in attempting to sell a mask that had been smuggled from Egypt. At that time he was the equivalent of a, how do you say it?, low-level messenger boy, for those who control the antiquities trade here in Italy."

The word *Egypt* struck me like a welcome slap, knocking away the last cobwebs of Emilio Brazzi's chloroform cocktail.

So Egypt was where Alexander was buried after all. Of course it was possible that the mask was found somewhere else, and only funneled through Egypt to Switzerland. But somehow that route seemed too roundabout to be practical.

My first thought was to press the cardinal at once for more information, but I decided to let this new information sink in a bit first. Instead I pried a bit more about his nephew.

"You mean the Mafia?"

"If you wish to call them that. But please allow me to continue."

"Excuse me, sir, but I have to ask a question: how was it that Emilio was included in that meeting with Zanski back in the 1980s? Wasn't that a bit above his pay level?"

The old man smiled again, and again his skin crinkled. "I was getting to that, my dear. The organization, Mafia if you insist on calling them, are in charge of any antiquities coming and going from Italy. Schott was ostensibly the owner of the mask, but he always had to be careful to stay on the right side of those people. That meant every part of the dealings had to be watched, if you will, by one of their own. My nephew was chosen, I believe, because he was a new and unknown member of the organization, and as such, it was thought he would attract less attention from the authorities who keep an eye on every move of the known illegal dealers here in Italy. As you know, my country wishes to guard its treasures very carefully, and the government is always on the lookout for important pieces leaving the country. In addition, my nephew had already worked for Schott on some lesser negotiations."

"I understand all that, but who actually brought the mask into Switzerland in the first place? And how do you know it came from Egypt?"

"I am not at liberty to tell you the details surrounding the journey of the mask, so please have the good manners not to press me, but I will tell you as much as I can. In the first place, the mask never came into Italy at all. That is really what is important for us here at the Vatican. It went directly from Egypt to Switzerland, and from there taken by Zanski to who knows where? The unfortunate association with my country in this matter arises simply because it is the Italian underground network that controls most of the illegal trade all over Europe, and thus, people assume these objects all originate on Italian soil. Some do, of course, but by no means all. And definitely not that mask.

"And currently, as you probably know, all sorts of Middle Easterners have involved themselves in the business, smuggling through the same underground conduits that service the drug traffickers. But thirty years ago it was the Italians who had the monopoly on the artifact trade."

"Then the Mafia never had direct ownership of the mask?" I asked.

"Definitely not."

"How can you be so sure?"

"Emilio was told so by someone higher up in his organization on the day he was assigned to accompany Schott to the meeting at the Credit Suisse. They sent him as a, how do you Americans say it?, watchdog, to make sure Schott didn't try to undercut the, as you call them, Mafia."

"So even though the Mafia had no actual contact with the mask, they were still entitled to their cut?"

The cardinal shrugged. "That's the way things work." He cleared his throat before continuing, "That mask, the one my nephew showed to the Warner people, is, of course, the one you are seeking. The Mask of Alexander the Great, is what we at the Vatican are seeking as well."

He hesitated, taking a breath and waiting for my reaction, then elaborated, "Normally the affairs of the underground do not concern us here at the Vatican, but at first because my nephew was involved, I became interested. I did not approve, mind you, since things of this world are not my normal concern, but I took it upon myself to learn what he was doing because I wished to steer him from this unclean path. Our family is a poor one, as I have told you, but a respectable one, and although I live in decided comfort here, many of my relatives have very little. Selling that mask would have enabled Emilio to buy land for his family and permitted him to leave the life of crime and return to respectability and godliness. I knew this and prayed and watched over him."

"You said 'at first' your interest in the mask was because of Emilio. What else?"

"An unfortunate occurrence came about recently that makes

the mask of vital importance to the Catholic Church. Please do not misunderstand. We do not want to possess it. Just the opposite. You may have read about an English fellow who claims that the mummy buried in the tomb of San Marco in Venice is actually that of Alexander the Great. Most probably he is what you Americans call a crackpot, but one can never be too careful."

This was what Barry had been talking about. When he originally told me about the switched mummies, I was skeptical, but now, hearing the same thing from the cardinal, the theory took on a new gravitas.

Cardinal Brazzi was explaining. "This bizarre body switch was supposed to have happened sometime during the Middle Ages, exactly when is uncertain. But, to conclude, if that mask we are seeking, which was quite obviously part of Alexander's funerary trappings, turns up here in Italy, it will fuel that rumor and give cause to exhume Saint Mark. And that we do not want."

"I'm not sure why you would be so adamant against opening Saint Mark's tomb, anyway. If you are so sure it is the saint who is in there, what would be the harm in proving it to the world?"

"You may laugh, my dear, at the superstition of an old man, but I have learned in my long life to take no chances." His eyes took on a dreamy look. "Our dilemma stems from the very nature of Alexander himself. Powerful in life, and apparently as much so after death. He was known to have been worshipped as a god with a fanatical following. What if, by some chance, his protectors actually managed to effect the switch. And he is, as that Englishman believes, safely resting in Venice?"

I thought a minute. By now the effects of whatever drug Emilio had used on me had completely worn off and my mind was totally clear and listening to the Cardinal with full attention. "OK, but what makes you think the mask might be here in Rome?" I asked.

"It is only speculation, but the fact that you are here searching for it . . ."

"How did you know I was looking for the mask?"

"Ah, Miss Guthrie," he shook his head as one would at a dim-witted child. "You must have guessed that kind of information travels rapidly here in Italy."

I changed the subject. "I know that Henry Templeton was also your nephew. How did he figure in the search for the mask?"

"Henry had no part in the affair initially, but later he joined Emilio's search for it. They looked for it for years, both together and separately. Henry was sure the Warner would still be interested and able to pay the asking price."

"Which was . . . ?" I held my breath, waiting for the answer.

"Somewhere in the area of one hundred million dollars."

If I had been looking in a mirror, I would have seen my eyes widen. In a matter of a few minutes, I had learned that the mask which presumably had been dug up in Egypt, also had a current dollar value that was higher than any archaeological find to thus far hit the art market.

The cardinal was still explaining. "Back in 1985, when the Warner was involved in purchasing the mask, Emilio contacted his cousin Henry, who was still a student. With you, I have heard." He paused momentarily and looked at me for verification. I nodded.

"Even as a student, Henry had knowledge of what was occurring in the museum. He watched Zanski's every move during that man's last days at the museum. Then, when he himself took over the position as curator of antiquities at the Warner, he continued to look for the mask."

"Was the Warner behind him in this search?"

"No. Although an employee of the museum, Henry was still primarily loyal to his family. His plan in searching for the mask was, how do you Americans say it? A side hustle, to help his cousin."

"I, and I think a lot of other people as well, always wondered how he got the job, as curator I mean. Not to imply he wasn't qualified." I was quick to soften the implied insult, not that I needed to protect the feelings of a man who had essentially had me kidnapped, no matter that he was a pillar of the Church.

"I am not sure about that. Neither Emilio nor Henry discussed it with me. But I would suspect the museum thought Henry's relationship with Emilio might be an advantage in their acquisitions. And convenient also, in the event that something could go wrong, as it did. They had a perfect scapegoat upon which to heap the blame."

"I always thought Henry was too smart to jump into that kind of trap."

"Sadly, my American nephew was much like his cousin Emilio. He was ambitious, and I am not proud to say, often unscrupulous, continuing the path of his predecessor Zanski, procuring illegally excavated objects for the Warner. Of course, this benefitted his cousin here in Italy, and through that connection with Henry and the Warner, Emilio rose in the hierarchy of the underworld. I would not have chosen such a path for either of my nephews."

Cardinal Brazzi stopped a moment and shook his head.

"Emilio I can understand because he had a family to care for, but Henry was another case altogether. His mother had married well, and he himself was both unmarried and had secure and respectable employment. May God rest his soul." He crossed himself.

"I am sorry for your loss," I murmured. "This is a fascinating story, but you still haven't told me why you brought me here."

"As I told you initially, I need your help. Should you find the mask here in Italy, I need you to bring it to me so we can transport it out of the country to, say, Greece, and swear you found it there."

"Why would I do that?" I felt bullied.

"Well," the cardinal raised his eyebrows, which were thick and grey and badly in need of trimming. "Why would you not? Whether the mask is brought to light in Rome or Greece would be of little consequence to you. We here at the Vatican would make all the arrangements for the transport of the mask out of Italy where you could 'find' it and reap all the rewards."

"What if I am not after rewards?"

"Then what is it, my dear, that you are after?"

A man of God should certainly understand my determination to return the mask to the body of Alexander. I confessed as much.

When I was finished, the cardinal looked as if he were about to laugh. It was not at all the reaction I had expected. "You cannot be serious. Yours is a very noble thought, to be sure. But you have no idea where that body might be, unless of course you believe it to be in the tomb of Saint Mark."

"I know I don't have much chance of getting the mask back where it should be, but that doesn't make me want to surrender it to a museum—or to you. And, yes, the tomb of St. Mark could be a possible resting place for Alexander's mummy." I stopped and thought for a minute. "But frankly at this point I don't think there is much chance of me turning up either the mask or the mummy, so you really haven't much to worry about. And," I was overcome with the futility of my whole quest, "for all we know, the mask could have been separated from Alexander's body long ago."

"A distinct possibility, but I am afraid that once again points to the body switch with St. Mark. It would never do to have a body that is believed to be a Christian saint buried with funerary trappings of a pagan, thus the mask and probably the other Egyptian regalia as well, were left in Egypt."

"Possible," I agreed, not sure what to make of this theory.

"And what about my request for your help?"

This was a man who held great power. Having him on my side was a definite plus.

"I understand your position, Your Eminence, and I will try to honor what you have asked should I, by some remote chance, find the mask. I really have no idea where this search is taking me, but I believe you and I have the same goal: to do the right thing."

Cardinal Brazzi reached over and took my hand.

"To us, the Church, that mask is a pagan symbol whose ultimate disposition is of little interest. The Church is the rock upon which so many of the faithful are supported. To disinter St. Mark would shake that foundation and do an unspeakable injustice to a great number of people. So yes, the right thing, from my perspective, is to prevent that from happening."

"I see your point, Your Eminence, and I will honor your position." I changed the subject. "One question, please, Your Eminence. Barry Epstein has received what he thinks are veiled threats. Are your people behind those?"

He gave me a puzzled look. "I have heard of nothing in that area. Sorry, but I cannot help you."

I hadn't exactly expected a confession, but there was no harm in asking.

I had no idea what time it was, but it had to be getting late. Gren would be back from Orvieto by now and looking for me.

I got up from the soft bed and looked around for my handbag and cell phone. The cardinal noticed and shook his head.

"Not quite yet, my dear, there is something else I must tell you."

I waited while he composed his thoughts.

"You must be very careful. You may laugh at this, but I had a dream—a dream that you were in grave danger. Do not trust anyone, not even those closest to you."

The cardinal's words frightened me. I sat there, on this luxurious bed, in one of the most opulent buildings of the world, utterly lost and terror-struck. People were stalking me, there was no one I could trust, and probably worse things were to come. How had I gotten here?

The cardinal seemed to sense my thoughts. This last hour with him had done much to overcome my initial mistrust of the man. But how did I know if I could believe him? After all, he had had me kidnapped and then admitted to a plan to misdirect an important antiquity, and the Church did not have a terribly stellar reputation.

He spoke again, even more quietly, "You will prevail. I saw it in the dream. But yet, you must be vigilant."

Hotel Hassler
Rome, Italy
An hour later

CHAPTER 53

GREN WAS WAITING IN THE HOTEL LOBBY when I got out of the cab at the Hassler.

"Where have you been? It's not like you to forget to call."

"Actually, I was at the Vatican."

Gren looked at me, puzzled at first, and then concerned. "You look awful. Did those priests attack you or something?"

"Yes, something." I tried to sound as vague as possible. I had not decided how much of this whole business to share with him.

"Your hair's an absolute mess. Come here and let Daddy pat your fur into place."

He gathered me in his arms and began to smooth my hair gently.

"Whoa! What's this?" His hand stopped for a moment. "A goose egg. Where did that come from? Sit down. You obviously have a lot to tell me."

"Do you think I'll die from my hematoma?" I asked, stalling for time.

"Don't think so; it's in the wrong place. We can get it checked out if you're worried, but only *after* you tell me where you got it."

"Could we sit down? This may take a while."

"Of course!" He led me by the hand to a pair of tapestry-covered armchairs discreetly placed out of the flow of lobby traffic. He pulled the chairs closer together so that our knees were touching, then he looked at me expectantly.

"I have kept a lot from you, Gren. For several reasons, not the least of which is your own safety."

His eyes widened. "Dramatic, but go on, please."

I told him just about everything: the mask, the threats to Barry, Zanski's puzzling reference to me, my growing belief that Henry's death was no suicide. I finished up with my adventure at the Vatican. It was against my better judgement to trust him, but somehow I did—at least more than I trusted the cardinal's warnings.

"So you really *did* spend the day there. I should have believed you when I smelled the frankincense perfume in your hair. Fascinating. Fascinating, but scary. These are very dangerous people you are mixed up with, and that includes your former husband. What do you plan to do next, and how can I help?"

I was glad I had told someone at last. Here in the safety of the Hassler lobby with Gren holding my hand, the memory of Brazzi's stalking and conking me out in the Colosseum became a bit less vivid.

"I'm not sure exactly who my enemies are at this point. I do know that Barry originally thought I might know where the mask is. But he was up front about it, and I doubt he would have ever hurt me anyway. But then there's whoever is stalking him, and therefore knows about me—and that's who I am afraid of."

I winced, feeling another stab of pain go through my head. "Barry's always been such a big mouth that even without trying, he could have put me in danger."

"Oh, Parthi, my poor baby. I would do anything, anything to

get you out of this."

"You just being here is a huge help."

Gren was silent a moment, gently caressing my matted hair. It made me feel safe, like I was some stray kitten who had been rescued from a storm. He eventually broke the companionable silence.

"Do you know anything at all, Parthi? Try to remember anything Zanski might have told you that could be a clue to where he hid the mask."

"You're assuming he hid it somewhere and didn't take it to Russia with him."

"Pretty good chance it's somewhere west of Russia. It doesn't seem that the Mafia got it back, because it hasn't surfaced during all this time, and those boys like to move stuff fast."

He stopped his train of thought for a moment and looked at me closely. "You still don't look so well, my dear. I'm going to take you to your room and order some comfort food."

If, at last, he had chosen this particular night to seduce me, it was bad timing. My head ached and I smelled of Colosseum urine and Vatican incense. However, I wasn't up to protesting anything, so I meekly allowed him to propel me into the elevator.

I closed my eyes as the comforting whir of the well-oiled machine lulled me into relaxation. I was suddenly very tired.

The elevator stopped with a refined jerk, and the doors slid open.

Gren took my elbow and led me in the direction of my room, "Do you have your key?"

"No, I left it at the desk when I went out."

"Wait here. I'll get it for you. I'll only be a minute."

I nodded, at that point not really caring whether or not I ever got into my room. The carpeted floor in the hallway looked quite inviting. I sank down, stretched my legs out in front of me, and rested my back against the cool stuccoed wall.

Gren eyed me dubiously, "Are you sure you're all right like that? You don't look very comfortable."

"I'm fine, really. I'll just close my eyes until you get back."

I had no idea whether I was asleep or not, but the next thing I was conscious of was someone staring at me. Or was I dreaming? The figure—at least it seemed to be a figure—was peering around the corner of the hallway. The image was there for only a second, or so it seemed, and since I was three-quarters asleep, I couldn't be sure.

I jerked my head up, and at that same moment heard the rush of footsteps from that same area of the hallway. I jumped up and ran toward the retreating footsteps fast enough to glimpse the figure of a tall man fiddling with the doorknob of room 710. Strangely, he had no key in his hand, and I knew for a fact that that room was occupied by an elderly German woman. He turned toward me for a second, and in shocked disbelief, I recognized Christos, the Warner Museum guard. What was *he* doing in Rome? I was about to say something when he turned abruptly and ran in the opposite direction.

It took me a moment to sort through the fuzz in my brain and try to make sense of what I had just seen. What was a guard from the Warner Museum doing in a posh Roman hotel, why was he watching me, and why, especially, did he run when I saw him?

Gren returned a minute later, key in hand. "Your room is back there. How did you get down here?"

"I saw someone. Christos from the museum. He was staring at me. Then he ran."

Gren winced, then he put his arm around me and led me back up the hall toward my room.

"I think we need to talk," was all he said as he fitted the old-fashioned key into the ornate lock.

Once inside, he led me to the bed, lifted my legs up, and slipped off my shoes.

"Just lie here a minute and catch your breath. There is something I have been meaning to tell you, but it was never the right time, and even though now is probably the worst time I could have picked, if I don't explain it all to you, you'll worry even more."

"What are you talking about?"

"Please don't tell me you haven't noticed that, as enticing as you are, I have kept physically very much away from you."

That embarrassed me. Of course I had wondered, but wondering to myself and discussing the subject with Gren were two different things.

"Well, you are very much a gentleman."

"And a gay one."

Would the surprises of this day never end? I was not sure how to react. To be honest, I had been more attracted to him of late, but perhaps I was just tired, or maybe Gren's revelation was not a complete surprise to me, because I felt oddly unemotional about this confession.

"But you've been married, and more than once," was the only comment I could muster up.

"Ah, yes. I am very much in the closet. Still."

"In this day and age? And in the art world? Gay is pretty

much a norm."

He shook his head. "Yes, but not in my family. My mother is still alive and controls the purse strings. She made it clear that if I 'deviated' in any way from what she considers acceptable Hopkins behavior, I am cut out of her will entirely. And honestly, I'd have a hard time surviving on a curator's salary."

"A lot of people do," I pointed out pragmatically.

"But not in the Hopkins way."

"So you maintain the family tradition of being beyond money?"

"Exactly; it's the Hopkins way."

"What about the wives? How did they feel about your sexual preference?"

"I never deceived any of them. My marriages were, well, alliances of convenience on both parts. Honestly, I tried my best to be straight. Succeeded pretty well. But there was always Christos . . ."

"Christos? What's he got to do with this?"

"He's the man I'm involved with. Have been for over thirty years. We met in Egypt when I was there on one of the pater's excavations about the same time you and I were working on our degrees. It was my father's last excavation, the one where he died. Christos was a waiter at a café we used to go to when I could drag Dad away from the site."

"But how did he get to Los Angeles, to the Warner?"

"Somehow, he managed to get to the States on his own and called me when he got there. I was pretty flattered a man would go to all that trouble and take those risks just to be with me. I managed to get him a visa, and recently the museum gig when I took over Henry's job. That meant we could be near each other, even in the daytime, without raising suspicion about our relationship."

"From his name I would have thought Christos was Greek. What was he doing in Egypt?"

"He was born there. Ever since Alexander there have been a large number of Greeks living in Egypt. All over the Middle East, actually. They remain quite apart from the Muslim majority."

"But why was he staring at me?"

"Concern, probably. You must have looked pretty pathetic crumpled up in front of your door, and he's a very kind man."

"Then why did he run?"

"Who knows? Afraid of being discovered, I imagine. He knows that until Mumsy dies, we have to keep our relationship entirely secret, and since he doesn't know you, he couldn't be sure you wouldn't blow the whistle."

"And you brought him here with us?"

He looked a bit sheepish. "Yes. Coming here with you was a perfect cover for us. Everyone would think you and I were a couple, and while you were here safely in your own room, he and I could spend time together."

"I feel sorry for you, Gren. It must be awful loving someone and having to hide it from the world."

"It won't be forever, I hope. Yet I do sometimes wonder what will happen once Mumsy is gone, and we can come out into the light. The class difference may do us in."

I thought a minute. Gren was a lot of things, and one of those was a pure snob. I couldn't imagine him in an open relationship with a menial worker, male or female. However, I refrained from comment.

He answered my silence with a change of subject, "I've ordered some soup to be sent up. It should be here in a minute or two. I think I should go and join Christos, if you don't mind. He must be worrying about the fact that you recognized him."

"I understand. I think I will just have the soup and get some sleep. I really am tired."

"That's probably a good idea. Anyway, I do look forward to you two getting to know each other when you're up to it. He's a fascinating man. Has a lot more education than one might think. Pretty much self-taught. He seems to absorb everything like a sponge. He's given me lots of good insights into what is going on in the museum."

The romantic in me could not do anything but wish them the best.

Gren kissed me lightly on the forehead and walked toward the door.

As it closed behind him, the thought struck me that he had put my door key in his pocket after letting us in. I probably wouldn't need it until morning, but in the light of the unexpected things that had happened today, it seemed like a good thing to have with me.

As quickly as my achy head would allow, I slipped off the bed, walked barefoot across the suite, and opened the door.

The hallway was empty except for two silhouetted figures that I could not identify because of the tricky angle of the setting sun. The lower parts of both men's bodies were pressed together, their hands groping buttocks. Their faces were in profile, but even in the fading light I could make out tongues darting, entwining. I stepped back into the room and eased the door shut.

Hotel Hassler
Rome, Italy
The next morning

CHAPTER 54

The next morning, I decided to have breakfast in the hotel dining room.

When I checked at the desk, I found that Gren had left me a message that he would be gone all day. Ostensibly another museum conference, but I also wondered if time with Christos didn't figure in there somewhere.

I sat alone at one of the small tables for two at the edge of the Palm Court, the most informal of the Hassler's eateries, but posh, nonetheless.

Being among well-dressed people laughing and chatting as they sipped espressos and nibbled on croissants helped erase the stress of the previous day.

That was, until I noticed a man coming toward me. His shirt was open, revealing an oversized gold medal advertising that he was protected by this saint or that. I could not identify the exact deity but offhand I suspected the Virgin Mary.

There was no mistaking him. It was Emilio Brazzi. A small scream must have accompanied the recognition, because I noticed a few heads bob up from behind newspapers and stare my way.

"What do you want?" I hissed in something of a stage whisper.

He first bowed, then looked at me with the benign face only an off-duty Mafioso can muster. “Please don’t be frightened. I am so sorry about yesterday. But you gave me no choice. My uncle demanded to speak with you, and I was afraid you would run away.”

“Why didn’t he just call me, or send a note, or anything more civilized than kidnapping?”

“I think he told you that in his position that would have been impossible.” He spoke with exaggerated formality that I suspected was not the vocabulary he normally used.

“All right. I accept your apology. Now, please let me have my breakfast in peace. I still have a headache from our little scuffle in the Colosseum yesterday, and seeing you is aggravating it. Either leave this minute or I will call security.”

He looked horrified. “Please, please do not do that. I only want to speak to you for five minutes, then I will never bother you again, I promise.”

In a well-filled and brightly lit dining room, I was quite brave. “OK. Five minutes.” I made a point of noting the time on my iPhone.

“May I sit down?”

“If you must,” I conceded ungraciously.

A waiter hovering on the periphery, who was probably thinking this was just another lovers’ quarrel between a tourist and a local, hastily approached and pulled out the chair opposite mine.

“Will the gentleman be joining you for breakfast?” He looked at me.

“He won’t be staying,” I answered with a scowl.

Brazzi shrugged, obviously expecting my reaction. When

the waiter had left, he began, "My uncle is, of course, concerned about the mask and its implication for the Vatican. My own reason for coming here this morning has nothing to do with that. I must talk to you about Henry."

He looked genuinely miserable. Like a sad little boy. A far cry from the cold-blooded enforcer who had dragged me out of the Colosseum yesterday.

"I know that you and Henry were cousins."

"But you don't know the whole story. At least I don't think you do."

His English was a bit rough, but very fluent. "You see, we were very much like brothers. His father's family was not so proud of their son marrying my aunt, a Sicilian, and one from the lower classes as well. Your country was not welcoming to Italians at that time, you know."

"I knew something about that. But remember, there was prejudice against the Irish and the Jews as well."

"I don't know about those other people, so I speak only for us Sicilians. And it was not only you Americans who treated us like dirt. It was our own people as well. Because we were poor. Money is the power that separates people."

Cynical as it was, I knew Brazzi had a point.

He went on, "In our grandparents' day, all over the south of Italy, the rich landlords had the right to *prima nocta* with any betrothed woman."

"What was that?" I asked.

Brazzi stammered a bit as he answered. For a tough guy he seemed uncharacteristically puritanical in discussing sex.

"A landowner had the right to take the virginity of any of his workers' brides. That had happened to my grandmother, and my sister was so afraid of the same thing that she stowed away on a boat to America. And I think you know the rest of the story. She was lucky. Married her American boss and left the whole dirty life in Sicily behind her. But she did not forget us. She made it possible for me to spend summers in Cape Cod with her family, no matter what her husband's family thought."

It was hard to believe that a rough customer like Brazzi had been exposed to Bostonian polish. Obviously, none of it had rubbed off on him.

Brazzi had stopped looking at me. He stared off in the distance as though I were not there at all.

He continued speaking, more to himself than to me. "None of our family ever forgot what it was like to be poor. My uncle went to the Church, as you know. I wanted to be successful too, but . . ." His voice trailed off.

"What happened?" I prodded. His story intrigued me, in spite of myself.

My voice brought his attention back. "I guess I was just a fuck-up."

He glanced quickly at me to see my reaction to his vulgarity. When I did not react, he continued, "I knocked around in Sicily as a kid, quitting school and hitting the streets. I loved soccer but was too poor even to buy a ball, so I and a couple of guys used to kick around some old heads we dug up on the farm."

"What kind of heads? Dead people?" My thoughts ran to the byproducts of Mafia hits.

Brazzi laughed. "No, Signora. Marble heads from the time of the Romans. One of the capos in the village saw what we had and offered us good money to bring him more, and, as they say in the movies, the rest was history."

"And that's how you got your start in this business?" I asked, amazed.

"Yes, Signora, and I don't regret any of it. I'm a family man, you might know, and it feels good to give my kids things I only saw in movies or in Henry's house."

"Back to Henry. What was his real story? I knew him when we were at the Warner together, but I never felt I really knew him at all. He pretty much kept to himself."

Brazzi nodded. "Yes, Henry was that way. But not cold like you think. He was just serious. He never could think of anything but his work. He wasn't gay or anything, just focused on being a top man in the museum world." He laughed, but not in a humorous way. "It was his way to be an overachiever like all of us in the family."

"So I guess it just came naturally that you and he went into business together? Your uncle told me something about that."

"Not at first. In the beginning he wanted to stay squeaky clean. But then I got married and needed more money, and he knew it would help me out if he threw some Warner business my way."

"Nobody could ever figure out why he would take that kind of risk after seeing what had happened with Zanski."

"Ah, you have to understand the Italian way. It's all about *la famiglia*, first, last, and always."

I nodded. "It all makes more sense to me now."

I had been waiting to get back to the subject of antiquities. I was sitting with a man who could shed some light on how the mask might have gotten into Schott's hands, and I was not about to miss this opportunity.

"Your uncle seemed to think I was somehow involved in this business with the mask. I confess I did know two of the key people who were with you in Geneva that day when you and Schott showed it to the Warner buyers. So what can you tell me about where it came from?"

Brazzi raised his eyebrows, then shrugged his shoulders and turned his palms upward in that characteristically Italian gesture I had come to recognize. "Just that some guy brought it from Egypt."

"Was he an Egyptian? Your uncle mentioned the mask came from there. Did Schott say anything to you about who the seller was?"

"People like us don't talk much about things like that, but OK, it can't hurt to tell you what I know. I am pretty sure that guy he got it from wasn't anybody in my organization. If he was, I would have heard about it on the street. So whoever he got it from must have been somebody on the outside, but who?" Again the shoulder shrug, "your guess is as good as mine."

"So you have absolutely no idea who that was?" This was important information, and I wanted to make sure.

"None. But the big boys knew Schott had gotten his hands on a hot find and they wanted a piece of it."

"Naturally."

"But now that I'm thinking of it, there was one thing really odd about the deal. Schott told me he'd given the seller a down payment, and the guy was supposed to come back as soon as the sale was made to the Warner and get the rest of his money. Well, he never showed up."

"But the deal never did go through, so that could explain it," I reasoned.

"Yeah, maybe. But it was still weird that the guy never showed his face again. If it was me, I woulda been there day and night trying to squeeze my money out of Schott. Either that or get my mask back."

I thought about that for a minute. "You don't suppose one of your boys got annoyed that an interloper was cutting into their territory and, as you would say, rubbed him out?"

"Always a possibility," Brazzi nodded. "Anyway, we'll never know now, and what does it matter? What we need to do is find the mask. I have promised my uncle, and," he added a bit sheepishly, "I would not exactly turn down a commission from the Warner or any other museum."

He hesitated a minute, looking at me. "What's your stake in this, anyway?"

That was direct. "I don't know that I have a stake, really. But I'm not interested in the money, if that's what you're asking."

"How could you not be? I mean, a thing like that will go for the big bucks, enough for everybody."

"I'm just odd, I guess. Or superstitious. Maybe that mask is something we should not even have."

He looked at me like I was either lying or out of my mind. "Maybe I hit you too hard yesterday. You know you're sticking your neck out, don't you, with so many people knowing you're looking for that mask? And you tell me you don't care about the money?" He scratched his head with longish manicured fingernails.

I just smiled. How could he possibly understand my obsession to get that mask back to the body it was designed for?

I changed the subject. "You were telling me how you got started in the antiquities business. But how does all that actually work? I mean from ground to gallery?"

Brazzi waggled his right index finger in my direction. "Supposed to be hush hush, but hell, everybody knows anyway, so I guess I ain't spillin' no beans. It goes down like this: the guys in the field, literally that is, dig up the stuff. Open tombs and so forth. This happens mostly in the countryside around the villages. Then there is a capo, a boss, in the closest town and they bring the goods to him. From there it goes to a bigger fish who has contacts outside of Italy—Switzerland, usually. And you know the rest: the guys in Switzerland clean it up, give it a phony ancestry, then into the gallery it goes, and," at this point Brazzi snapped his fingers dramatically, "poof, you're lookin' at it tomorrow in some hotshot museum or mega-rich guy's house."

"Sounds like a pretty well-oiled underground railroad."

Brazzi's shoulders seemed to puff up a bit. "You bet."

"I've heard about that trade for years, but I never wanted to think about it," I said. "Doesn't it ever bother you that you're stealing from the dead?"

Again, the upturned hands. "Naw, why should it? Them people are dead and don't need their stuff anymore."

I looked at him closely and detected the merest crack in the bravado. I probed further.

"The digging gets done at night, doesn't it? Does it ever get, well, spooky, to be opening someone's grave and robbing it?"

"OK, OK. I get your point, but you gotta remember our organization drops more than a few euros in the church collection box. Do that, say a few prayers, and Christ wipes away all sins."

He crossed himself for emphasis. "They were fucking pagans, anyway, the guys we're digging up. So what's the difference?" He tightened his arm muscles in a way that brought a ripple to the tight pecs beneath the thin silk shirt. "And remember, my uncle is one of the head honchos in the Vatican, so you can just bet the man upstairs listens to him."

No use arguing with that logic.

"Now, Signora, I have answered your questions, and it is my turn to ask you something." Brazzi had returned to his formal use of the English language.

"OK. Go ahead. Ask."

"My children are grown and I have made enough money to keep my wife and me in comfort for the rest of our days. I am ready to get out of this business and go straight, as you Americans say. Maybe grow a few grapes and make a little wine. Henry also was ready to retire. That brush with the law frightened him pretty bad, and then don't forget the saintly Boston Templetons. They were mad as hell when he got arrested and it was splashed all over the papers.

"For sure, Henry wanted to get away from all that. He had me looking for places over here that he could buy and live closer to the family. It was all arranged. On top of that, my uncle put the heat on the government boys, and they were making a deal with the Warner to drop all the charges.

"That is why I know he did *not* kill himself. And why I am here with you today. My heart bleeds, and I must know what happened. Because of my problems with the law . . ." He stopped talking for a moment to make sure I understood.

"I cannot go to America to try to find Henry's killer myself. If I could, I am sure I could discover what went down with my cousin. And make whoever did him in pay but good. But I cannot, so I am asking you. Do you know what happened?"

"Not exactly, but Barry Epstein, like you, is pretty sure Henry did not commit suicide. No offense meant; we had thought maybe it was the Mafia."

"No good Catholic commits suicide. It is a mortal sin. Please promise me you will let me know if you find out anything about who caused my cousin's death. It was most likely someone within the museum world, and since you know that world better than me, I am asking for your help."

"Why should I promise you anything?" It seemed more than cheeky for yesterday's kidnapper to be expecting favors from me today.

"Perhaps because it is the right thing to do."

THE REST OF THE WEEK WAS UNEVENTFUL. I shopped, ate, rested, and in general acted the part of the typical tourist.

I saw little of Gren and Christos. Now that their relationship was out in the open as far as I was concerned, there was no longer the need to create the illusion of romance between Gren and me.

I was a little sad, I suppose. I was getting older, and the chances of love becoming fewer. Maybe I would be alone forever. Probably I would die alone. That was something I did not want to think about.

To pick up my spirits, I decided to have my hair done. I hadn't been able to do a very good job of shampooing it myself because Brazzi's bump was still too painful for me to completely undo the clump of matted hair that surrounded it.

There is nothing like a European beauty treatment to lift one luxuriously from any and all doldrums. I had chosen a small but elegant salon just off the Via Veneto.

As the beauty operator, a slim woman with the look of a young Audrey Hepburn, massaged my scalp (at least that part Brazzi had not come into contact with), I felt myself floating away on a soft, spongey cloud. The mask, Gren, Barry, and all my other problems were on hold, temporarily, at least.

An hour later, hair shining, hands paraffined and massaged, and even a few out-of-place hairs plucked from my eyebrows, I emerged into the fall sunlight.

Los Angeles, California
The next week

CHAPTER 55

BACK IN LA, however, my relationship with Gren resumed much as it had been before we went to Rome.

Christos had reverted to his role as museum guard, and I again occupied center stage in Gren's public life.

It was fun being the girlfriend, albeit a pseudo one, of the acting antiquities curator of the Warner.

I enjoyed having someone I could share ideas with, and Gren's relationship with Christos did not seem to get in the way of our emerging friendship. There were also the perks of a renewed relationship with the museum. Rather than feeling the old pain of a career gone wrong as I had during those final days as a Zanski student, the new Warner seemed a place of energy and excitement. One of those latter perks came in the form of a text from Gren on Wednesday morning: "Can u come to museum ASAP? Explain when u get here."

Naturally, I went. Barry had stopped badgering me about my progress in finding his supposed tormenter, and no one had frightened either of us in the last five days. I was thinking it might be time to go back to Boulder.

"Can you believe this?" Gren asked as I entered his office twenty minutes later. "They have an education department here, and yet they saddle me with pulling antiquities for some school group visiting tomorrow."

"No assistant yet?" I asked.

"Nope. Drat the luck. With the number of people who would give their eyeteeth to work here, you'd think at least one would suit the profile the trustees are looking for."

"Don't you get to hire your own assistant?"

"Well, yes and no. I technically get to choose, but as usual, the board has the final say."

"Tough. What can I do?"

"I guess act as my assistant, at least for today. I'll make it up to you, dinner or something. I've got meetings all day and it would help if you could go to the storeroom and select a few objects—not too fragile, mind you, or too valuable—that the docents can let these kids handle. Just two or three will do, perhaps a lamp and a kylix—but why am I telling you? You know just what will work for them. Probably better than I do."

He stopped a minute and put his hand on his chin. "You'll need a badge so security will not question your being there. Christos will fix you up."

"Is the storeroom where it used to be?" I asked. "I thought I read somewhere the entire basement storage was being redone along with the rest of the museum."

"It is, but nobody seems to have done anything about it yet. I suppose they'll get around to it sometime."

Minutes later, with a plastic-coated identity tag bearing my name, photo, and the word *Antiquities* in large letters hanging from a cord around my neck, I entered the antiquities storeroom. It was the first time I had been there since my final days as a student in 1985, but nothing seemed to have changed.

The room was furnished with glass shelves beginning at waist height and continuing to the ceiling. Below were pull-out bins that I knew to contain pottery sherds and other ancient miscellanea. The bin with my long-neglected votives was most likely still there as well.

First, I would do what Gren had asked, and pick the objects for tomorrow's elementary school field trip. Then, and only then, if there was time, would I delve into my past.

It took very little time to select five relatively indestructible objects that would give the children a personal relationship with the ancient world: a round Roman lamp with a scene of battling gladiators on the discus; a small unguentarium, the kind of vessel designed to hold perfumed oil; a late-Roman red bowl; an Egyptian ushabti, a faience statuette whose function was to take the place of a living servant in a tomb; and lastly, a chunk of mosaic flooring from an unidentified Roman villa. That should do the trick.

I wasn't sure if I was ready to see if my votives were still as I had left them twenty-eight years ago. I had not heard of anyone else studying them and they weren't the sort of thing that would be put on display, so there was a good chance they were still there. Waiting for me.

If I didn't at least look at them, I would probably regret it in the years to come. I took a breath, squared my shoulders, and walked toward the familiar place in the bank of bins. My bin was unmarked but unlocked. I pulled it out.

The votives were as I had left them, with some of my study notes in yellowing sheets on top.

Hard to believe I had once thought this was to be my life. Out of habit, I began to separate the whole pieces from the fragmented ones. The bin seemed fuller than I remembered, although the top pieces, the ones bearing the likeness of the hunting goddess Artemis from her temple at Ephesus, were still as I remembered them. Curious.

Almost without thinking, I began to remove the statuettes from the drawer and arrange them on one of the long tables that occupied the center of the room. I had removed about three quarters of the contents of the bin when my hand touched something that felt like cardboard. I quickly removed the last figurines and found that a square of what was indeed cardboard had been used to create a false bottom to the bin. I wedged my fingernail between the edge of the cardboard and the wooden side of the bin. It came out easily.

Underneath was an object wrapped in what seemed to be more than one layer of protective cloth. My heart began to beat faster. Even before I carefully removed the wrapping, I knew what it was.

I had found the Mask of Alexander.

Now what should I do?

Basement storeroom, Warner Museum
Beverly Hills, California
Minutes earlier

CHAPTER 56

The dark-haired woman whom he now knew as Parthi was alone in the storeroom. The Mask Hunter had quietly followed her there after Grenville had asked him to give her a badge for entry into the visitor-prohibited areas of the museum.

He waited and watched her enter, noticing that she had left the door partially open, a stroke of good luck for him. He stood quietly at the entrance, watching, keeping just out of her range of vision should she turn in his direction. But he had nothing to fear in that department. She seemed to be totally absorbed in her task, carefully taking artifacts from storage compartments and transferring them to the work table in the center of the room.

Today her hair was pulled back into a ponytail and she was dressed in stretchy black pants and a long-sleeved T-shirt. Alexander's coin hung on its golden chain around her neck.

As he watched her, the Mask Hunter imagined all the things he would like to do to her. First, he would lock the door securely. He knew the positioning of each security camera, and there was little chance they would be discovered, but he was a careful man. She would be expecting him, smiling encouragement. He would lift her gently onto the table and pull the T-shirt over her head, kissing her nipples as he removed the garment from her body. They would grow firm as he worked magic with his tongue. She would moan softly, her body writhing in anticipation of what was to come.

He would leave the precious medallion of the god Alexander to glow against her bare skin. He had waited too long to hurry this delicious moment, so he would delay easing the pants over her slim hips, choosing instead to caress her gently, but with enough pressure to stimulate her through the fabric. That she knew what was to come next, and with a body that knew how to respond, would heighten the pleasure for both of them when the final moment came.

Then abruptly, the Mask Hunter's reverie was cut short and his attention diverted from the woman's body to something she held in her hand. She had removed a wrapped object from the bin that contained scraps of small statues. It was larger than anything else she had taken out thus far. From her body language, he knew she was holding her breath.

Doing the same, he watched as she removed the cloth wrappings. Could it possibly be, after so many years of searching: the sacred mask?

But it was. There was no doubt about it. Although he had never seen it, the golden-eyed man knew that the object she was holding was the answer to his quest.

He was still for a moment, flooded with the emotion of finally having found the mask and the practical question of how to take it from her without killing her. This was a question he had long pondered and now that the time had come, he still had no answer. He was torn between his mission to retrieve the object that would ensure the eternal life of Alexander and his very human desire to preserve the life of the living woman before him. Indecision flooded his thought. He did not move.

Basement storeroom, Warner Museum
Beverly Hills, California
The same time

CHAPTER 57

I carefully removed the layers of cotton sheeting that wrapped the mask and gazed down at the face of the man who in life had conquered his known world, and in death continued to capture worlds he could not even have imagined existed.

The gold had tarnished little over the years, although a few dings on the side of the face attested to its years of travel. The face, albeit stylized, bore a marked resemblance to the coin I wore around my neck. However, the ram's horns were absent, and the flowing hair restrained. With their deep-set romantic aura, the eyes were the same, but the nose bore signs of restoration, either ancient or otherwise. The head was crowned with a delicate wreath of oak leaves, giving a somewhat incongruent appearance to the otherwise pharaonic-appearing facepiece.

I continued to peer down at the actual mask that had once protected the mummfied face of Alexander the Great. It is true what one heard about such moments taking the breath away.

What had Zanski been thinking to put it here? Knowing something of the way his mind worked, it was logical that he would have held the mask as a trump card to ensure his job at the museum should the trustees continue to harass him. Growing up under the thumb of the KGB had taught him that trick.

Obviously, my bin was to be only a temporary stashing place until the right moment for him to dazzle the trustees and emerge the eternal hero.

But that moment never came. He never came back, and, ironically, neither did I, until now. For him death had intervened, and for me the reluctance to face a painful past.

Yet now that I had the mask in my possession, what to do with it? How could I get it back to its rightful owner? Who should I reach out to?

Barry first came to mind, but knowing his character, there was no way I could trust him.

He would undoubtedly take it and sell it to the highest bidder. This mask deserved a better fate than that. If I even breathed a word to him, it would be impossible to explain why I did not want him to have it. I could see his face now, alternating between anger and disbelief, shouting something like "How in the name of hell do you think you're going to return something to some guy who's been dead for millennia, and as far as we all know, left no forwarding address? You really do belong back in that loony bin."

Right now, I had to do something. Could I trust Adam? Probably he and the entire troop of trustees were little better than Barry. Interpol? No, with my luck, that would backfire, and the mask would be impounded forever while Greece, Italy, and Egypt fought over its ownership.

Overall, my best bet was Gren. Although not as well-heeled as he made himself out to be, he didn't seem to be fueled by greed, and of late he and I had formed a surprisingly close bond. So why did everything in my gut shout *no*?

I needed time to think.

"Goodbye, Alexander," I whispered as I prepared to rewrap the mask. "I'll be back soon."

Basement storeroom, Warner Museum
Beverly Hills, California
The same time

CHAPTER 58

Christos did not hear Grenville approach until he felt the tap on his shoulder.

"Shall we go inside?"

Christos reacted with a start. "Oh, hello. I was just about to go back upstairs. I came down to check if Parthi needed anything." He hoped Grenville would not hear the strain in his voice.

"Most of the visitors have left for the day, and Carlos is on duty anyway. Come with me." Grenville's voice was neutral. He put his hand on Christos' shoulder and gently propelled him through the partially open doorway.

Basement storeroom, Warner Museum
Beverly Hills, California
The same time

CHAPTER 59

"Find anything interesting down here?" Grenville asked.

I was so taken aback by the men's sudden appearance that I couldn't speak.

Gren continued in a conversational tone, "Odd thing happened just now. I was walking past the security station and glanced at the cameras for this area. And what do you think I saw?"

Again, he did not wait for a reply.

He crossed the room and removed the mask from the bin. "To think it was right here, under our very noses, for all these years. And it took you to find it for us, you clever girl."

"Shall we call Adam and tell him the good news?" I asked.

He laughed. "Is that what you expect? I don't think so."

I pivoted my head closer to him, not sure I had heard him correctly, but afraid that I had. "What did you say?"

"I think you heard me, my dear."

His amiable facade was gone, as though it had itself been a mask. That idea would have been ironic in less troubling circumstances. However, just now, he reminded me of a cobra in the instant before the strike.

"I am sorry to have to do this to you, Parthi. I really do like you. A lot. But this belongs to me."

I tried to control my voice. "What do you mean?"

The expression in Gren's narrowed eyes needed no interpretation.

"You don't really think I intend to turn this over to the museum as a gift, do you? Do you have any idea what it's worth and how many years I've waited to get my hands on something like this? I knew my father was on to something big just before he died, but he wouldn't even tell me where he was digging. My own father. How's that for family?" He punctuated his words with a snort. "This is what he meant when, in that last journal entry, he said he had found HIM!"

The thought crossed my mind that perhaps Gren's father had had some idea of his son's character, and that was the reason for the estrangement, but mentioning it at this point would only antagonize him.

How could I have been so stupid not to have seen through Gren? I had not liked him originally but allowed his recent charm to cloud my vision. I should have called Barry after all. Too late now.

I still had not moved, frozen by his menacing demeanor.

Gren was holding the mask. Then he turned away from me. He put it down gently and grabbed my arm with his right hand.

"Don't move. Don't make a sound, or this will be more painful than it has to be."

He wrapped his left hand around the Alexander necklace I was wearing and pulled tight. The gold cut into my neck. I winced.

"What do you plan to do now?" My voice was more of a

squeak than a human sound.

"Simple. Although it pains me, truly it does: dispose of you, then smuggle the mask back to Switzerland, where Brazzi will put it back in the same vault it was in thirty years ago. Since you were thoughtful enough to tell me that tidbit about the Vatican's stake in the mask when we were in Rome, I'm pretty sure Brazzi and his uncle will be only too anxious to make a deal with me. Then I will negotiate its sale to the Warner. Just like Zanski planned to do. Although this time there will be two payouts for me: Brazzi in cash for finding it, and the Warner in the form of promotion to senior curator for negotiating the deal for them."

All this time Christos stood watching, but he did nothing.

"A big win for me," Grenville continued. "I'll keep the job as long as it amuses me, then retire to Alexandria. Live like a mogul. You should enjoy the irony of this: me living like a king in Alexander's own city, thanks to him." He stopped a moment, regarding me with an undisguised sneer. "Yes, a big win for me, but not for you, lovely one. But then, somebody always has to lose."

I shuddered. Knowing that he didn't plan to let me live to tell about this made my legs weak. The rest of my body was stiff, caught in the vice of Gren's grip.

There was silence. At last, Christos spoke, taking a step toward Grenville. "I cannot let you do that. The mask is the sacred property of Alexander the Great and must go back to him."

Grenville looked puzzled. "What are you talking about?"

Christos continued in a calm voice. "I was planning to wait until Parthi left the basement, then take the mask and slip away before anyone knew it—especially you. You were always a means to an end, and now I can fulfill my ancestral obligation of preserving the remains of Alexander the Great."

Even though the chain around my neck was constricting me, I was still able to swivel my head slightly in Christos' direction and was surprised to see the steely look that had replaced his normally benign demeanor.

Grenville did not respond but reached into his jacket pocket and pulled out what looked to be a 9mm Beretta.

"After I saw your little discovery down here, I thought I might need this. You should know I also took care of the cameras, so there'll be no record of what happens here in the next few minutes," Grenville chuckled. "I got into the habit of keeping this baby at the ready doing business with the bad boys in the antiquities trade."

Before Grenville could say another word, Christos swiftly struck his gun arm, knocking the weapon to the floor. The surprise caused Grenville to release his hold on my neck.

Grenville's face was a purple rage as he lunged at Christos. In one motion, his fist undercut Christos' chin, knocking him to the ground. Grenville stood over him triumphantly. "You made a bad choice, my boy."

While Grenville's attention was diverted, I reached down and snatched the gun from the floor. Suddenly aware of this, Grenville turned toward me. His eyes were flashing, although his voice was calm. "You won't shoot me, my dear. I know you. You haven't the guts."

He took a step toward me, reaching for the gun. I stepped back.

"Now, put the gun down. I'll take the mask quietly and no harm will come to any of us."

Did he actually believe I was stupid enough to trust him this time? I held the gun steady in both hands.

"Don't come any closer," I warned.

He lunged. That was his mistake. The gun went off.

Then Grenville was on the floor. There was blood everywhere. The shot had blown off a piece of his skull. Had I even pulled the trigger? I suddenly felt a wave of nausea.

On the floor close by, Christos was stirring. I turned my back on the grisly spectacle as he rose shakily to his feet. My own knees wobbled, and I was near the point of joining Grenville on the concrete floor. Christos crossed the room toward me, put his arm around my shoulder, and led me to a chair. I was shaking. He gently caressed my cheek. "It's all right, Parthi, you had to do it."

He glanced briefly at the corpse. I followed his eyes. "Did you love him at all?" I asked.

"I am a very good actor. How could I love anyone who cared only for himself?"

One more question was burning in my mind. "What about Henry Templeton? Did he really kill himself?"

"I had been watching him for years, both him and his Mafioso cousin. If he ever knew anything about the mask's whereabouts, anything at all, he would have acted on it. Both of them, like Grenville and I, and your Barry Epstein, and later the Pope himself, were all looking for it, although quite separately, and with entirely different aims. But to answer your question: I believe it was Grenville who killed Henry Templeton."

Still keeping my vision averted from Grenville, I slowly regained my sense of reality and recalled what Christos had said about returning the mask to Alexander.

"So you actually know where Alexander is buried?"

"It is safer if you do not know too much, but yes, my mission is to reunite Alexander with his mask."

Did this man actually know where Alexander's tomb was, when people had been searching for it for centuries and found nothing?

"We don't have much time. Although the walls down here are thick enough that the gunshot would not have been heard by anyone upstairs, we still need to work swiftly."

I thought a moment, then I picked up the gun and wiped off my fingerprints using the wrapping from the mask. When I was sure the gun was clean I handed it to Christos.

He understood.

He walked toward the pool of blood encircling Grenville's body and stepped in it. "I'll leave these shoes in my locker for the police to find."

He started toward the door. "As soon as the night watchman realizes the cameras have been disabled, security will begin searching the museum for any disturbance. I must leave now." He moved toward the door, then stopped and turned back toward me. "Come with me."

I closed the distance between us. I looked into his deep amber eyes, and for a moment, I was tempted. An image of myself living out my days in peace and love and simplicity flashed before me. But I knew it wouldn't work. I shook my head sadly. "No, my friend, I must stay here. And you must take the mask and complete your promise to Alexander."

He nodded. "I understand. But know that I will be watching over you. You too have become a servant of the great god Alexander, and you will be rewarded in the land of Osiris. And if you are ever in difficulty here on earth, I will be there."

With those words he left the room.

Despite the horror of a dead body in the room, and my response to it, I was fascinated by the revelations of the past few minutes. The golden treasure Grenville had placed on the table seemed to float before me. In my shocked state it seemed alive, encouraging me to stay strong.

Learning that the location of Alexander's resting place, if not his actual tomb, had been known all along by a fanatically loyal dynasty of protectors was astounding. And that not one of them, through the centuries since Alexander's reburial, had revealed its location—in spite of their own poverty and the lure of the wealth it would provide—was equally amazing.

I could only speculate how the mask had left Egypt. Tentacles of the underworld were everywhere, and after Benjamin Hopkins' death, anything was possible.

Director's office, Warner Museum
Beverly Hills, California
The following day

EPILOGUE

It was a cloudless fall day in Los Angeles. The characteristic haze—some called it smog—that usually blanketed the city was nowhere to be seen. The view from Adam's office on the top floor of the Warner Museum stretched from the tall downtown buildings to the ocean in the distance. I sat in a wing chair facing the director's desk. Adam himself paced the room, deep in thought.

"In a few minutes the press will be here, and I'll have to divert all my energy to damage control. I've asked you to be here because they will obviously want a statement from the last person seen on the security camera in the storage room before the system was disabled."

"What do you expect me to say?" I asked.

I was making every effort to act the shocked bystander who had just learned that a murder had taken place perhaps only minutes after my leaving the museum basement.

"This will only be a formality. It seems pretty clear what happened: Grenville and the museum guard must have waited until you left the basement before entering. Who knows what their plan was? Or why either one or both of them disabled the camera system?" He stopped for a moment, shrugging his shoulders. "But this is what I am pretty sure happened: Christos shot his lover, Grenville Hopkins, in a fit of jealous rage over what he mistakenly thought was a romantic relationship between you and him. The guards have already been interviewed, and they were pretty clear that Grenville and Christos had been an item."

Adam continued, "It is absolutely imperative that we maintain the illusion that this tragedy is a personal drama and in no way connected to the recent scandal involving Henry Templeton, or to antiquities at all.

"From the look on your face, Parthi, you still have no idea of the realities of the antiquities world. What we have is an imperfect system, to be sure, but one that best preserves priceless cultural material. This has been true from the beginning of archaeology. Just where do you think the Elgin Marbles would be today if Lord Elgin hadn't had the foresight to preserve them in the British Museum? Most probably crushed into lime to make concrete. The same is true about all the great artifacts of the world, at least those that have survived, largely because of their being rescued by us westerners. I may look and sound like a snob to you, totally dismissive of the fact that the countries of origin have certain rights to the creations of their ancestors. True, of course, but they also have responsibilities, and historically they don't have a very good track record on that score."

He stopped talking and looked at his watch. "As much as what I am saying needs to be said, this is not the time. I feel passionately about what we do here at the Warner, and I am hoping that you can see my point."

I did not, so I changed the subject, asking, "Do you know what actually happened to Henry?"

"Technically no, and I prefer not to speculate. But off the record, I knew and worked with him for almost thirty years, and I knew him as a strong and pragmatic man. The likelihood of his committing suicide was very slim. However, that cannot be my concern. It will be up to his family whether or not to look into it further."

"What about Christos, the guard? Won't the authorities try and find and extradite him for Gren's murder?"

"Up to them. I'm sure they'll try, but my guess is that he had this planned pretty carefully, including the escape route. I'd be surprised if they catch him."

"So what exactly do you want me to say today?" I asked, returning to the subject at hand.

"Just what you told me: you were in the basement doing some work for Grenville, finished it, and left. You saw nor heard nothing. Grenville and the guard must have come in some time after you left. No matter how tempted you are to be a heroine and speculate on what you suspect about Henry's death and any possible connection to this, please think it through first. There is nothing to be gained by bringing even more scandal to this museum."

Although it seemed so wrong, I wanted to get this over with, and I agreed. According to plan, only Adam and I attended the police interrogation and subsequent press conference.

All things considered, both were faster and easier than I had anticipated. Adam did most of the talking. I would not have been a very convincing liar anyway. In the end, they all appeared satisfied with the idea of a crime of passion, seeming to eagerly buy into the stereotype of a violent Middle Easterner.

Naturally there was the added sensationalism of the antiquities curator at the Warner having been the victim of a lurid homosexual crime. That alone would sell newspapers. They had no need to probe more deeply.

BARRY WAS WAITING FOR ME when I walked out of the Warner conference room. "Well, there you have it, kiddo. Case all wrapped up. Seems like you almost got yourself too close to the apex of a love triangle. Your lousy choice in men almost got you killed."

"Don't forget, you were my first lousy choice." I changed to a more serious tone, "I'm just glad it's over. The antiquities world is every bit as treacherous as I remembered it."

"No regrets about not publishing those figurines?"

"None. But I did open that storage bin when I was in the basement, only because I thought it might make me rethink my career choice."

I had no intention of telling Barry or anyone else what I had found there.

Barry had obviously noticed I was lost in thought. "Pondering what might have been?" he asked.

"Not really. Actually I feel free at last from the whole thing."

"Wish I did. I'm still out all that cash I put down for that damn mask all those years ago, but all in all, I guess I'm no worse off than before this started, and at least I can take a walk without looking over my shoulder."

"You take walks now?"

"Figure of speech."

"I feel a little bad about Henry. Even though he chose to bend the law the way he did, he still didn't deserve to die. And it wasn't a good death, either, with the world thinking he was more of a criminal than he actually was, and a coward to boot, killing himself rather than owning up to his actions."

Barry smiled. "I have a feeling the Italians may have something to say about that. You are going to tell Brazzi what went down, aren't you?"

"How could I not? After all, I did promise him I would find out what I could, and even though he's a Mafioso, a promise is a promise." After a slight pause I added, "And, remember, they were blood."

"Speaking of blood relations, this gets Cardinal Brazzi and the whole Vatican off the hook too, doesn't it?"

"Very conveniently. With no mask of Alexander the Great on the horizon, there will be no pressure to disturb St. Mark."

"I keep wondering who killed Henry. And despite everything, I wish I had that mask to sell. Where do you suppose it is, and will it ever turn up?"

I thought a minute. "I'm actually glad we never found the mask. I wish you felt that way too. There are so many treacheries beneath the glamour of the art world. It's not a nice thing, the actuality of what goes on in museums, I mean. On the outside, everything is so wonderful, inspirational even, but behind the scenes, it's totally different. Especially in antiquities."

"Well, what do you expect when what you're hoping to dazzle the public with are the products of robbing from the dead?" Barry was never one to mince words.

"Chilling, isn't it, when one looks at, let's say, a Greek vase. How many people actually realize what they are looking at was made to comfort the dead, not impress the living?"

"Yup, sweetie. Those suits in the museums are not much different from the Mafia guys, or than I was."

"You know, even though you nearly got me killed, this experience hasn't been all bad for me. It opens up a space for me to have a future."

I was quiet for a moment, then smiled. "For once in my life I wasn't a coward."

"If you say so, baby. As for me, I made a lot of dough in the past, and maybe I will again in the future. So I guess this time I need to take my lumps. After all, it's only money."

But it was more than money. I tried to get that across to Barry. "Don't you find it almost surreal that after all these years, Alexander is still on the move?"

"Hadn't really given that much thought. So where to now?"

"The airport, I guess."

On our way there—thinking about Alexander—I kept hearing Bonnie Tyler, in my head singing about good men and gods and fiery steeds. Weren't we all holding out for a hero?

Alexander had been found after so many had been searching for him for so long. Humming to myself, I knew Bucephalus, too, was out there somewhere waiting for me.

ABOUT THE AUTHOR

Anna Wilmans received a PhD in Archaeology and Ancient Art History from University of Southern California in 1986 and has participated in excavations in Israel, Turkey, and Greece. She is a published author of scholarly articles, book reviews, monographs, and several commissioned biographies of living artists.

Her more recent adventures in archaeology include investigation of the Chumash population of California's Gaviota Coast, to be fictionalized in the next Parthenia Guthrie novel.

She is a lifelong lover of animals, especially horses and wildlife. She currently owns a Mustang, a Quarab, and a Welsh Pony and is establishing a foundation to protect California mountain lions.

She is a member of the Archaeological Association of America and a Fellow of the Explorers Club.

The Mask Hunter is her first work of fiction.

Forthcoming Novels
in the Parthenia Guthrie series:

The Bead

Parthi accepts a commission to redesign a historic California ranch house and becomes embroiled in a web of greed, murder, and intrigue set against a backdrop of the last pristine stretch of Gaviota Coast threatened by land developers, wildlife poachers, and family dysfunction.

A Death in Kenya

Parthi travels to Kenya, the land of her birth, to uncover the truth about her father's supposed suicide years earlier.

The Stalking Scarab

Parthi is called to Egypt to investigate a string of suspicious deaths attributed to the age-old curse of Tutankhamon's Tomb. She is reunited with Christos Laventis, the Mask Hunter, to solve this case.

www.ingramcontent.com/pod-product-compliance
Lightning Source LLC
LaVergne TN
LVHW020658110826
845149LV00012B/2034

* 9 7 9 8 9 9 0 7 4 8 0 2 6 *